THE BOYFRIEND

JOHN NICHOLL

Boldwood

First published in Great Britain in 2025 by Boldwood Books Ltd.

Copyright © John Nicholl, 2025

Cover Design by Head Design Ltd.

Cover Images: iStock

A CIP catalogue record for this book is available from the British Library.

Paperback ISBN 978-1-83561-269-9

Large Print ISBN 978-1-83561-265-1

Hardback ISBN 978-1-83561-264-4

Ebook ISBN 978-1-83561-262-0

Kindle ISBN 978-1-83561-263-7

Audio CD ISBN 978-1-83561-270-5

MP3 CD ISBN 978-1-83561-267-5

Digital audio download ISBN 978-1-83561-261-3

This book is printed on certified sustainable paper. Boldwood Books is dedicated to putting sustainability at the heart of our business. For more information please visit https://www. boldwoodbooks.com/about-us/sustainability/

Boldwood Books Ltd, 23 Bowerdean Street, London, SW6 3TN

www.boldwoodbooks.com

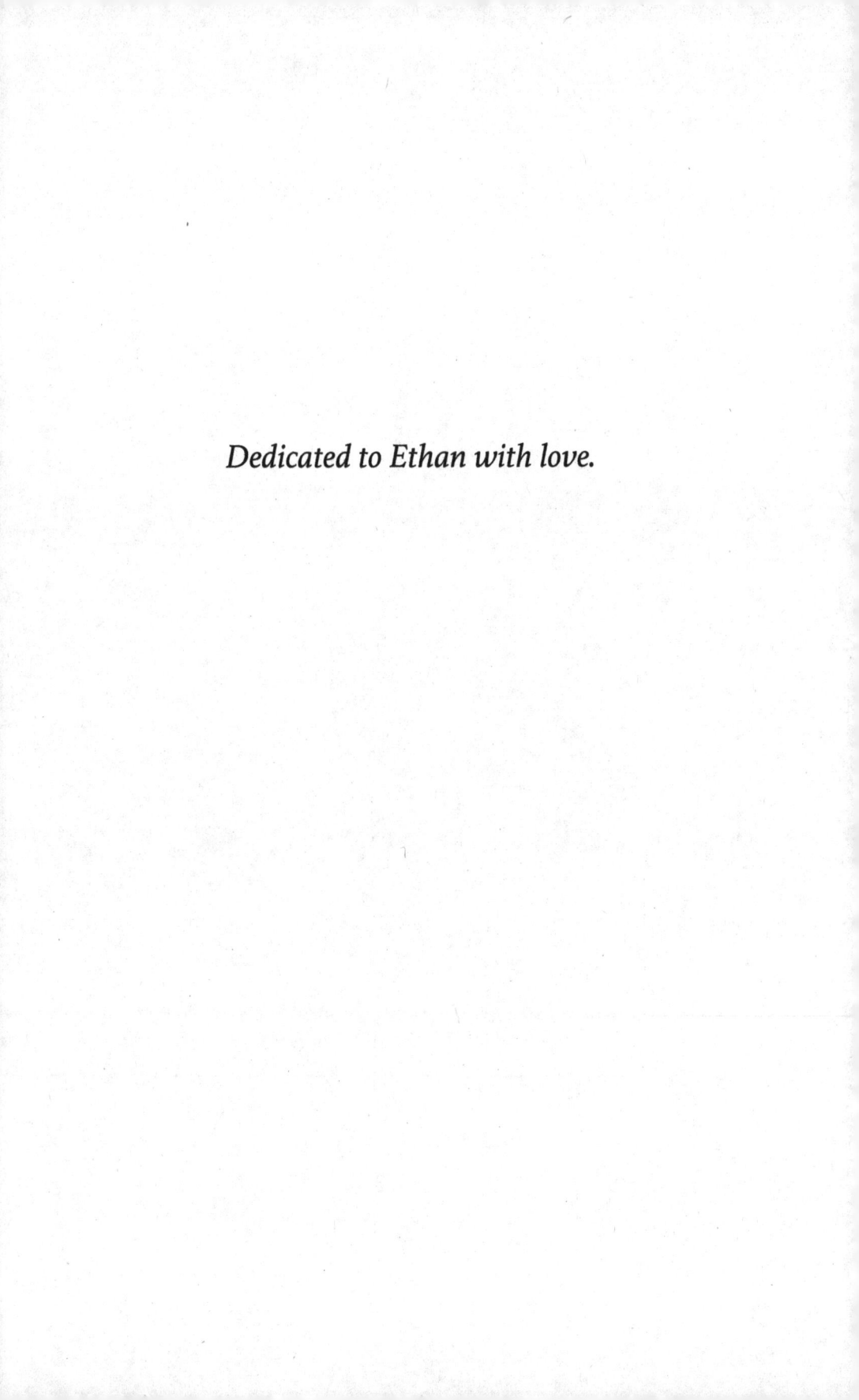

Dedicated to Ethan with love.

1

Twenty-year-old Anna Edwards looked up from the floor with tear-filled eyes as her boyfriend stood over her, far too close for comfort. She swallowed hard before speaking, not quite able to comprehend the enormity of what he'd done. His actions were so seemingly at odds with his past behaviour. As if he was a different man – someone she didn't know at all.

'Why, Mark, why?' she asked. 'Why would you do that to me? To someone you're supposed to care for?'

Mark Shady glared down at Anna, with the hint of a sardonic smile playing on his lips. And before he even responded, she thought that maybe she was witnessing his true nature for the very first time. There'd been hints before. In recent days. Things she'd minimised or ignored. But never at the start. And never anything like this.

He pulled up the zip of his tailored trousers. 'Such a drama queen,' he said, slowly shaking his head as if she'd said the most ridiculous thing he'd ever heard. 'Such a fuss about very little at all. I told you to lay still, not to fucking move. Simple enough instructions, even for a halfwit like you. But no, you couldn't even manage that. Sometimes, I wonder what I saw in you in the first place. I thought you students were supposed to be intelligent.'

Anna touched her swollen bottom lip, then looked at her two bloody fingers, tears flowing freely. And even then, after all that had happened, a part of her thought she could appeal to his better nature. To reach out and find the man she'd thought he was. The seemingly kind, generous, and thoughtful person she'd fallen for. As if the rape was an abomination. Totally out of character. Something he'd instantly regret if she made him understand.

'You hurt me, Mark. I said no. I shouted no. You pinned me down and covered my mouth. Look at the state of me. Can't you see I'm bleeding? You did that. *You!*'

He took a single step back and stared down at her. 'Is that it? Are you finished? It was just a bit of fun, that's all. You really are a miserable cow. Any more complaints before I shower to wash your stink from my body?'

Anna sat up now, her distress turning to anger.

'*Fun?* What the hell are you talking about? You were violent and nasty. Why are you being so cruel?'

Shady laughed – he actually laughed – and she knew in that instant that nothing she could do or say would ever get through to him. She opened her mouth as if to speak but couldn't find the words. He wasn't the man she'd thought he was at all. Not even close.

'You've got ten minutes,' he said as he walked towards the first-floor flat's bathroom door. He stopped with his hand on the door handle. But he still didn't look at her, continuing to talk as he opened it. 'I want this place immaculate and you gone. And take all your shit with you. All of it.'

Anna rose slowly to her feet. 'What... what you did was a crime. You must realise that. What makes you think I won't go to the police?'

He broke into a brief smile. And now he was looking at her, studying her with accusing eyes as if she was in the wrong, not him. As if she was the criminal. His voice had a mocking tone. 'Tell who-ever the fuck you want to. It would be your word against mine. Who are the police going to believe? A successful local businessman like me who could have any woman he wanted, or a hysterical, needy little tart like you? I'd tell them you like it rough. Begged for it. And you got exactly what you wanted.'

Anna reached for her clothes as she began to cry again.

'But that's not true. I really... I really thought you were a nice guy. Why be so horrible? I thought you loved me. You said I was your soulmate. That we'd be together for ever.'

Another smile.

'Well, there you go. That just goes to show what a great liar I am. Think about that before you con-tact the pigs. They wouldn't take you seriously. Not for a minute. Now get dressed, tidy this place up, get your things together, and then fuck off. You're starting to bore me. I should have dumped you long before now.'

Anna began hurriedly dressing as he closed the bathroom door. And within five minutes, she was out of there, standing in the street, mobile phone in hand, and calling for a taxi.

* * *

Shortly after, Anna stood in the West Wales Police Headquarters car park, staring up at the red brick building for almost ten minutes before finally finding the resolve to enter. She'd thought about her first meeting with Mark, her initial attraction to him, the attention he gave her, the unexpected flattery that raised her mood when she needed it most. And for a time, she silently pondered, he'd seemed a keeper, almost a dream come true with his smouldering good looks and seemingly warm personality. Until today, until those awful events, when everything changed for ever. When the real Mark, the man he truly was, revealed himself for the first terrible time.

And even then, as she slowly climbed the wide steps towards the smoked glass doors in her reluctant search for justice, a part of her wanted to turn and run, to never speak of the rape, to push it to the back of her mind and try to ignore it as if it had never happened at all. But somewhere deep down inside, she knew she couldn't do that. Because some things she would never forget, however hard she tried. She silently told herself she had to tell her story whatever the future held. To make people understand what she'd been through. To convince those in positions of power that she was telling the truth. Nothing but the truth. Because what Mark had done was wrong. He'd used her as if she was worthless. And he deserved to be punished. Surely that wasn't too much to ask?

2

NINE MONTHS LATER

Detective Sergeant Raymond Lewis shook his head and frowned as the jury's foreman announced a not-guilty verdict in a sing-song Welsh voice. And for the briefest of moments, as he sat there, the detective thought he might start weeping – right there and then, in front of everyone, as he sometimes did in his dreams.

Months of work down the drain. Interviews, interrogations, statements, and forensics. And for what? Mark Shady. Innocent! The worst decision in the world. And as bad as it was for him, Lewis knew it would be so much worse for the victim. Shady would be cheering, elated, and celebrating, and

Anna would be crushed, despondent, and very likely heading for depression.

Lewis could have cried for Anna. A skilled defence barrister had torn her life to pieces. Made her seem the guilty one. As if her skimpy mode of dress had somehow invited the rape. Justice? Fucking justice! One rule for men and another for women. As if consent meant nothing at all. It had always been so. No wonder there were so few convictions. Where was the justice in that?

Lewis grimaced now, still considering the awful unfairness of it all and quietly seething as Shady sought him out with a fixed, gleeful stare, looking him in the eye and giving him the finger. It was all so horribly predictable, thought Lewis as he turned away, resisting the impulse to shout out a string of hateful expletives or, better still, to knock the stupid smirk off the other man's face with a powerful, well-aimed blow. That would be natural justice, like in the old days, when he was a young copper. Before everything changed, cameras everywhere. The dirty bastard wouldn't be so full of himself then.

Lewis pulled his green polyester tie loose at the collar as he made his weary way towards the exit at the back of the court on heavy leaden legs, still deep in thought, trying to make sense of it all. Seconds seemed like minutes as he crossed the busy room, head down, focused on the wooden floor, keen to avoid Shady's further triumphant attention, his latest victim, or any of her family members – her mother, father, or older brother. How would they feel, poor sods? Like shit, that's how. He would talk to them. That time would come. All a part of the job. But for now, he couldn't face it, his emotions too raw. He didn't feel good about that. He knew it was another failure. A dereliction of duty. But so be it. That's how it was. He wasn't Superman. He was flesh and blood like everybody else. *Come on, Ray. One foot in front of another. Focus on the floor. Nothing lasts forever. It will all be over soon.*

The detective felt overheated and sweaty despite the January cold as he made his way out into the chilly, grey Swansea street, his blood pressure rising to a savage high as his mind continued racing, fixated on events. Not guilty! Shady! Like fuck he was. The bastard should be languishing in a cell and rotting for years to come. But no, he was walking free. Released back into society as if he'd done nothing at all.

As he hurried away from the court building, Lewis asked himself if he'd done right to encourage Anna to go to court at all. Rape allegations were notoriously hard to prove, however committed the witness. And this case had been no different. Not guilty! A scumbag like Shady. It really didn't get any worse than that.

Lewis decided he badly needed a drink before heading back to Carmarthen, just the one, something to take the edge off, as he made his way towards the nearest pub, a watering hole he knew well, only a few minutes' brisk walk away if he picked up his pace.

The pencil-thin, middle-aged barman clearly recognised the ageing detective as he pushed open the heavy door and entered the quiet, white-painted room, raising his hand and nodding in friendly greeting. 'How's things?' the barman asked, then added, 'Long time no see,' as Lewis approached the bar, slightly out of breath, his chest rising and falling as he perched his not-inconsiderable bulk on a high stool he found far from comfortable. The barman was friendly enough and welcoming. But Lewis wasn't in the mood to chat.

'Half a bitter,' he replied with a tobacco-ravaged rattle, wishing he could order a pint. And maybe a whisky chaser or two to wash the beer down.

A surprised look flashed across the barman's

face. 'Are you sure? You've never struck me as a half-man.'

Lewis had rarely felt less sure in his life. But the law was the law. The days when a copper could get away with it were long gone. The new breed nicked their own. Where was the loyalty? Another unwelcome change in a world that felt more alien by the day.

'Driving.' That was all Lewis said in reply, just the one word, almost spat from his mouth.

The barman nodded his understanding. 'Red Dragon?'

Lewis could almost taste the yeasty dark liquid on his tongue. It wasn't his favourite bitter. But it came close. Nectar from the gods.

'Yeah, that'll do nicely,' he said, looking the other man in the eye.

The barman drew the beer with what seemed a practised ease and handed Lewis the glass, filled to the top with just the right amount of frothy head.

'Cheer up,' he said, resting his elbows on the bar, 'it might never happen.'

Lewis gulped half the glass, swilling the beer around his mouth, appreciating the familiar flavours for a second or two before finally swallowing with a satisfied sigh that only momentarily raised his mood. 'Already has, mate, already has.'

'Bad day?'

Lewis tilted his head back, drained what was left of his drink, and then stood, grimacing slightly as his inflamed joints stiffened and complained.

'Absolute shit show, as it happens,' he said as he banged his empty glass onto the bar and went to walk away.

'Hang on in there, mate,' the barman called after him as if they were friends. 'That's what my old mum used to say. Things'll get better. Hope to see you again soon.'

Lewis didn't reply as he approached the door, pushing it open with an outstretched hand and looking up at the dark sky as it started to rain. He shook his head again, furrowing his brow. It seemed God was mocking him. As if the day wasn't already bad enough, he was about to get soaked to the skin.

He pulled up the collar of his coat to no good effect, strode out with purpose, then picked up his pace, very quickly out of breath as he hurried towards his police car. But the effort, he told himself, was worth it as he began to pant like an overheated hound. It was time to head west for home. And a pint or two at the rugby club. Yeah, why the hell not? The drink was reaching out to him, calling. Welcome, alcoholic oblivion beckoned. Far from the first time and certainly not the last. A therapy of sorts. His kind of medicine. Something he'd relied on for years. Far better than any antidepressant tablets he'd ever been prescribed. Yeah, he'd throw down one welcome drink after another. And for a time, he'd forget Shady and all the bastards like him. The men who offered nothing but misery. He'd choose to forget until tomorrow, until he was back at police headquarters, back on duty. And then, well, it was a case of getting on with the job.

3

Lewis was enthusiastically tucking into a large fried breakfast when Detective Inspector Laura Kesey entered the West Wales Police Headquarters staff canteen at just after eight the following morning. Bacon, eggs, sausages, beans, mushrooms, and hash browns were piled high on his plate and all covered in copious amounts of tomato sauce, which didn't come as any surprise to the DI. A blob of sauce had run down from one corner of the big man's mouth, settling on his stubbled chin. Like a massive red-faced toddler needing a bib, Kesey thought to herself, shaking her head with a grin. Typical of the man. Such things seemed to define him. No change there.

Kesey waited for a second or two, just inside the canteen door, watching her sergeant as he sat there, seemingly unaware of her arrival, focused on nothing but his food, as if the fatty fare was the most important thing in the world.

Kesey shook her head, sighed, and then headed to the serving counter, standing behind two recently appointed probationary uniformed constables she thought looked young enough to be sixth-form school boys. She silently asked herself if they were so very young or if she was getting old. She wasn't sure, concluding it was probably a bit of both. She was nearly forty, after all. Middle age beckoned. And time passed so very quickly. Where did all the years go?

Kesey ordered a cup of strong black coffee and a single slice of wholemeal toast with a little sweet local honey, exchanging cheery pleasantries with the usual blonde-haired woman behind the serving counter before joining Lewis at his table at the back of the room.

The DS looked up with bleary, red-veined eyes, silently acknowledging her arrival with a subtle nod of his balding head before forking a large slice of salted bacon into his wide-open mouth and chewing, washing it down with a slurp of milky tea and burping. He often suffered indigestion, one of his many ailments. Hardly surprising, Kesey thought, given his excesses. He just didn't look after himself like he should. Not for as long as she'd known him.

Kesey sipped her hot coffee and frowned.

'And a good morning to you, Ray,' she said sarcastically in her Birmingham accent, which bordered on monotone. 'You're always so cheerful first thing. Thanks for the lovely welcome. It's just the start of the day I was hoping for. You're like a beam of sunshine in my life.'

Lewis took another slurp of tea, leaving a milky moustache above his top lip.

'Don't even start,' he said with a throaty rasp. 'I didn't have a great night. You're lucky I'm here at all.'

Kesey raised a hand, pointing at his face.

'You've got some sauce on your chin. About an inch below your lip.' She didn't bother mentioning the milk.

He put down his knife, wiping away the sauce with a paper tissue taken from a side pocket of his worn wool jacket, which Kesey noted looked well past its best, much like himself. She took a small bite of toast, savouring the sweet honey. A treat she sometimes allowed herself.

'I can see the diet's still going well,' she said, scowling at his plate and rolling her eyes.

'Oh, for God's sake, not this again,' Lewis replied in west Wales tones. 'How many times, woman? You never stop banging on about it. A man's got to eat.'

Kesey let out a snorting laugh that had nothing to do with humour. It was a conversation they'd had several times before. It never got her anywhere. His eating habits hadn't changed in the slightest. But she had a duty of care, and she thought of Ray Lewis as a friend as well as a colleague. She felt she had to keep trying. Just maybe, one day, he'd listen, as unlikely as that seemed.

'Yeah, but a man doesn't have to eat all that greasy crap,' she said. 'You've had one heart attack. And you know what your consultant said. Lose some weight! That stuff's the last thing you should be eating. I can almost hear your arteries screaming for help from here.'

Lewis let out a long audible breath, as much a groan as a sigh.

'Yeah, yeah, you've told me often enough.'

She was quick to reply, making no effort to hide her frustration.

'Then why don't you listen?'

He pressed his lips together.

'Have you heard what happened yesterday?'

Kesey knew he was changing the subject. It was a tactic he often used when the direction of a conversation unnerved him even slightly. But she decided to let it slide, thinking she'd said enough. She'd done her bit. And it wasn't as if he was going to listen anyway.

'In court?' she asked, sitting more upright, suddenly interested. Happy to focus back on work.

'The bastard got off.'

Kesey's eyes narrowed as her body stiffened. 'What? Shady, not guilty, again? You've got to be kidding me.'

'I wish I was,' Lewis replied, putting down his fork and grimacing, rubbing the back of his neck.

Kesey rarely swore, but the time seemed right. 'Oh, for fuck's sake!' she said with venom.

'He'll be back in that pizza place he runs and targeting his next victim before you can blink. And that's if he hasn't already got someone in mind. He goes from one to the next. One ruined life after another.'

Kesey blew out the air. 'I really thought we had him this time.'

'Yeah, I had my hopes,' Lewis replied with a look that said a thousand words, none of them good. 'It never used to be this hard. Everything's changed, and not for the better. Victims don't get a fair deal any more. Not like the old days. It's all weighed in the criminals' favour.'

Kesey dropped her chin to her chest before raising her head a second later, looking her sergeant in the eye. She thought he looked suddenly older, worn down by life. It seemed the pressures of the job were getting to him. And she could understand why. They were getting to her too.

'That's the third time Shady's got off in court,' she said. 'Three young women raped, all in similar circumstances, all with a similar MO, and we still can't make it stick. It makes me sick.'

Lewis cleared his throat before speaking with feeling.

'And don't forget about the four cases that didn't even get to court. And no doubt, more victims haven't even come forward. Shady's into double figures, for sure. I'd bet my life on it. He's a one-man crime wave.'

'I haven't forgotten any of them, Ray,' Kesey quickly replied. 'Believe me, I haven't. I interviewed three of the four myself. All young, pretty, and local. One lives in my street. I see her in karate classes. No one wants to nail Shady more than me. And this time, I really thought we had him. The CPS seemed confident. I thought he was looking at a long stretch.'

Lewis sighed with a sneer, pushed his empty plate aside, and then wiped his mouth with a sleeve.

'It's the system,' he began, back on his soap box, stating the obvious. 'And the bastard knows his way around the law pretty damn well. He reads up on it, legal textbooks, the lot. He told me that himself. And he took pleasure in the telling, with obvious pride. He thinks he's untouchable. That we're all mugs. That he can do whatever the fuck he wants to any woman he fancies and get away with it. And up to now, it seems he can.'

Kesey nodded. 'I know, Ray, I know.'

'It's all a game to Shady,' Lewis continued, now in full flow, speaking more quickly and rushing his words. 'If the bastard's arrested, he knows exactly how to play it. He says all the right things, never implicating himself in any crime. And if he is charged and ends up in court, he pays for a good barrister. Chooses well. He's got no moral compass, no concept of right and wrong. But he's also devious with a high IQ, convincing in the witness box, and he doesn't get rattled even under heavy pressure. He holds his nerve with confidence. The man's a psycho who targets girls with vulnerabilities, studies them, gets to know them well, and then uses any weaknesses against them when he needs to. It's all planned; I'm certain of that. Nothing happens by accident. He identifies anything that can undermine his victims as credible witnesses and makes sure he mentions it on tape and in the witness box. "She's promiscuous, she's got mental health issues, she's got a history of lying, it's personal, revenge for me dumping her" – that sort of thing. And it works for him. Has done every time. That's his MO right there.'

Kesey swallowed a mouthful of fast-cooling coffee and nodded again. 'I know, Ray, I know. You've told me. We've discussed it all before.'

'All the girls think he's all right at first. No, no, better than all right, they think he's kind, thoughtful, generous with money, a successful local businessman, boyfriend material. He makes certain of that. Quite the actor. He makes every girl think they're special. And all the time, the bastard's planning. He's scheming with his evil ways. He builds them up to knock them down, maximising the impact. I think that's all part of his pleasure, the waiting, the anticipation. None of the victims sees the real Shady until he decides it's time to pounce. And then, well, it's too late. He gets them alone, makes sure there are no witnesses, and sometimes somewhere they find unnerving – an abandoned building, a dark graveyard, somewhere like that – and then he does his thing. It's the force he enjoys, the power; it's all about the dominance, the lack of consent. That's what turns him on. I'm certain of that. That's what gives him his kicks. And he does everything he can to humiliate his victims too. Tells them they're ugly as he assaults them, that they smell, that it makes him sick to touch them, that they're not good enough for him, that it's like screwing a pig. That he was only ever with them in the first place because he felt sorry for them or as a bet with his mates.'

Kesey listened in contemplative silence, ignoring the impulse to look at her watch or the clock on the wall. None of what Lewis had said came as any surprise to her. It wasn't the first time they'd discussed the case in such detail. And she could have said much the same herself. But she let her sergeant talk nonetheless, knowing he needed to say it, to vent and get it off his chest. Because Lewis was a more sensitive man than his gruff appearance and persona suggested. Not many people knew that, but she did. The realisation came with time as they became more comfortable in the other's company. She now considered him a hard but complex man with a warm heart. So different from her first impressions several years before. Justice mattered to Lewis. Victims mattered to him. Particularly women and children. And failure ate away at him like a dog with a bone.

Now she glanced at her watch. There were things she needed to get on with – something that couldn't wait. It was time to move things along.

'Have you seen Anna since the verdict?' she asked only a second after he'd finished speaking. 'Have you spoken to her?'

Another sigh, louder this time, as he averted his eyes to the wall. 'No, not yet; I'm planning to pay her a visit at her parents' place once I've caught up with some paperwork. She moved back in with them after the rape, at their smallholding near Brechfa. And she still hasn't gone back to university. She had a few mental health problems as a teenager, even before encountering Shady – an eating disorder, self-harm, that kind of thing. She was on the mend, but there's been severe anxiety issues since the rape. It's set her right back again and undermined her progress. Hardly surprising. Everything that happened hit her hard. She's going to be in pieces after the verdict.

And there's every chance Shady will already be making things worse. Calling her a liar on social media, saying she's a fantasist, a girl with a grudge, or both, that sort of thing. Anything to increase her suffering. He won't let it go. Not for a single second. All part of the game. He's a sadist. That's his thing.'

Kesey was quick to reply. 'You need to speak to her as soon as possible, Ray. Do it this morning. Forget the paperwork. That can wait.'

Lewis raised his eyebrows, looking less than persuaded.

'It's the file for the Roberts case – the burglary. You said you needed it as soon as.'

'Not till tomorrow,' Kesey replied, suspecting her sergeant was looking to delay the visit, if only for a few hours.

'If you're sure,' he said.

Kesey stood, checking her watch again, pushing up the sleeve of her jumper, making it obvious. A child protection planning meeting at a local social services office was calling, and she was finally losing patience. Lewis had a habit of repeating himself. As if he thought just by talking, he could change things.

'Yeah, I'm certain,' she said. 'As of now, seeing

Anna is your number one priority. So get it done. And let me know how it goes when you get back. I want to be kept in the loop on this one; no surprises.'

'Okay, will do; message received.'

'I'm out this morning, but I should be in my office by two at the latest. I'll see you then.'

Not for the first time, Lewis raised a hand to the side of his head in a mock salute, something she knew was his way of lightening the mood. There was no disrespect in it, as she'd first thought years before. If anything, there was affection.

'I'll be there, ma'am, anything you say, ma'am, at two o'clock sharp. Your wish is my command.'

Kesey stifled a laugh, not wanting to encourage him, because it didn't take much. 'And I don't want you paying Shady a visit,' she said insistently, her smile disappearing as quickly as it appeared. 'I know exactly what you're like. And that last complaint nearly put an end to your career. The force has changed, Ray. Keep your hands off him. You can't get away with that sort of shit any more. You've only got a few months till retirement. You don't want to blow it now. Not when you're so near to a full pension.'

He rose stiffly to his feet, avoiding her accusing gaze.

'I'd cut Shady's balls off if it was up to me. Hang 'em from his ears like Christmas decorations. Stick his severed cock in his dirty mouth to make him choke.'

Kesey frowned hard, thinking she'd like to do much the same herself but not willing to admit it.

'I know you would,' she said. 'You've said it often enough. By all means, enjoy the fantasy. But you can't lay a finger on Shady. You know that. So stay away.'

Lewis tilted his big head to one side and scratched his nose.

'Right, duty calls, I'll be on my way then. Places to go, people to see.'

'Did you hear me, Ray?'

Lewis walked away, responding without looking back, speaking a little louder than he had been, a sharp edge to his tone. 'Yes, Laura, loud and clear, you've made your point.'

She hurried after him, not ready to let it go, following him out of the canteen and into a well-lit corridor with closed doors to either side.

'For now, focus on supporting Anna and her family. Put her in contact with Victim Support. And help facilitate a criminal injury claim. At least then she'll get a few grand.'

Lewis replied as he continued walking one heavy footstep at a time. 'It's not money she needs, it's justice.'

Kesey considered arguing. But she knew he was right. 'Shady's time will come,' she said with feeling, looking Lewis in the eye. 'He will slip up. He'll get overconfident. He'll say something or do something he can't deny. They all do in the end.'

'Yeah, but how many more victims will there be before then? Girls who'll have their lives ruined. Ripped apart to meet that scumbag's needs. I'll see you later, Laura; I'd better make a move. Time's getting on.'

4

Lewis wasn't in the best of moods as he drove the approximately twelve-mile journey from police headquarters to Brechfa, a small village deep in the rolling green west Wales countryside at the top of the Cothi Valley. He stopped in a quiet layby after a mile or two on the A40, playing Radio Wales, his favourite station, on his phone, thinking the usual combination of eclectic middle-of-the-road music and humorous banter might cheer him up a bit despite the melancholy thoughts that were dominating his morning. But even that was a lost cause today. His lower back was aching. His head was still a little muzzy after the alcohol. Two prescription painkillers hadn't helped one little bit. And worse still, the Shady case was eating away at him. It had come to mind all too often during a disturbed night of very little sleep, and it still bothered him now. Lewis considered himself a black-and-white sort of man. There was right, and there was wrong, with very little, if anything, in between. And the injustice he encountered in his policing role was sometimes too much to bear.

Shady, he told himself, really was the scum of the earth. A loathsome parasite. And now he had to face the bastard's latest victim, and likely her devastated family too, with all the morale-sapping angst that would inevitably entail. He'd be in the spotlight. A target for their anger. As if he was the bad guy. As if he was to blame for the verdict. Like it was somehow his fault. What copper wouldn't be dreading the visit, however experienced, however good at the job? There was an inevitable shitstorm coming his way. Something that couldn't be avoided.

Lewis thought he'd rather be doing almost anything else as he signalled then pulled back onto the A40, leaving Carmarthen behind and following signs for Llandeilo. He knew the road well, having travelled it many times over the years, but the beauty of the Towy Valley still wasn't lost on him. Despite dark clouds, the falling rain, and his low mood, he could still appreciate the vista. He glanced to his right at the meandering river, recalling happier times when he'd picnicked on the bank with his ex-wife one sunny Saturday when they were young, full of life and in love. So long ago. And so much had changed. She'd left, he was alone, and the past almost felt like another life. As if someone else had lived it and there was only the now.

Lewis scowled, screwing up his face, then asked himself if he'd become more sentimental as he grew older, fast approaching a retirement he dreaded. And he decided that the answer was likely yes. Not that anyone cared. No one saw the real man he hid behind his gruff persona. Because none of that mattered to anyone but himself. What an old fool he'd become.

Lewis pushed his ruminations from his mind as he pressed his foot down hard on the accelerator, taking full advantage of a straight stretch of road to pass a tractor towing a trailer loaded high with logs. He wasn't in any hurry to reach his destination for all the reasons he'd already contemplated. But he told himself he couldn't spend his day dawdling. There were other crimes demanding his attention. And he had to see Kesey at two. She'd said as much. And she never appreciated him being late. One of the things that really pissed her off. There was no point in antagonising her when he didn't need to.

Lewis was half hoping there'd be no one in as he drove his unmarked police car along the long stone-strewn track leading from the main road to the Edwards family's smallholding, a large detached house surrounded by mature trees. But as he negotiated a final bend with a high hedge to either side, he saw the entire dwelling for the first time. And his heart sank because someone was there. There was an old, rusty, black four-wheel drive pick-up truck and a much newer, bright red three-door hatchback parked on an area of muddy grass to the left of the front door, and a light was shining bright in a first-floor room to the far right of the building.

Okay, he said to himself as he parked, switched off the engine, and pulled up the handbrake. It was time to get on with what he was here to do. Take whatever flack was coming his way and then get out of there as fast as his feet could carry him. All part of the job.

Lewis exited the car without bothering to lock it, then hurried along a narrow path towards the front door as the rain suddenly turned to icy hail, small balls of frozen water stinging his face and making him blink. He stepped into a stone porch with several pairs of muddy black and green wellingtons to one side, glad to get out of the inclement Welsh winter weather, considering it a small victory, but still dreading the morning's events to come. He stood stiffly and began knocking on one of the door's two frosted glass panels with gradually increasing force, ignoring the bell for no particular reason. And all too soon for his liking, the door was opened wide by a middle-aged, grey-haired woman he immediately recognised as Doreen Edwards, Anna's mother. Entirely predictably, in Lewis's opinion, she had a sullen, angry look on her ruddy, heavily lined face. And if anything, she looked older than when he'd seen her in court the previous day. Much older than her years. It seemed events had taken their toll.

'What the hell do you want?' she asked with a strong Welsh accent, hands on hips, looking Lewis in the eye, almost spitting her words.

The detective took a single step back, not in the least bit surprised by her words but slightly shaken by the intensity of her reaction. Dealing with criminals was one thing. That was the easy bit. But victims and their loved ones, well, that was quite another.

'I'm... I'm sorry things worked out as they did,'

he said with feeling. 'I was hoping for a quick word with Anna. I... I know it all must have hit her hard. The jury got it badly wrong. It should have been very different.'

Doreen's expression didn't change as she crossed her arms over her chest. Lewis thought it was likely more angry resentment than loathing, but he wasn't entirely sure. Maybe there was hatred too.

'Oh, so you know how hard it's been for my poor daughter, do you?' she asked, her tone rising in pitch, not quite to the point of shouting but close. 'Is that so? And do you know that Anna has done nothing but cry since the verdict? Do you know that she's up in her bedroom now, bawling her eyes out because you've turned up here like a bad smell, reminding her of everything she's trying her best to forget? Is that what you know, Mr Oh-So-Clever Policeman? Because it doesn't seem you know very much at all to me.'

Lewis stood there for a beat, swallowing hard, searching for the right words, anything that might placate her even slightly. But even then, he knew nothing he could say would make much difference. Words didn't change anything, not fundamentally. But all he could do was try.

'If you could just let me in, please, love? We

could have a proper chat then, and I could talk to
Anna about anything she's particularly worried
about. An injunction wouldn't be a bad idea.
Keeping Shady away. And Victim Support can be
very helpful in cases like this. I won't keep her long.'

Doreen kept her eyes on him, fixing him with a
steely glare that seemed to peer into his very soul.
She didn't seem to blink at all. 'You did a lot of
talking before the court case,' she said, her pitch
and tone less aggressive now, but her words still uttered with assertion. 'And what good did anything
you said do us? No good at all, that's the truth of it.
What makes you think Anna would ever want to
talk to you again? You're lucky my husband isn't
here. He'd have seen you off our land long before
now.'

And who could blame him? Lewis thought. Maybe
it would have been better if he'd left it a few days
before calling or even not come at all. He was about
to give up and leave when Anna suddenly appeared
on the staircase behind her mother, slowly descending towards the red-tiled hallway, dressed in
faded blue jeans and a loose green jumper that
looked several sizes too big for her slight frame.
There were dark circles around both her sea-green

eyes. Sadness seemed to define her. Sorrow seemed to seep from every pore.

Lewis forced a thin smile as Anna looked him in the eye, and to his surprise, she said, 'Let him in, Mum,' in a voice resonating with raw emotion as she reached the bottom step, which creaked slightly under her weight.

The mother pulled her head back, eyes wide, staring as if her daughter had said the most ridiculous thing she'd ever heard.

'You want to invite him in? Are you sure?' Doreen asked with narrowed eyes, still not standing aside. 'You burst into tears when you saw his car coming down the lane. And now you say you want to talk to him. Please don't feel pressured into doing something you don't want to do. That's the last thing you need. I'm worried about you, *cariad*. I don't want you to get upset again. I don't know how much more you can take.'

Anna raised an open hand to her face and wiped away a tear as Lewis watched her. Looking over the mother's shoulder, he thought the girl looked broken, a shadow of the person she'd once been. But there was dignity about her too – an inner strength and determination he'd noted before. He admired her for that. Despite everything and everyone, she was still here.

'Let him in,' Anna said again. 'There's no point in putting it off. He's here now, so best get it over with. He wouldn't have come if it wasn't important.'

'Okay, have it your way. But I hope you don't end up regretting it. I don't want you in floods of tears again.'

Anna held one hand with the other. Lewis thought to stop it trembling.

'Thanks, Mum.'

Doreen Edwards and her tearful daughter led Lewis into a comfortable, well-furnished, pale-yellow-painted lounge to the left of the hall. There, he was invited to sit on one of two tan leather armchairs located to either side of a three-seater sofa festooned with variously coloured cushions. There was a roaring matt-black wood burner in the ancient hearth, blue-yellow flames dancing behind the glass.

Anna sat, but her mother remained standing.

'Cup of tea?' Doreen asked, shifting her weight from one foot to another.

Lewis nodded, forcing a smile, thinking the mother's mood was finally softening, and he was keen to keep it that way. And a cup of sweet tea was always welcome.

But it seemed Anna wasn't in the mood for refreshments. 'If you could leave us alone, please, Mum. There are things I need to discuss with Sergeant Lewis alone. Let's leave the tea for now.'

Doreen looked at her daughter with evident concern, asked her if she was sure, and called her *cariad* again, the Welsh word for love.

'Yes, thanks, I'm sure,' Anna replied, hugging her trembling body with both arms, clinging to herself as if her life depended on it, one thin leg crossed over the other. She wiped away another tear from her pale face and waited until her mother left the room before speaking again, sitting facing the detective but now looking at the floor.

Suddenly, Anna looked like a rabbit caught in the headlights, a startled look on her face as if close to panic. 'Have you s-seen social m-media?' she stuttered, her voice barely more than a whisper.

Lewis hadn't. It was a part of the modern world he hadn't yet embraced. He thought it a waste of time and effort. But he suspected he knew what was coming next. For a moment, he thought she might start sobbing as she had during her interview that first time he'd met her months before, her chest heaving as she gasped for breath.

'No, love, I haven't been online,' he said, pushing the memory from his mind and trying to sound as supportive as possible as he leaned towards her. 'What's happened? Is there something you need to tell me?'

Anna rushed her words now as if desperate to expunge them from her mouth for fear that she might be unable to say it if she delayed.

'Mark has posted about the trial and me on Facebook, Instagram, and Twitter. He's put a photo of himself with a big toothy grin on his stupid face, with one of me looking sad and upset right next to it. And there's even a video on YouTube of him dancing up and down and cheering with a glass of bubbly in his hand, as if he's won the lottery or something. And almost a thousand people have liked it already. And some are sharing it. It's going to go viral. Everyone is going to see it. It's like another nightmare come true. Doesn't he think he's hurt me enough? He really is a total bastard. He must hate me so very much.'

Lewis nodded, feeling genuine sympathy for the girl. Like many female victims her age, Anna re-minded him of his daughter.

'Oh, shit, I'm so sorry, love. Yeah, what a bastard. That's one word for him. I can think of a few more. I've called him most of them.'

Anna paused, took a deep breath, then continued, tears welling in her eyes again as she fought to retain control. 'I've reported it to the various sites, but it's all still there. Because it seems Mark has posted everything in a way that doesn't break the rules. He's clever like that. Speaking in the third person, never naming me, and not using the word rape, just saying that people sometimes make things up to get revenge and that needy people sometimes allege things that aren't even true. He tagged me and a load of other people, all my friends, and even the university. And everyone will know he's talking about me because of the photos and everything in the media. I sometimes wish I'd never reported the rape. I thought I was doing the right thing. But nothing good has come of it. All it did was make things worse. All the waiting for the trial for months on end, then having my personal life torn apart in court as if I'm a lying tart, and now this, all the awful publicity. And for what? A not-guilty verdict. What was the point of it all? No doubt Mark's laughing at me. Laughing his head off. And everyone is going to think I'm crazy. Just a demented girl who made up a story.'

Lewis emitted a long, deep, audible breath, feeling well outside his comfort zone but wanting to say something constructive. He could feel her pain. She'd expressed it so well. And it was written all over her face.

'You did the right thing, love,' was all he could think to say. And he said it with as much conviction as he could muster. But even then, he knew she had a point. And he suspected he didn't sound entirely persuaded despite his best efforts. The whole thing stank.

Anna glared at him now, red-faced, tears running down both cheeks as if she could no longer hold them back. 'The right thing? Did I? *Did I?* Are you sure? Because it doesn't seem that way to me.'

Lewis shifted in his seat, struggling to get comfortable. He suddenly became acutely aware of his aching back as his tired muscles stiffened, and he thought there was some truth in what she'd said. Her words almost sounded accusatory, as if she felt it was at least in part his fault. And maybe it was. He was a part of the system that let her down, a cog in the machine. What the hell could he say to that? He had to say something.

'You tried your best in very challenging circumstances, love. And the jury should have believed you. I don't know what they were thinking. You should be very proud of yourself. You were an absolute star in that courtroom. No one could have done more.'

Anna screwed up her face. 'But the jury didn't believe me. They thought every word I said was a lie. That rather than being a victim, I was some vindictive, scheming shrew who made everything up to get revenge on an innocent man just because he'd dumped me. As if any woman would do such a crazy thing. I had bruises, facial injuries, and even that wasn't enough to get a guilty verdict. Mark claimed I enjoyed rough sex, asked for it and craved it. And they believed him, not me, *him*! How totally fucking ridiculous is that!'

Lewis shook his head with a deep frown. He'd never heard her swear before. And it sounded somehow strange coming from her mouth.

'More fool them,' he said. That was all the detective had – the best he could offer. And he knew it wasn't enough – not even close.

Anna held her hands wide in front of her, palms forward, fingers spread as if pleading for something very different in her desire to rewrite the past.

'More fool them? Is that supposed to make me feel any better?' she asked, her shoulders slumped over her chest like a deflating beach toy. 'Because if it is, it doesn't. The whole world thinks I'm some kind of lying masochist. Kind words don't change a thing.'

Lewis searched for something positive to say. Anything hopeful, something that could improve the situation even slightly and make her feel better. But he knew there was only so much he could do. 'I'll contact the various social media companies for you as soon as I get back to the station,' he said with feigned enthusiasm. 'I'll make it official and see if I can get all that crap taken down asap. And I'll ask someone from Victim Support to contact you in the next day or two. See if they can sort out some compensation. It's a civil thing, all decided on the balance of probabilities rather than reasonable doubt. The not-guilty verdict doesn't affect your right to the money. You should be looking at about eleven grand if all goes well. I think that's the current figure.'

Anna paused for a few seconds as if deep in thought, finally looking Lewis full in the eye.

'It's never been about money. I never cared that Mark was well off. That was never important to me.'

Lewis nodded his acknowledgement. He'd never thought it was.

'I know that, love,' he said. 'But every little helps. And the cash will help pay the legal bills if you go for an injunction. It's got to be worth talking to your solicitor. See what she can do for you. Something keeping Shady away with a power of arrest would be best. At least then we can nick him if he gets too close.'

Anna let out a brief snorting laugh that was one of the saddest sounds Lewis had ever heard.

'Do you know, when I first met Mark, I thought he was really wonderful,' she mumbled through tears. 'He seemed like such a nice guy – so kind, so generous, and gentle – one of the nicest men I'd ever met. It wasn't just his good looks. No one could have seen how it would turn out – not me or anyone else.'

Lewis knew she'd never said a more valid word. And he wanted her to understand he knew it too. That he didn't doubt her for a second. 'That's how he wanted it, love,' he began, holding her gaze. 'Shady played you from the start. That's what he does. He knew exactly what he was doing. He was biding his time. Anticipating the end game. That's what he likes. It's his thing. And he's good at it.'

Anna fingered the dainty gold chain hanging around her neck.

'I realise that now. I saw it when it was too late. It was only then that I understood what he was. It's a pity the jury didn't see it too.'

Lewis was quick to reply. 'Yeah, absolutely, a real shame. I only wish they had. You did a great job in that witness box. I'm still baffled they managed to get it so horribly wrong.'

Suddenly, Anna's expression hardened as she lowered her hands to her lap. 'If my brother gets his hands on Mark, he'll beat the crap out of him. I know he wants to. And he could do it without any problem at all. He's a boxer. A Welsh champion who could go professional. Mum's told him to stay away from Mark. To stay out of it. And Dad agreed with her. He usually agrees with everything she says. But a bit of me hopes Dylan beats Mark up and gets away with it. At least then, the pig would know how he made me feel. There'd be some justice in that.'

Once again, Lewis silently pondered that he'd love to do the same. To smash Shady to a blubbering mess of blood and snot with a flurry of powerful blows as the scrote begged for mercy, all his arrogant self-confidence gone. 'Best not, love,' he said with an empathetic look. 'I'd have a quiet word with your brother if I were you. Ask him to leave it alone. He'd only risk being banged up in Swansea nick with a criminal record for violence. That would be the end of his professional boxing career before it's even started. Shady would have the last laugh. And nobody wants that. Least of all me.'

She snapped out her response. 'Oh, so some people do get sent to prison, then? Not Mark, of course; that would be too much to ask. Not a rapist who's attacked an innocent girl and ruined her life. But maybe my brother, if he chooses to take revenge. Wouldn't that be an irony? Where's the fairness in that?'

Lewis felt his entire body tense, thinking her words a good point well made. An eye for an eye sometimes made sense to him. And particularly where sex offenders were concerned. And it did now. If Anna had been his daughter, he'd have ended Shady, put him in the ground and risked paying the price. But the law was the law, and he was an officer. So best keep his opinions to himself.

'Do you want me to talk to your brother for you?' he asked. 'I could put him in the picture. Tell him you talked to me. Warn him off for his own good.'

A quick reply as Anna shook her head. 'No, no, absolutely not. Please don't. Dylan's lost all trust in the police. And he wouldn't be happy I've talked to you. He'd think I've spoken out of turn.'

Lewis nodded with a slight movement of his head and said, 'Okay.' Just the one word, thinking maybe it was time to leave. That he'd done his bit and said enough. Because the look of relief on Anna's face told him all he needed to know.

He was about to stand, relieved the morning's meeting was reaching a timely conclusion, when Anna said there was something else she needed to mention, stopping him in his tracks. He settled back in his seat, hoping that whatever she was about to say wouldn't take too long.

'Mark posted about you too,' she said. 'On social media. I saw his post on Facebook last night.'

Lewis's eyes narrowed. 'About me?'

Anna nodded twice. 'Yeah, and what he wrote wasn't very nice.'

Lewis gritted his teeth. 'What sort of thing are we talking about?'

She avoided his gaze. 'Well, there's a photo of you outside Boots the Chemist in Carmarthen with an odd look on your face. I think you must have been coughing or sneezing. That's how it looked to me, anyway. And there's a short poem. Just a few lines.'

Lewis screwed up his face as his blood pressure soared to a savage high. 'A poem?'

'Not a nice one,' she replied in a whisper. 'Mark likes that sort of thing. He thinks it's funny. He used to make up little verses about me when we were to-gether. Flattering ones at first. But, of course, that changed. They became quite mean towards the end. And then cruel. Anything to knock my self-esteem and confidence. I think he liked to upset me. No, I know he did. It's only now, looking back, I can see what he was doing.'

'And this poem about me is on Facebook, yeah? Is that what you're telling me?'

'That's right. Just a silly thing. I was in two minds about telling you. But I thought you'd want to know.'

Lewis felt his chest tighten. And for some rea-son, his ears felt hot. 'Can you show me?' he asked.

Anna fetched a silver-coloured laptop from where it was charging on a pine shelf to the right of the room's only window. As Lewis watched her cross the room, he noticed she'd lost weight she couldn't afford to lose. She had to be, what? Seven, maybe seven and a half stone at most. No wonder her mother was worried. If she was his daughter, he would be too.

'It should be easy enough to find,' she said as she returned to her seat. 'He tagged me and quite a few others, the same as he did in his posts about me. It's obvious why.'

Lewis watched in brooding silence as Anna opened the computer on her lap and began tapping the keyboard with fast-moving fingers. He noticed all her nails were bitten low.

'Ah, yes, there it is, still there,' she said. 'And it's getting quite a bit of attention – even more so than some of the posts about me last time I looked. People seem to think it's funny – well, most of them, anyway.'

Lewis resisted a strong impulse to swear.

'Can you pass it over?'

Anna did as he asked, resting the laptop on the low coffee table immediately in front of him as he took his black-framed reading glasses from the inside pocket of his jacket. He perched the spectacles at the halfway point of his nose before picking up the computer, carefully studying the bright screen with a scowl that spread across his face. And as he stared, he couldn't quite believe the evidence of his eyes. There was a photo of him, all right. There it was, undeniable. Just as she'd said. A picture taken after his return from Swansea to Carmarthen the previous day, after he'd parked his car, as he'd hurried past Boots on his way to the rugby club. And Anna was right; he was sneezing, head back, mouth wide open, dark mercury fillings in full view. Shit! Damn Shady. The twat must have followed him. And the photo was awful. He looked old, grey, fat, and ridiculous. So different to the man he felt inside. A laughing stock for all to see.

Lewis dragged his eyes away from the bright colour image, reading the short rhyme written above it:

> *Sergeant Lewis*
> *What a dork*
> *20 stone and made of pork*
> *I'm free, the judge wore a wig*
> *And Porky Lewis is just a big fat pig*

Lewis sat there, quietly seething for a second or two before slowly closing the laptop and placing it back on the coffee table, asking himself why the post was getting to him quite as much as it was. He'd been called a lot worse over the years, but never so publicly and never in such a humiliating way. That was probably it. And worst of all, the stupid rhyme held some truth. Shone a light on his decline. There was the explanation right there. And the boys at the station and rugby club would love it. They'd be taking the piss for God only knew how long. He imagined a new nickname, Porky, or something similar. And he'd have to take it on the chin. Pretend it wasn't getting to him. Or he'd never hear the last of it till his dying day.

Lewis rose stiffly to his feet, keen to hide his feelings of indignity. He was frustrated by what he saw as his over-the-top reaction and angry that he'd let a tosser like Shady get to him at all. More than that, he knew Anna was dealing with much worse – so much worse.

'I have reported it for you,' she said. 'I did as soon as I saw it. I thought you'd want me to. I can't believe so many people think it's so hilarious. It just seems ridiculous to me.'

'Thanks, love. That's very kind of you,' he replied with genuine gratitude. 'But you concentrate on your own problems. You've got more than enough to deal with without worrying about me. And I'll make sure the compensation is sorted out for you as quickly as possible. Is there anything else you want to say, anything at all, or anything I can do for you before I'm on my way?'

Anna stood, her pretty face pensive. He could see the tension in her haunted eyes before she spoke, as if what she was about to say truly mattered. 'Well, there... there is one thing I... I haven't told you about. I haven't told anyone. Not even my mother. I, I, haven't had the courage until now. But Mark's already dating someone new. He's changed his Facebook profile from single to in a relationship. And I'd hate another girl to go through what I went through, or worse. I think you need to know about everything he did to me. If something awful happened to the new girl and I hadn't spoken out, I couldn't forgive myself.'

Lewis reached out, touching Anna's arm for a fleeting moment an inch or two above the elbow. 'Okay, I'm listening,' he said with genuine concern. He'd noted the tension in her voice, the evident angst.

Anna let out a groan and was about to speak again when the lounge door suddenly opened, Doreen peering around the frame.

'Is everything all right in here?' she asked. 'Are

you both ready for that cuppa? You've been talking for almost twenty minutes.'

Anna was quick to reply. 'Sergeant Lewis is just about to leave, Mum. We're done for today. And I'm... I'm getting tired. I need to rest.'

Lewis glanced at Anna, thinking the timing of her mother's arrival couldn't have been worse. Although, a part of him was glad to be getting out of here.

'You didn't want to discuss that one last thing before I go?' he asked, suspecting and half hoping the answer would be no.

Anna dabbed at her face. 'No, it's nothing, forget it; I've taken up enough of your time.'

'No rush,' replied Lewis, feeling he had to. 'I've got as long as it takes.'

Anna appeared to be considering her response when her mother interceded. 'Didn't you hear what my daughter said, Sergeant? She's tired. Isn't that obvious? I really don't know why you've come here bothering us anyway. It's time for you to go.'

Lewis turned, looking back at Anna as he reached the front door, his hand on the brass handle. He thought she looked conflicted, standing there in her loose-fitting jumper, opening her mouth but then closing it as if there was something she still wanted to say. As if her mother's well-intentioned intervention had been ill-advised.

'You know where I am,' he said, looking directly at Anna. 'And you've got my number. If you need to talk, arrange to see me at the police station or give me a ring day or night. I'll always help if I can.'

And with that, Lewis left, glad to be out of there but still asking himself what Anna would have told him had she had the chance. He spotted Dylan Edwards, a heavily muscled man in his mid-twenties with short-cropped black hair, coming out of a stone outbuilding on his left as he settled in the driver's seat and started the engine. Dylan stood stock-still, hands on hips as his mother had earlier, and stared at Lewis with unblinking eyes as the detective engaged first gear, pressed his foot down on the accelerator and drove slowly off. He flashed a quick smile before he left the younger man's sight, but it wasn't reciprocated. Dylan's dark expression didn't change, as if it were cast in bronze. Hardly surprising, thought Lewis as he drove back along the track towards the A40. The police had played their part in what was likely the worst period of the Edwards family's life. And it hadn't gone well. Shady was free. And now the scumbag was taunting Anna just because he could. So the family didn't have much to thank the force for, if anything at all. Maybe a bit of compensation would help? It would at least provide official recognition of Anna's suffering. The booby prize. It wasn't a prison sentence. But it had to be better than nothing. And it wasn't like he had much else to offer. Lewis consoled himself with that.

5

Mark Shady, the not-guilty verdict, and his cynical, mocking social media posts repeatedly came to Lewis's mind as he drove back to Carmarthen, sometimes breaking the speed limit despite the wet road. The detective pictured Shady's manic, grinning face in his mind's eye as clear as day, the predator's bright blue eyes, dark, slick hair, and those overly white Turkey teeth, gleaming like freshly fallen snow, too perfect to be real.

Lewis spent the entire journey on autopilot, obsessing about the man he now considered an archenemy of all that was good. He felt his whole body tense as he thought about Shady's objectionable personality, the absolute distress he inflicted on his many victims, and how he avoided conviction at the cost of others. He'd rarely detested a man more.

When he reached the pleasant west Wales market town he called home, driving slowly past Shady's restaurant at the lower end of Merlin's Lane and peering in through the tinted glass, Lewis briefly considered paying Shady a visit. But the detective quickly decided the time wasn't right to mark Shady's card, however tempting the prospect. He could see two, maybe three people through the partially open window blinds. And the last thing Lewis wanted or needed was potential witnesses if he were to bend the rules. Witnesses with camera phones who could record everything he said and did. As if he was the criminal, he was the bad guy. Not like the good old days when people respected the police and kept their noses out of his business. Another modern world development he didn't welcome or appreciate. He would talk to Shady. It would happen. He was determined about that. But now was not the time.

The intermittent rain had stopped by the time Lewis arrived back at police headquarters just before eleven. The sun had broken through the grey clouds and bathed the entire area in a soft winter light that had gone some way to raising his spirits, if only briefly. At least, he said to himself, he wasn't going to get soaked again. It was a small win, but a win nonetheless.

Lewis exited the car with a throaty groan, trudging across the car park, picking his way past the many puddles until he reached the broad steps leading to the entrance he knew so very well. And once again, as he approached the glass door, Shady's immature poem came to mind. And Lewis was already anticipating the inevitable reaction to the various social media posts as he entered the modernist building. He could almost hear the tittering laughter, some to his face from long-serving colleagues who had the confidence to mock him and some behind his back from those who didn't know him so well. Nothing in a small town stayed secret for very long.

Lewis reminded himself that he didn't mind a joke as he nodded his acknowledgement to the middle-aged female civilian staff member at reception before heading further into the building. But there was a limit, he told himself; a bit of fun was one thing and scorn quite another. And the source of the hilarity had to count, didn't it? Shady? Of course it did. Nothing the bastard said or did was very funny at all.

Lewis decided on a quick lunch after a couple of hours' paperwork: a plate of much-needed stodge to raise his flagging spirits, something warm and tasty. He still had a slight hangover from the night before and thought another canteen visit would do him some good. It would set him up nicely for his two o'clock meeting with Kesey and whatever else the afternoon would bring.

A long-serving female sergeant, seated close to Lewis as he stood impatiently waiting at the serving counter, looked up at him with a mischievous grin and a wink. The two had trained together many years before, but they didn't have much in common other than the job. They were acquaintances more than friends. But that didn't stop her from commenting, as he knew she inevitably would.

'Fame at last, Ray,' she called out, a glass of water in hand, raising it to shoulder level as if toasting success with sparkling champagne.

Lewis turned stiffly to face her, swivelling his head and looking down with a deep frown he couldn't have hidden if he'd tried.

'Oh, you've seen it then?'

She let out a girlish giggle, which Lewis thought was misplaced given her age. 'Everyone has,' she replied with another laugh. 'You know what it's like. News spreads like wildfire in this place.'

He shook his head slowly, his lips pressed together. 'Oh, great, no surprise there.'

'I'd report it to Facebook if I were you,' she added, the grin leaving her face. 'Get it taken down. That's what I'd do.'

It's a bit late now, thought Lewis, reaching the front of the short queue, keenly anticipating his meal.

'Yeah, I know, I will,' he said, keen to bring the conversation to an end.

Lewis ordered baked beans, double egg, and chips, one of his favourite meals. He washed it down with a mug of milky builder's tea, sweetened with three heaped teaspoonfuls of white sugar, having recently cut down from four. Lunch was welcome, as always. It filled a gap. One of the few pleasures he had left. But as he sat there brooding, he was beginning to regret going to the canteen at all despite the toothsome fare. The number of supposedly humorous comments sent his way quickly became irritating. Although, he did his best not to let it show. Because that would only encourage some of his fellow officers. He knew that full well. And he knew he'd do much the same if it was one of them in the spotlight. As annoying as it all was, it was best to sit there and get it over with. It was the police way. A bit of piss-taking meant you belonged.

Lewis rushed his meal, one large mouthful after another followed by generous slurps of sugary tea. He'd been a fast eater for as long as he could remember, but today was speedy even by his standards. He pushed his empty plate aside, burped at full volume, and then stood, planning to do a bit of overdue computer work before seeing Kesey as scheduled. No doubt she'd have a joke or two for him too. Something else he'd have to put up with, like it or not. All part of the job. Such was life.

Lewis pushed open Kesey's office door a few seconds before the arranged time, knocking once and entering without waiting to be asked.

Kesey put down her pen, pushed a thick sheaf of papers aside, and gave a slight nod of welcome.

'Okay, let's get it over with,' he said, standing before her cluttered desk. 'I know you've seen it. The bastard used the force hashtag – that and a few others.'

'Several officers, and even your rugby club!'

Lewis frowned hard. 'Come on, spit it out. I know you must have something else to say for yourself?'

He could tell Kesey was stifling a laugh before she spoke. And he had a good idea what was coming next. 'No, I think you looked very smart in that big red padded coat. You were quite the man about town. But why did you have your mouth wide open? Were you trying to catch flies?'

Lewis resisted the impulse to smile as he sat himself down. He hadn't realised how ridiculous the coat looked until he'd seen the Facebook photo. But it had been warm on a cold winter day, so the style still didn't bother him a great deal. He'd told himself he was all about substance, that he'd never been a looker. So what did it matter? The coat did its job.

'Is there anything else you want to add while you're at it?' he asked, crossing one leg over the other, trying to look a lot more relaxed than he felt. 'I'm sure there must be something. I bet you can't wait to tell me.'

'Porky! Now, there's a name to conjure with. I think it suits you rather well. Not that it's very original. Wasn't there a cartoon character with a similar name back in the day?'

Lewis raised himself in his seat, both feet now planted firmly on the floor, his body language betraying his true feelings, as it often did.

'Yeah, yeah, laugh all you want. Hilarious, as always. But I'll tell you one thing. I'm going to nail that Shady bastard the first chance I get. If he thinks he's getting away with taking the piss, he's very sadly mistaken. I'll get him if it's the last thing I do. He won't be laughing then.'

All of a sudden, Kesey looked more serious. 'Oh, here we go again.'

Lewis stiffened. 'What the hell is that supposed to mean?'

'You know exactly what I'm talking about.'

'Do I?' he asked, a little put out despite having had similar conversations before.

'Have a quiet word with Shady by all means, but please be careful. He's not an ordinary criminal. You know the way his mind works. He was taking the piss, yeah, that's obvious. But maybe there's more to it than that. He may well be looking to provoke you into doing something you shouldn't do. Any excuse for him to make an official complaint. And I know what you're like. Don't go over the top. And remember, Shady's little joke doesn't break any laws. You don't want to play into the bastard's hands. He'd love that. And I could do without the paperwork.'

'There's a few things I'd like to break.'

'Don't do anything stupid, Ray. That's all I'm saying. Use your head.'

He shrugged, momentarily raising one shoulder.

'Trust me, I will,' he said, not entirely convinced he would. 'I know the score. The devious little git isn't going to get the better of me.'

Kesey looked across at him, still sat there with a scowl on his face. She shook her head and sighed.

'Okay, right, let's move on,' she began. 'I've said my bit. How did it go at the Edwards place?'

Lewis asked himself how much he should say. Should he give her the full unedited details or just the highlights? There was no telling which she wanted. It could be one or the other, depending on her mood and the case. It changed from one day to the next.

'Not great,' he replied, thinking she'd respond. If she wanted to know more, she'd say so. That was her way.

'Not great, how?' Kesey asked. 'Can you expand on that for me?'

Lewis gathered his thoughts. 'I saw Anna and her mum. The father wasn't in. They're both gutted, obviously; it goes without saying. Shady got off. Why the hell wouldn't they be? And he's been posting some really unpleasant shit about Anna on social media. Far worse than his crap about me. It wasn't enough for the bastard to rape the girl. Now he's got to publicly humiliate her too, for all the world to see. What a total prick! We've got to find a way of putting him away.'

Kesey nodded with a frown. 'I saw that. I want you to take screenshots of everything before contacting the various sites. And have a word with the CPS; Liz Aitken would probably be best. I don't think Shady's posts constitute any offences as they stand. But let's see what Liz says. It could be seen as criminal if we build up a picture.'

Lewis thought it unlikely but didn't say so, moving the conversation along. 'There's more bad news. Anna told me Shady's already in a new relationship, no doubt grooming his next victim. Maybe I should have a word with the unlucky woman. Warn her off. Tell her who she's dealing with. Put her in the picture. It's highly likely she'll have already heard things about Shady, seen things online and maybe on TV. But you know what he's like. If he can convince a jury he's innocent, he can convince her too. I could try to put that right.'

'He was found not guilty, Ray. There's nothing on his record sheet. And there's been no civil proceedings, no injunctions, nothing. You need to remember that. If kids were involved, we could justify it under child protection procedures. But otherwise, I can't see it.'

Lewis let out a snorting laugh.

'Oh, yeah, the bastard's as innocent as a newborn baby. I'm not likely to forget.'

Kesey looked at the screen of her desktop computer, tapping a few keys.

'Ah, yeah, there you go,' she said with a nod, pushing her fringe away from her eyes. 'Shady's posted a photo of himself and the new girl on his restaurant's Facebook page. Slim, blonde, and young like most of the others. She only looks, what? Eighteen or nineteen maybe, certainly no older than twenty.'

When Lewis stood to look, his expression quickly darkened. He looked sullen, even for him. 'Oh, shit, I know her; that's Mike Flowers's daughter, Carly. He's a DC in the Pembrokeshire Division. She's in her first year at Trinity Uni, studying English, I think, with a teaching career in mind. Although I could be wrong. I was only half-listening when he told me. He's going to love this. His little girl in a relationship with an evil scrote like Shady. It doesn't get any worse than that. Are you going to tell him or am I?'

Kesey let out a breath. 'How well do you know Flowers?' she asked.

Lewis lowered himself back down into his seat. 'Well enough. We've shared a few pints over the years. We're big rugby fans. Both went to the Wales–Ireland Six Nations game in Cardiff last year with a few of the lads. His nickname's Daisy, for obvious reasons. I consider him a friend.'

Kesey nodded. 'Okay, that's clear enough, and I've never met the bloke. So you talk to him. It would be better coming from someone he knows. Give him a ring. Do it today. And let me know how it goes.'

'Will do,' he said with a nod.

Kesey checked her watch, something he knew she often did when about to end a meeting. 'Anything else?' she asked, the sheaf of papers already back in hand.

'I think Anna has something else to tell me,' he said, rising slowly to his feet, placing his hands on the arms of the chair to aid his movement. 'I'll keep you posted if she gets back in touch and it's anything interesting.'

'Bit late now,' she said. 'The trial's done.'

'Yeah, I know, but anything she says could be useful for future reference.'

Kesey nodded, looking less than persuaded. 'Okay, fair point. Thanks, Ray, I'd better get on. These statements aren't going to read themselves.'

He turned on reaching her office door. 'Any news on your promotion?'

She frowned hard. 'It's not happening.'

He pulled his head back. 'What? I thought it was nailed on.'

'So did I, Ray, so did I.'

'What the hell happened there? I'm guessing Halliday had something to do with it. The miserable git!'

She glanced at her watch again, pushing up her sleeve.

'I'll tell you all about it another time when I'm less rushed.'

Lewis knew his DI was closing the conversation, avoiding further discussion and not wanting to share. And he respected that. It was her prerogative. Kesey was ambitious. She wasn't like him, satisfied with his status and role. Missing out on her promotion would have hurt. And any further questions would be unwelcome at best. She might choose to explain when ready, or perhaps not at all. But now, it was time to go.

6

When he entered his shared CID office a few minutes later, Lewis kicked his grey metal wastepaper bin with such force it bounced off the nearest wall with a resounding clang. Everyone else was out, which pleased him. The day had already been a challenge even by his usual policing standards, and he strongly suspected it was about to get worse. At least now he could have a private conversation without listening ears. And, he pondered, there were definite advantages to that.

The detective lowered himself onto his overburdened black leather swivel chair, bemoaning the phone call he was about to make and his aching lower back, which never seemed to let up. As he settled in his seat, shifting his weight in a hopeless attempt to get comfortable, he imagined how he'd feel were it Flowers ringing *him* to say his own daughter was in a relationship with a slimy little prick like Mark Shady. It would be a bad dream come true.

Lewis leaned back, took off his shoes, rested his feet on his desk, and picked up his office phone with fat sausage fingers. He'd decided against a coffee for the time being because it was best to make the call. Yeah, get it over with. It had to be done. He was the bearer of bad news, whichever way he looked at it. There was no point in delay.

Lewis dialled Haverfordwest Police Station's direct number from memory and only had to wait a matter of seconds before receiving an answer. 'It's DS Ray Lewis, headquarters. I need a word with Mike Flowers.'

'Daisy's out at the moment, Sarge. Can I take a message?'

Lewis swore silently under his breath.

'I'm in all afternoon. Tell him to give me a ring. And it's important. Tell him that for me. Asap. It's not something that can wait.'

'Will do, Sarge.'

Lewis did a bit of paperwork, a part of the job he hated, made a coffee with extra sugar to raise his flagging spirits, and then only had to wait about twenty minutes or so before DC Flowers returned his call. Lewis was chewing a chunk of rich dark Swiss chocolate and reading through a burglary statement relating to the Roberts case when his phone rang. He recognised Flowers's Cardiff accent as soon as he spoke, for some reason thinking he sounded almost Italian, perhaps even more so than Welsh. So different from his own Carmarthen tones.

'All right, Ray. It's Daisy. I'm told you need to speak to me. What can I do for you?'

Lewis manoeuvred what was left of the salty-sweet chocolate around his mouth with his tongue for a second or two before swallowing. He quickly decided to get straight to the point rather than engage in small talk. It was terrible news, the worst. Why delay the inevitable? There was no way of softening the blow.

'It's, er, it's about your Carly, mate. She's fine; nothing has happened to her. I want to be clear on that right from the start. But there is something you need to know.'

Flowers responded with an urgent tone, his concern evident. 'Oh, God. Okay, Ray, I'm listening.'

'Take a look at the Facebook page for the Shady Shack Pizza Restaurant in Carmarthen. It's named after the owner. A nasty little fucker called Mark Shady. He's got a long history of sexual offences against young women, all about your Carly's age, and none of them proved. And your Carly is in a relationship with the slippery bastard. There's a photo of them together on the restaurant page. And they look far too close for comfort. Arms around each other's shoulders, smiling. I thought I'd better give you a heads-up. I'd want someone to tell me if it was my daughter we were talking about. Sorry to give you the bad news. I know it can't be easy to hear.'

There was a brief silence. Then what sounded like a long exhale of breath blown through the mouth. Lewis could picture the other man grimacing even before he spoke: the concern on his face, the stress of it all.

'I know all about it, Ray. And all about Shady too. That Anna Edwards case you dealt with got a good deal of publicity. You must know that. It was all over the local papers, front page, and on the Welsh evening news a couple of nights running. I've tried talking to Carly, and so's my missus. Of course we have. But the girl doesn't want to listen. I'm tearing my fucking hair out, to be honest. I know Shady's a nasty piece of work. But Carly's completely besotted with the bloke. Thinks he's the best thing that's ever happened to her. Actually used those words. And nothing me or the wife says makes any difference at all. It's like we're banging our heads against a brick wall. She was such a good daughter growing up. A right daddy's girl. She used to listen to everything the missus or I said. But these days, it's as if we're the enemy. Like we're somehow out to harm her life.'

Lewis broke off another large chunk of dark chocolate, looking at it lovingly but resisting the almost overwhelming temptation to lift it to his mouth. He realised he was salivating, wiping his lips with a hand. Sometimes, he observed, the anticipation could be almost as good as the eating – not quite, but close.

'Oh, shit. Kids, eh,' Lewis said with feeling, momentarily thinking back to his own daughter's troubled teenage years. 'The Edwards girl thought Shady was the bee's knees too, before, well, you know what I'm talking about. Before he showed her who he really is. He's one manipulative bastard. Cons his victims into thinking he's one of the good guys before finally showing them different. One of the most devious gits I've ever had the misfortune to deal with. And there's been a few.'

There was another pained sigh at the other end of the line before Flowers spoke again.

'I can't believe how naïve Carly is, even after growing up a copper's daughter. Be careful who you trust; I told her that time and again when she was a kid. People aren't always what they seem. Not everyone is nice. Some are evil bastards, like Shady, who'll do you harm. But she thinks me and her mother are worrying about nothing. She keeps saying Shady was found innocent, that the Edwards girl made everything up for the attention.'

Lewis made a face. 'That couldn't be further from the truth.'

'I know that, Ray. I don't need any convincing. But try telling Carly that. I've tried to tell her of the reality. But I'm just not getting through. And the more I say, the worse it seems to get. She put the phone down on me last night mid-sentence. And didn't even answer when I rang again. That's not something she's ever done before. She was as good as gold before meeting him. Like I said. You couldn't hope for a nicer girl. I can't believe how much she's changed. And it's all happened so very fast. Crazy!'

It all made sense to Lewis; the pattern fitted. There was Shady's MO right there.

'That's what Shady does: isolates his targets by

turning them against friends and family. Not an easy situation. I bet the bastard's loving this. That's the sort of bloke he is. Everything is a game to him. And if there's a copper involved, that won't rattle him. Not one little bit. If anything, he'll see it as a challenge to overcome. And he'll still think he can win. The man thinks he's invincible, a classic psycho. Only his needs matter. His and nobody else's. The quicker he's off the streets, the better for everyone. And the happier I'll be.'

Flowers sounded close to panic when he responded, the pitch of his voice uneven.

'A target? You think Carly's a target? You think Shady's planning to rape her? He's that bad?'

'I'm sorry, mate, I shouldn't have used the word. Force of habit. You know what it's like.'

There was another brief silence, three or four seconds at most.

'No, you're right,' Flowers said dejectedly. 'That's exactly what my Carly is. A fucking target! I'll ring her again tonight. See if she'll talk to me. She's an intelligent girl. I know she'll see sense in the end. She'll see Shady for what he is once the shine wears off. But how long is that going to take? And what if something horrendous happens before she finally gets the message? It doesn't bear thinking about. I

can't believe all this is happening. And it's all happened so very quickly. Although, I think they were
first in contact when he was still on remand.'

Lewis furrowed his brow.

'Really? You think?'

'She hasn't said as much.' A short snorting
laugh. 'She hasn't told me very much at all. But
that's the only sense I can make of it. He's a good-
looking bloke who plays the victim. And Carly's a
sucker for a sob story. I had a word with a guard I
know at Swansea nick. Dai Williams, he's from my
village. He's a good bloke. And it seems several
women wrote to Shady while he was banged up on
remand. Dai didn't have the details, no names, or at
least none he could remember. But he did say it's
something Shady used to boast about to anyone
who'd listen – other prisoners, the guards. He used
to call the women his fan club, the Pink Pussies. Apparently, he thought it was funny. The fucking
wanker!'

Lewis nodded his head, thinking it all rang true.

'That sounds like Shady,' he said. 'Exactly the
sort of thing he'd revel in. He loves himself. Anything to feed that big ego. I'd love to bring it
crashing down. And one day I will.'

A little groan at the other end of the line. Almost

as if Flowers was in physical pain. 'Yeah, what a
lovely guy! A right charmer.'

Lewis gave a cough, clearing his throat, and
wished he could light up a cigar to complement the
chocolate. Chocolate, coffee, and nicotine – what a
combination. 'Just keep trying to get through to her,
mate,' he said, focusing back on the conversation.
'That's all you can do. And maybe send a text if she
won't speak to you, or let the missus do the talking,
woman to woman. She might have more success
than you. It has to be worth a try.'

'I keep getting pictures in my head. Horrible pictures. To me, Carly's still my little girl. And it's my
job to protect her. But how the hell do I do that if
she thinks I'm the bad guy? No one loves her more
than me. Not even her mum. What part of that
doesn't she understand? Shady's got her looking at
everything upside down. I'll tear the dirty bastard
apart if he ever hurts her. Beat him to a pulp, job or
not.'

Poor sod, thought Lewis, considering the call
even more challenging than he'd anticipated. And
he'd forgotten how much Flowers liked to talk.
Daisy never was the strong and silent type.

'Do you want me to have a quiet word with
Carly for you?' Lewis asked. 'I'd be happy to, if that

helps, off the record. I could tell her about all the other allegations we've investigated. Anna Edwards wasn't the only one Shady assaulted. And the stories were all very similar – far too consistent to be a coincidence. They can't all be making it up. I could tell your Carly that, explain it. Just say the word.'

Lewis heard what sounded like another groan before Flowers spoke again. 'I only wish it was that simple. But it is not. Shady's convinced her the police have got some sort of vendetta against him. That it's personal, vindictive. And he's talked about you. Told her you're out to get him for no good reason. Even that you put ideas into all those women's heads. That you're willing to do anything and everything to convict an innocent man because of some crazy argument the two of you had when he made you look a fool.'

Lewis clenched his hands into fists, digging short nails into sweaty palms.

'That's total bollocks!'

'Yeah, I know that, Ray. But try convincing Carly. Shady's had her watching all sorts of conspiracy crap online: the anti-vax stuff, the moon landing, holocaust denial, a one-world government, chemtrails, amongst other things. And she's falling for it all, swallowing the lot. The more I say, the less she believes me. She thinks I'm a part of it all, and you are too. If you turn up, well, that's just going to make things worse. In her eyes, it'll prove what Shady's told her is true. That we're out to get him. That he's the victim.'

'Oh, for fuck's sake, why do people fall for that shit?'

'Beats me,' Flowers replied with feeling.

'Maybe you should have a word with Shady?' Lewis asked. 'Face to face, up close and personal. To let him know you're keeping a close eye. Tell him that you'll nick him if he crosses a line. It might do some good.'

Another groan. 'I already have, Ray. I threatened the bastard. Told him I'd punch his lights out if he didn't fuck off and leave Carly alone. And he laughed at me. The bastard actually laughed! Said that he had a hidden camera and had recorded everything I said. And that he'll show Carly the film if I ever bother him again. He even threatened to post it on social media to end my career.'

Lewis screwed up his face. 'Oh, shit, that's typical of the scrote. Exactly the sort of thing he'd do. Do you think he's really got the recording? He could be full of crap. It's the sort of bullshit he'd come up with.'

'Hang on, let me close the door. One of the brass is hanging about in the corridor... There, that's better... I doubt Shady's got anything on me. We were outside in a quiet car park. It was dark, cloudy, gone eleven at night. And he couldn't have known I was following him until I got out of the car and approached him. I was careful. I guess he could have had a small hidden device somewhere on him. It's not impossible. But why would he? Why would anyone? And even if he had, why would it be on? I could see his hands the entire time.'

Lewis silently contemplated that, knowing Shady as well as he did, it wasn't beyond the bounds of possibility. He could have guessed Flowers would turn up at some point, anticipating his arrival and preparing accordingly. The snake would do anything, however unlikely, to gain an advantage. But it seemed a long shot nonetheless. Daisy was probably right. It was likely an empty threat.

'I'd go and see him again if I were you, mate. Ask him to show you the recording. If he's got it, he will. He couldn't resist winding you up. At least then you'll know what you're dealing with. And if not, if there's nothing to show, you're off the hook. You'll know he's full of shit. My feeling is, if he had you recorded, he'd have already used it against you. At

the very least, he'd have shown your Carly long before now. He couldn't resist playing his winning
card. He'd be creaming his underpants. That's the
sort of bloke he is.'

'Yeah, I've been thinking along the same lines.
But he could be playing the waiting game. Building
up the tension. Can I take the risk of antagonising
the bloke? That's what I'm asking myself. I could be
inviting trouble.'

Lewis rolled his eyes, shaking his head slowly.

'If Shady did record you, you're already screwed
unless you can get your hands on it and destroy it.
And if not, which seems likely to me, you need to
know. It's got to be better than doing fuck all. He's
got you by the balls, as things stand. You're not going
to stop worrying. And that achieves nothing at all.'

There was another brief silence.

'I'll give it some thought,' Flowers finally said.
'You're probably right.'

'Of course I am,' Lewis replied. 'You know it
makes sense.'

'Am I right in thinking Shady lives above the
pizza place?'

'Yeah, he's got a flat up there, two bedrooms. I
searched the place. Waste of time. Didn't find any-

thing helpful. Shady made sure of that. Why do you ask?'

'Oh, no reason. I was just wondering, that's all.'

Lewis asked himself if there was more to it. 'Okay, mate,' he replied, recalling that Flowers sometimes had a tendency towards indecisiveness. 'Give me a shout anytime if you need to talk. You know where I am. And let me know when you're next in Carmarthen. We'll go for a pint at the club. As I recall, it's your round.'

Lewis was about to end the call and focus back on his chocolate bar when Flowers spoke his name tentatively, sounding hesitant.

'Ray...'

'Yeah?'

'You will keep all this to yourself, won't you? About me threatening Shady? About the recording?'

Lewis shrugged in frustration because some questions didn't need asking.

'Of course I will, mate. No worries, it goes without saying. You never told me anything. This conversation didn't happen. Everything is between you and me.'

Flowers's relief was almost palpable, even at the end of the phone line. 'Thanks, Ray. I appreciate it.

And I'll think about what you've said. Do you want me to let you know what happens?'

'Yeah, of course, keep me in the loop. But nothing in writing. Not even encrypted. Give me a ring or, better still, face to face.'

'Okay, noted. And thanks again. Not everyone would have done the same.'

Lewis put the phone down and drained the last of his coffee. He quickly finished his chocolate bar, then put his shoes back on. Standing stiffly, he left the room and approached Kesey's office door, knocking twice before opening it and entering. She'd asked for an update; he knew she wouldn't let it go, so he'd give her one. And he'd already decided to stick as close to the truth as possible without incriminating Flowers. It was easier that way. Kesey could be extremely astute. He'd be less likely to be caught out.

'Have you got two minutes for a chat, boss?' he murmured, surprised to feel uncomfortable with a deception he saw as necessary. Kesey was a stickler for the rules – standing orders, everything by the book – and she never appreciated his ways and means, not even when they paid off. So some things were best kept to himself.

The DI looked up from her piles of red-tape paperwork with tired eyes.

'Yeah, but make it quick.'

'I've spoken with Mike Flowers. It's all good. He already knew. And he's spoken to his daughter. Let her know the risks. We've done our bit. We can't do any more.'

'Anything else I need to know?'

Lewis began retreating towards the door.

'No, that's it. Thought I should let you know. Right, I'd better make a move. I can see you're busy. If there's nothing else, I'll leave you in peace.'

Kesey's eyes narrowed.

'You seem a bit flustered, Ray. In more of a hurry than usual. What aren't you telling me? There's something up. I know there is. I can read you like a book.'

Lewis put his hand on the door handle, wondering what the hell to say. He searched for an adequate response. He'd given Flowers a commitment and wasn't about to betray a friend.

'No, I, er, I was just thinking about your promotion again, that's all. I know it meant a lot to you. Becoming a chief inspector and all that. I thought it was a cert. It's been playing on my mind.'

She glared at him. 'Not now, please, Ray; I told you I'll tell you about it when I'm ready. Close the door after you. I need to get on.'

7

Lewis was sitting at his desk, focused on his computer screen and drafting an overdue email to a local CPS lawyer, when his phone rang just after eleven the following morning. He briefly massaged an aching knee, digging in his thumbs, then picked up the handset after the fourth insistent ring.

'CID.'

'Morning, Sarge. It's Ben at the front desk. You'll never guess who I've got sitting here waiting to see the duty officer...'

Lewis shook his head with a sigh. It seemed the young constable never failed to build up his part. He was always bubbling over with enthusiasm, like a puppy, sometimes over very little at all.

'Come on, Ben, spit it out, lad. What's this, twenty questions or what? Talking to you is a bit like being on *Mastermind*.'

'Mark Shady. He arrived about five minutes ago. I thought you'd want to know.'

The sergeant's eyes widened. All of a sudden, he was interested. 'Shady? What the hell's that maggot doing here?'

'Someone threw paint stripper all over his nice flash Merc.'

Lewis let out a loud and hearty laugh. 'What, and he wants our help? After all the shit he's done. What a comedian.'

'I think he's after a crime reference number for an insurance claim. Sorting the car's going to cost a good few quid. I had a quick look to cheer myself up. Whoever did it's gone the whole hog. The car's only about a year old, forty grand's worth, and in a right state. Looks like Jackson Pollock had a go at it. It's going to need a total respray.'

Lewis made a face.

'Pollock? Who the hell's he? Is he local?'

'Sorry, Sarge, he's an American artist. Jack the Dripper. Died in the fifties. One of my interests. I studied art and design at university.'

Lewis shook his head again, thinking that any

copper with a few O levels was considered an academic when he'd started the job. So much had changed, and not for the better.

'Get a grip, Ben, for fuck's sake,' he said. 'Keep Shady there. Make some excuse if you have to. I'll be down in five minutes. And don't mention my name. I don't want the bastard spooked and doing a runner before I get to talk to him.'

'Okay, Sarge, understood.'

Lewis made a brief toilet visit and then headed to the recently repaired lift, a few short steps along the corridor. He waited for less than a minute with fast-growing impatience, stepped into it, and pressed the button for the ground floor, all the time thinking Shady's unexpected arrival far too good an opportunity to miss.

Lewis strode into the public waiting area with a glower to see Shady sitting there, wearing an expensive-looking light-grey business suit with a white shirt and navy tie, slightly loose at the collar. The exact same outfit he'd worn on the day of the recent not-guilty verdict. Lewis wondered if that was more than coincidence. A reminder to Shady of his triumph. A trophy of sorts. The deviant git! Yeah, that was probably it.

Shady looked up from his mobile as Lewis slowly approached.

'What the hell are you doing here, *Mark*? I would have thought this is the last place you'd want to be.'

Shady screwed up his face. 'Oh, shit, not you, of all people.'

Lewis grinned, feeling that, for once, it seemed he had the advantage. 'I'm told someone's vandalised that expensive motor of yours.'

Shady nodded twice but didn't say anything.

'It's not surprising when you think about it,' Lewis continued, filling the silence. 'You've got to be one of the most hated men in town. There must be any number of people with a grudge – fathers, boyfriends, brothers. You're lucky it's just the car that got damaged. It could have been you. Maybe next time it will be.'

As Shady remained seated, legs stretched before him, the detective thought he was trying to look as relaxed as possible. But a definite flash of anger when Shady spoke betrayed his true feelings. He wasn't nearly as composed as he was trying to make out. And to Lewis, there was some satisfaction in that.

'I'm innocent, remember that. *Innocent!* I've got

no criminal record at all, not even a parking ticket,' Shady snarled after slotting his phone into an inside pocket of his tailored jacket. 'Get that into your thick head. I'm just an ordinary member of the public. A taxpayer who funds people like you. I pay your salary. So show me some respect.'

Lewis glared down at him. 'Good luck with that.'

'I know you lot are going to do fuck all about the car. You're never going to find the culprit. You couldn't find your arse with both hands. But I need the damage paid for. So needs must. I want a reference number for the insurance, and then I'm gone.'

Lewis felt himself tense. He'd had much worse said to him many times over the years. But there was something about Shady that never failed to get to him. He had no redeeming qualities, not a single one. The man was evil personified. The scum of the earth.

'Where's the car now?' Lewis asked.

Shady pointed towards the exit. 'In the car park. Where the hell else would it be?'

Lewis cracked his knuckles. 'Show me.'

'What the fuck for? The pig on the counter has already seen it. I just need the paperwork. That's it. There are places I need to be.'

'Just show me the car, Shady. I need to see it for

myself. The quicker this is done, the quicker you can piss off. So let's just get on with it, shall we?'

Shady stood, sighed exaggeratedly, straightened his tie, and then led the way, with the detective walking close behind. Lewis waited until they reached the damaged vehicle at the far side of the car park before speaking again. He studied Shady as closely as possible, looking for any signs of weakness, then jabbed a finger towards his face, just inches away.

'Now you listen, and you listen well. I want all that shit you put online about me and the Edwards girl taken down today. Am I clear? *Today!* Or this car won't be the only thing you've got to worry about.'

Shady stepped towards Lewis and laughed, holding his gaze, not looking away. 'Me, worried? You've got to be kidding me. What are you going to do, Porky? It's the best joke I've ever heard. Absolutely hilarious. I've got off every single time you've nicked me. And that's how it's going to stay. I'm cleverer than you. You must have realised that by now. I win, and you lose. I can do whatever the fuck I want and get away with it. So I'm taking nothing down. Not about you and not about that sad little tart. I might even post some more. That wasn't the only photo I took of you. And you look just as stupid in all the others. I couldn't stand to live if I looked like you. I'd crawl off into a dark corner and die. The shame would be too much.'

Lewis gritted his teeth, looking Shady in the eye. He would so have liked to have pinned him to his car bonnet by his throat. 'You think you're so fucking clever, don't you? I've dealt with a lot of scumbags like you over the years. And they all lost in the end. It would be a shame if someone spread rumours that you're a dirty little grass, *Mark*. That you're on the police books, giving information about local criminals to make a few miserable quid. Some right-hard cases in the area wouldn't appreciate that one little bit. I wouldn't like to be in your shoes if that ever happened. Those good looks you're so very proud of would be splattered all over the place. There'd be no pretty young things after that.'

For the first time, Shady seemed rattled. He was trying to hide it. But it was there. 'You wouldn't do that!'

'Wouldn't I? Try me,' Lewis quickly replied.

Shady snarled his response, eyes narrowed to slits. 'Make this personal, make me an enemy, and you'll seriously regret it. That's a promise from me to you. Cross me, and there's a raging tempest coming *your* way. You're no match for me. I'd destroy you. And don't ever make the mistake of thinking those are empty words. You have no idea what I'm capable of.'

Lewis somehow held himself back as a red mist threatened to descend. He resisted the almost over-whelming impulse to hit out, strongly suspecting that Shady was looking to provoke precisely that. A public assault in a location on a surveillance camera would suit his purpose well.

'Your time will come,' said Lewis at touching dis-tance, the men's noses almost meeting. 'You'll slip up. Get overconfident. Make a mistake. Your kind always do. And then you'll be banged up for years. Locked in a cell for twenty-three hours a day and guarding your arse in the showers. You'll be an old man by the time you get out. And that's if you get out at all. Pretty boys like you don't do well in prison. You're going to find that out soon enough.'

Shady looked back at Lewis with a serpent-like coldness, the two men standing there like prize fighters at a weigh-in.

'You've got a daughter, haven't you, pig? Bron-wen, isn't it? Yeah, that's her name. A big fat oinker with plenty of tasty crackling covering her bones. And she still lives locally. Not too far away. That wasn't difficult to find out. Not in this town. And I quite like the taste of piggy girls. Nice and juicy. I'm dating one now, as it happens. A right little hottie who loves a bit of it. She couldn't wait to shag me as soon as I got off. A bit of contact when I was on remand and she was gagging for it. Can't get enough of me. I might film myself screwing her sometime soon. Maybe put that online. And send it to her dad. I'm sure he'd appreciate that. And perhaps when I'm done with her, I'll spend some time with yours. Have a bit of fun with her. So, no more threats of rumours, eh? You back off, and your girl stays safe. Have we got a deal?'

Lewis snarled, eyes popping. 'You do not go near my family!'

Shady stepped away to open his car door, looking up at the detective as he climbed into the driver's seat. 'Touched a nerve have I, Ray? I can see our nice, friendly chat has got to you. You want to be very careful getting so stressed at your age and carrying all that weight. I'll see you again. Maybe now's not the best time to sort out the insurance after all.'

8

Lewis woke with a sudden start as his mobile rang out on the small oak cabinet to the left side of his double bed. It felt almost as if he was lying in quicksand as he slowly rolled over towards it, still half asleep with a muzzy head after downing several cans of strong German lager only hours before. He reached out stiffly and swore as he checked the time, asking himself who the hell would be contacting him at gone two in the morning.

The detective held the phone to his face, coughed, farted, scratched his big belly, then said a grumpy 'Hello' as his sore eyes gradually adapted to the semi-darkness of the room.

'DS Lewis? Is that you?' a woman asked in faltering tones.

The detective slowly raised himself into a semi-seated position, propped up on four feather pillows, having recognised Anna's haunted voice as soon as she spoke.

'It's twenty past two in the morning, love. What's the urgency? Can't it wait?'

When she replied, he realised she was weeping. There was jerkiness, words between sobs, as he'd heard before.

'I had a nightmare a-about... about what Mark did to m-me,' she stuttered. 'And, and, you did say to ring you anytime, day or night, if I needed help. I was in two minds about calling at all. But I... I finally decided it might be okay.'

Lewis immediately regretted his initial response, chastising himself for his impatience. The girl was right; he'd invited the call. He only had himself to blame.

'Of course it's okay, love. You take your time. Tell me what you called to say. And please call me Ray. There's no need for formality.'

There was a brief silence, as if Anna was preparing herself for whatever was coming next.

'Mark, Mark, he... he did things to me towards

the end of our relationship. Things, things I've never spoken about. In the days leading up to the rape and then... and then on the day itself. I can see now they were warning signs, obvious red flags. So, why didn't I see that at the time? Why did I stay with him for as long as I did? How stupid am I? I should have run a mile.'

Lewis blinked his tired eyes when they began to sting. 'Back in the day when I started in the job, if we ever screwed up, Grav, my old DS, used to tell me hindsight's an exact science. And those were wise words. It's all too easy looking back when we know the outcome and the full facts. But not always so easy at the time. Nothing that happened was your fault, love. Don't ever go thinking that. Nothing at all. You were manipulated, groomed and controlled by a man who's skilled at it. And no one should ever blame you for that, not you or anyone else. Shady's the guilty one, him and only him. Now tell me, what did the bastard do to you? You can tell me every-thing. Don't hold anything back.'

There was another second or two's silence be-fore Anna spoke through her tears. 'It's so very hard to say it.'

'Just tell me, love. Get it out; that's best. You'll feel better once you have.'

There was the sound of muffled sobs, then a sniff. 'Okay, here goes. Mark, he... he liked to role-play,' she began. 'He called it our secret little game. But it didn't seem like a game to me. I dreaded it every single time. And he swore me to secrecy. He did things, awful things I didn't like at all.'

Lewis wondered where the conversation was going. And wherever that was, he needed the detail, however difficult, however painful. Experience told him open questions were best.

'Okay, I hear you,' he said. 'What exactly are we talking about?'

'I... I can't believe I'm even saying this. It seems totally insane. But it's true, absolutely true. He'd... he'd tell me to lay completely still on my back on the bed and to hold my breath for as long as I possibly could while he pushed my legs apart and climbed on top of me. I hated it so very much. Being used like that, like a piece of meat. I thought it was so bizarre. But Mark got more and more excited. He could hardly contain himself. Much more so than during normal sex. And he got really angry if I ever moved an inch or even took a breath. I wasn't supposed to move at all. He... he said that was the point of it all. The bit that turned him on. To feed a fantasy he'd had for a long time. And he said I was useless to him if I didn't comply. That he'd have to find a new girlfriend. Someone who'd indulge in his games. A fun girl who was happy to meet his needs.'

Lewis sat more upright, the unexpected disclosure driving sleep away. What the hell? 'Are you saying Shady wanted you to play dead?'

There was another brief silence, two or three seconds this time, no more than that.

'He... Mark never said as much. He never used those words. But, yes, looking back, I think that's exactly what he wanted. He used to tell me to practise holding my breath.'

'Okay, love, you're doing well, I hear you. Is there anything else?'

'What sort of man wants sex with a dead body? What kind of evil fantasy is that? It's sick and horrible and freaks me out even to think about it. I'm ashamed to say I gave in more than once when he'd plied me with drink or pot. I hate myself for that. I think I was in denial at first. That's the only sense I can make of it. Not willing or able to accept the true reality of what he was doing to me. Because I still loved him then. And I believed he loved me. I told myself there must be something I didn't understand. That I was naïve and he was mature, a sophisticated man. That maybe other people liked the things he liked too. How stupid was I?'

Lewis shook his head. 'You were under his influence, manipulated by a master. Don't blame yourself for a single second. You bear no responsibility at all.'

'Thanks so much, Ray, I'm so glad I rang. I'm not sure anybody else would understand. Not even my therapist.'

'Shady's responsible, him alone. Remember that and never forget it. Everything that happened was down to him.'

She began to weep again. 'There was always so much pressure and persuasion until I finally gave in. I felt I had to. And then... and then on the day of the rape, I'd had enough. I couldn't stand it any more. I was sober, and I said no. I told him I thought it was creepy. That I hated it. That I never wanted to do it ever again. And that's when he lost it, pushed me over, pinned me down, threatened me, pulled my panties aside, and, well, you know the rest.'

Lewis had been in the job a long time, and nothing shocked him any more – not even this. But his chest tightened as he thought of his daughter. Shady's recent threats came to mind – as if they were ringing in his ears. He now knew Shady may be even more dangerous than he'd realised – a potential killer in the making, a deviant whose behaviour was escalating. And that wasn't good.

He focused back on his call. 'I'm so sorry you had to go through all that. It must have been awful. But why tell me now, love? Why not before the trial?' he asked, suspecting he already knew the answer. It wasn't unusual for the victims to hold something back. And he saw that as his failing, not hers.

'I... I felt ashamed,' Anna replied ever so quietly, almost in a whisper. 'And I... I didn't want anyone to know. Especially not my family. I still feel shame. But I just can't get what happened out of my head. And the dreams are so horribly real. I get flashbacks. It's like I'm back there with Mark on top of me, holding me down. Ordering me to shut my stupid mouth and not to move. Today, I realised I had to tell someone if I'm ever to find peace. And you seemed the obvious person. You've always been sympathetic and ready to listen without negative judgement. You've tried your best to help even if we didn't get the desired result. So here we are. That's why I rang.'

'All right, love. I understand, and I'm glad you did. And, like I said, none of this is your fault. You've got nothing to feel guilty or shameful about. You're the victim here. I know I keep saying it, but I can't stress that enough. Are you willing to make a written statement? I'm hoping the answer is yes. It would be good to get all this down on paper.'

Anna's voice rose in pitch and tone now, her words rushed, almost blending into one. 'I'm not going back to court, if that's what you think. I'm never going through all that again. Not a chance in hell! I wouldn't ever have told you if I'd thought...'

'No, don't worry, that's not going to happen, love,' he said with conviction and some regret. 'That's all done and dusted. It's just that it would be helpful to put what you've told me on record in case something similar comes up in a future case. It builds a picture, like the pieces of a jigsaw. Shows what kind of man Shady is. The sort of things he does. And I'm not going to be around forever. It might be someone else doing the investigating next time. Whoever that is could read your statement if you're willing to make one. And that could prove important. Can you do that for me?'

'Do you think Mark might do it to the new girl? Or maybe something even worse?'

Lewis paused before speaking, thinking first of young Carly and then his daughter. He could feel the tension in his gut and chest. 'You weren't Shady's first victim, and you may not be his last. I wish it was different. But I have to accept that possibility. And he's one evil bastard. He's not like you and me. You know that better than most.'

'Okay.' That's all she said. Just the one word.

'You'll do it? You'll make a statement?' Lewis asked.

He imagined her nodding.

'Yeah, yeah, I will,' she said. 'When?'

'How about later this morning, at ten?'

'Could we make it half past? I said I'd help my mum clean the stable first thing. I think she's trying to keep me busy. It doesn't help, but she means well.'

'Of course we can. No problem at all. Half-ten it is. Do you want me to come to you?'

'That's probably not the best idea. Dad's going to be in. But I don't really want to come to Carmarthen either. Not when there's a risk of seeing Mark. I couldn't stand it. Not after everything.'

Lewis thought for a second. 'We could meet at Ammanford Police Station if that works for you? It's only about half an hour's drive from your place, on Foundry Road.'

She sounded relieved.

'Okay, yes. I can borrow Mum's car. I'll tell her I'm going to see my psychologist or meeting a friend.'

Lewis scratched his chin. 'There's plenty of room to park. Just ask for me at the front desk. They'll be expecting you. And there'll be a cup of tea waiting. We'll get the statement done as quickly as possible. It won't take us long. And then you can be on your way.'

'Thanks, Ray.'

He was grateful for the sentiment, thinking it generous in the circumstances.

'Any news re the criminal injuries application?' he asked.

'Not as yet.'

'I guess it's early days,' he replied. 'I'll give Victim Support another nudge if you haven't heard something by the end of the week. It shouldn't take them long. What about your solicitor? Have you thought any more about the injunction?'

'I've got an appointment on Thursday. Dad's going to go with me. Or maybe Mum if he's too busy.'

Lewis smiled, pleased she'd listened, acting on his advice for what it was worth. 'Good, glad to hear it,' he said, sounding as upbeat as possible. 'I'll see you later this morning, love. Now, it's late; try to get some rest.'

Lewis sat on the edge of his bed in his extra-large white vest and black socks for a few seconds after ending the call, thinking that sleep was likely beyond him. He rose stiffly, pondering that maybe pulling on some underpants and heading down-stairs for a cheese and onion sandwich and a gen-erous tot of neat Scotch in front of the telly wasn't such a bad idea. And perhaps a slice of fruit cake too, the one he'd bought in Asda. It was only a few days out of date. Maybe a week, or two at most. Yeah, why the hell not? Hunger called, and anything had to be better than lying awake in the dark, lost in melancholy thought for God only knew how long. Such things never got him anywhere. Once awake, that was it. And overthinking changed nothing at all.

He briefly considered picking up his mobile again to call Kesey at home to tell her about the night's events. But he quickly decided such a call was neither necessary nor appropriate. The DI needed her rest too. She'd told him that often enough. Further talk of Shady could wait.

9

Laura Kesey held a favourite pottery mug to her mouth with a slightly trembling hand, washing down two much-needed painkillers taken from her handbag as she awaited her sergeant's imminent arrival just before three that afternoon. She lamented that it hadn't been an easy day. And a chat with Ray was at least something she could undertake without undue stress. However challenging the nature of the subject matter, their close friendship and mutual professional respect made their interactions tolerable at worst and often even enjoyable. Ray had that skill. An easily likeable character. So very different to the time spent with the chief super.

As she put the empty mug down on her cluttered

desk and gently massaged her temples with two fingers of each hand, Kesey reminded herself that meetings with Nigel Halliday often left her with a headache. The pain usually started at the base of her neck and spread across her scalp. And today was no different. It was the inevitable tension the man created. The dismissive way he talked to her, his objectionable personality, and being so full of himself for no good reason at all. Why was Halliday such a total prick? She hadn't liked the man from the first time she'd met him, thinking him pompous and self-important. Not a real copper: an administrator, a penpusher. And her opinion of him hadn't changed a great deal since. If anything, she now liked him even less. He'd promised her a promotion, dangled it in front of her, called her back from a holiday in the sun when it suited his purpose, and then snatched the offer away again. Manipulative, a user, that's what he was. And she often hoped he'd return to London's Met, the force from which he'd come. But so far no luck there. Maybe, she pondered, one day that dream would come true. Her professional life would be so much better if it did.

Kesey drove all thoughts of Halliday from her busy mind, instantly back in the now as Lewis pushed open her office door and trudged into the room, pulling up a padded chair and sitting heavily opposite her untidy desk with a sigh.

'Coffee?' he asked, she thought more in hope than expectation.

'No time, Ray. I'm a bit rushed. You said you wanted to talk about Shady. Let's get on with it. What's bothering you this time?'

Lewis took a breath and then placed one leg over the other. 'I had Anna Edwards on the phone in the early hours.'

Kesey's brow furrowed as she raised her eyebrows. 'How did she get your number?'

Lewis shrugged, open hands in front of him. 'I gave it to her. What's the big deal? Does it matter?'

'Oh, come on, Ray. I've talked to you about this. Stop giving victims your personal number. Anna should be contacting you at work. Or she can speak to someone else if you're not available. Someone who's actually on duty. Give people the station's number, by all means. Or they can dial 101, or 999 if it's urgent. That's the way the system is supposed to work. You know that as well as me.'

He looked back at her with a bored look, no doubt deliberate. It was something else they'd discussed several times before. He hadn't listened then, and she thought it highly unlikely he would now. Sometimes she wondered why she even tried.

'Has the lecture finished?' he asked. 'I thought you were in a hurry.'

'Have you looked in a mirror today? You look completely exhausted. And you know your health's not great. The last thing you need is unnecessary calls in the middle of the night. I've told you this. You're your own worst enemy.'

'Are you done? Can we get down to business? It'll be time for you to go if we don't make a start.'

She snapped back her reply, fast losing patience.

'Just get on with it, Ray. I sometimes ask myself why I bother trying to help you at all.'

Lewis's expression hardened, and she knew he was in business mode. Their conversations often followed the same predictable pattern. He'd outline whatever concerns he had succinctly and professionally, one of his strengths, something she valued. There was electricity in the air. The mood had changed.

'There's things Anna hadn't told us,' he began, looking Kesey in the eye. 'Shady pressured her to play dead during sex. It turned him on. She had to lay there not moving and holding her breath. And he got seriously pissed off if she didn't comply.

That's what led to the rape. It was always going to happen sometime, but that's why then. That was the trigger point. The one time she said no.'

Kesey held her aching head in her hands, dropping her chin to her chest as Lewis paused, waiting for him to continue as she knew he inevitably would. And in those brief seconds of silence, she fully understood the potential threat a predatory male sex offender with such deviant death fantasies may pose. Painful experience had taught her all she needed to know. Women and girls who'd died at the hands of such destructive men, monsters in human form who offered the world only pain. Ray was right to be worried, and now she was too. And just when she'd thought her day couldn't get any worse. This put even Halliday's mundane musings in the shade.

'I think Shady could be even more dangerous than we realised,' said Lewis a second later as Kesey listened, focused only on him. 'No, no, I'm certain of it. One hundred per cent. There's no room for doubt. I've been looking again at his pattern of offending. The MO is similar in every case, but the rapes have become more regular, and he's already in a new relationship. He fantasises, targets a victim, grooms her, and then offends, as we've said before. Nothing new there, but now he can't wait as long as he did.

And he's having fantasies about the women being dead. The man's a killer waiting to evolve. If we don't stop him, I'd be willing to bet it's only a matter of time.'

Kesey made a face, wanting to look on the positive. She was never one to jump to conclusions without serious thought. For her, things were rarely as black or white as they were for Ray. Sometimes, threats ended in disaster. That was true. But sometimes, they came to nothing. Hopefully, in this case, it would be the latter.

'Yeah, maybe,' she said. 'I get what you're saying. It's a genuine concern. But let's not get ahead of ourselves.'

Lewis pulled his head back.

'The bastard's going to end up murdering someone. Isn't it blatantly obvious? What do you want me to do, draw you a picture?'

Kesey counted to three in her head, a technique she sometimes used to calm herself. And she told herself such things were necessary. Because sometimes she was the balance to Ray's excess, the yin to his yang. 'You know that profiler from Cardiff we used for the Sheridan case?' she asked.

'Yeah, the prat with the beard and round metal

glasses. And the worst comb-over I've ever seen in my life.'

She chose to ignore his use of the insult, already thinking her words would be lost on him. But she'd try nonetheless. Maybe this time, for once, it would be worth the effort. 'He once told me there's a big difference between fantasising about something and actually doing it. One doesn't necessarily lead to the other.'

Lewis made a face, looking far from persuaded and making it obvious. 'Are you clutching at straws, girl?'

'I'm saying nothing is certain where human behaviour is concerned, that's all. You must realise that after all your years in the job. It's complex. Shady's complex. Offenders like him always are. Not everything is as straightforward as you like to think it is.'

He shook his head. 'Look, we know Shady's a psycho. Not even the profiler would argue with me about that. He's a misogynistic sadist who enjoys hurting females, both physically and mentally. That's how the bastard gets his kicks. And he thinks he's invincible. That he can get away with anything. Because up to now, he has. And that's not me theorising. He told me to my face. One day, maybe soon, he'll kill unless somebody stops him. His fantasies will become too powerful for him to ignore. Role-play won't be enough any more. And he'll want to make his games real. That's my profile for you, right there. And I know I'm right. I'd bet my pension on it.'

Kesey drummed the fingers of one hand on the top of her desk, rat-a-tat, thinking it a convincing contention. Ray had a point. 'Let's just say you're right,' she said, glancing at her watch and thinking the hospital meeting might have to wait after all. 'For the sake of argument, let's assume Shady is thinking about killing someone. I have to accept that's a possibility. But what on earth do you suggest we do about it? We can't nick the man for a roleplay fantasy, however much we'd like to. And it's not like we can refer him to another agency for counselling help. He's not even in the system. He's a suspected offender, and that's it. As of now, legally, he's got a clean record. He's no more a criminal than you or me.'

Lewis shook his head with a look of disgust; no doubt, she thought, because he knew she was correct. Some things not even he could argue with.

'Do you have any suggestions?' she asked. 'I'm open to ideas. My options are limited, at best.'

He blew out air. 'We keep a close eye on Shady,

and we nick him for anything and everything the first chance we get,' he said a second later, a nicotine-stained finger raised to his chin. 'I'm told he likes a spliff and a bit of coke from time to time. I'll have a word with the drug squad. Point them in his direction. It's just personal use; more's the pity. It's just a slap on the wrist, even if he's caught. But it's got to be better than nothing. Maybe there's an in there. And I'll go back over all the rape cases that didn't get to court to see if we missed anything. I've already dug out the files. It's a long shot, but needs must. And I'll have another word with Daisy. Put him in the picture. I'll do that today. As soon as we're done here.'

Kesey allowed herself a grin, momentarily amused by the nickname despite having heard it before. 'How much are you planning to tell him?'

'Everything I've told you. You'd want to know if it was your kid, wouldn't you? He's in the job, same as us. It's only fair.'

'Carly, isn't it? His daughter?' she asked.

'Yeah, that's right.'

'Are she and Shady definitely still in a relationship even after her dad had a word with her?'

Lewis shrugged, raising and dropping his shoulders. 'As far as I know. I haven't heard any different.

And I'm sure Daisy would have told me if they weren't. He'd be doing cartwheels.'

'It might be an idea to establish that as fact before saying anything.'

He screwed up his face. 'Goes without saying.'

Kesey gave Lewis a pensive look. 'I don't know this Flowers officer like you do,' she said. 'But I know what it's like to worry about a child's safety. It's one of the worst things in the world. He's not likely to do anything stupid, is he?'

'Stupid?' asked Lewis, an expression of incomprehension on his face that Kesey thought contrived.

'Oh, come on, Ray, don't play the innocent. Something outside the law. You know exactly the type of thing I'm talking about.'

Lewis stood, using the arms of the chair to help himself to his feet. 'No, not a chance, Daisy's not the type. He's a follow-the-book copper, like you.'

She fetched her navy raincoat from where it hung on the back of the door. 'I hope you're right. The rules are there for a reason.'

'Yeah, yeah, so you keep telling me.'

She swallowed her frustration with his reply. 'We're done here,' she said. 'I think we've said all we need to say for now. I'd best make a move. But keep me updated if there's anything significant. No surprises.'

Lewis followed her into the corridor. 'Are you in in the morning?' he asked.

'I'm off the rest of the week. But Jan and I are having a get-together at the house for some friends on Saturday at seven if you fancy it? It's our wedding anniversary. You'd be very welcome. And there'd be a few guests you've met before.'

Lewis replied as they walked, approaching the stairs. 'Sounds good. I've got nothing else on. Do I need to bring anything?'

'Just yourself and a bottle of booze. There'll be plenty to eat. Jan's doing a buffet – a few sand-wiches, sausage rolls, and some nibbles, that sort of thing.'

He was slightly out of breath when he re-sponded. 'Are you sure she's okay with me coming?'

'Yes, I've spoken to her. But she doesn't want you getting too drunk again, not like the last time. I've told her you're a reformed man. You'll have to be on your best behaviour. Maybe drive rather than get a taxi.'

'Halliday's not coming, is he?'

She laughed. 'No, Ray, that's one person who's definitely not invited.'

'In that case, I'll see you there. And tell Jan not to worry. It'll be weak shandy all night. And I'll bring her a nice box of chocs as a goodwill gesture.'

Kesey took her car keys from a coat pocket. 'She'll like that. She loved those milk-free ones from the health food place in Lammas Street you got her at Christmas. Oh, and I meant to ask: has Shady taken down that social media stuff?'

Lewis tensed. 'Like fuck he has. It's all still there,' he replied with a glower.

'I'll contact the sites when I get a chance,' Kesey replied. 'Let's see if that does any good.'

Lewis held open a large glass door for her to exit. 'Thanks, boss,' he said. 'It's appreciated.'

10

Lewis hurriedly returned to Kesey's office via the lift once she'd left the building, knowing it was less likely he'd be disturbed there than in his shared CID room. Speaking to Mike Flowers again was a conversation he wanted to have alone. He made a strong, sweet coffee, ate the last chocolate biscuit from a packet in the DI's desk drawer, and was pleased to discover Flowers was in when he rang the police station in Haverfordwest minutes later.

'Hello, Daisy, it's Ray. How are things? Any news your end?'

'Give me a minute, mate. I'll go sit in my car and ring you back on the mobile. A bit of privacy wouldn't do any harm. It's hectic here. I don't know what's going on. No one tells me a thing. The place is buzzing.'

'Ask for DI Kesey when you speak to the switchboard. I'm at her desk.'

Lewis noted a concerned tone when Flowers responded. 'What? She's not there with you, is she?'

Lewis took a slurp of coffee, emptying the mug. 'Nothing to worry about. It's just me, she's out. Won't be back today. You can relax.'

Kesey's office phone rang minutes later. 'So, what's the news?' Lewis asked.

'Carly's finally talked to the missus; thank God for small mercies. She still seems to think I'm the enemy, but at least she's communicating with her mum. Only texts so far, but it's got to be better than nothing. That's progress in itself.'

'I'm assuming that means Carly's still dating that wanker?'

Lewis heard a sigh at the other end of the line. 'Afraid so,' Flowers replied. 'Still no joy there. But at least I know she's safe for the moment. She's in London for a few days. Something to do with her course. And it gives the missus a chance to keep talking to her without Shady sticking his beak in.

That's got to be good news. I'm trying to look on the positive side. What else can I do?'

'You haven't heard any more about his claims to have recorded you?'

'No, I think it's all bullshit. Not a word.'

Lewis hesitated, knowing he was about to temper his friend's upbeat mood. And there was no pleasure in that. 'There's something else I need to tell you, Daisy.'

'Oh, for fuck's sake, what now?'

'I've only just found this out. It's something the Edwards girl told me in the early hours. And it's important. Something you need to know. But if I tell you, it can't go any further. You can't tell Carly or even the missus. 'Cause if it ever gets back to Shady, he's going to know it came from Anna. And that would put her at risk. I can't let that happen. So you keep it to yourself and do what you will with it. Have we got a deal?'

'Course we have. Just tell me. It can't be any worse than what I'm thinking. And I know how to keep my mouth shut. Goes with the job.'

Lewis then outlined all Anna had told him, communicating his concerns and highlighting the dangers in terms Flowers couldn't fail to understand.

The DC said nothing as Lewis spoke. And even when Lewis had said all he had to share, there was silence. For the briefest of moments, Lewis thought Flowers might have ended the call.

'Are you still there, Daisy? Did you hear me?'

'Yeah, still here,' Flowers replied.

'Anything you want to ask? I know all this must have come as a shock.'

Lewis thought he heard Flowers throwing up and then a car door slamming shut before he finally replied.

'I've got to get Carly safe. Whatever it takes, one way or another. I'll tell the missus it's more urgent than ever, without going into detail. Maybe she can go up on the train to London. Plead with Carly to see sense. Talk to her face to face. If I stay well out of the way, it might work. Has to be worth a try.'

'Sorry to be the bearer of bad news.'

'No, I'm glad you told me. You're a good mate. Not everyone would have done the same, not like in the old days. A lot of the loyalty's gone.'

'The least I could do.'

There was the sound of Flowers spitting something from his mouth.

'I've got to ask, Ray, do you really think Shady's a likely killer?'

'Yeah, sorry, I do,' Lewis replied, wishing he could say something different. 'I've dealt with scum like him before. All the signs are there. I've never been more certain of anything in my life.'

11

That evening, Lewis stared at his mobile on the old pine coffee table in front of him for almost five minutes as he downed two cans of best bitter, carefully considering his best choice of approach when he finally made the call. Given Shady's recent implied threats, he knew he had to talk to his own daughter. It couldn't be put off for very much longer. But the conversation was never going to be an easy one. So, how much to say? Not an easy decision. It had to be sufficient to prewarn Bronwen and put her on her guard, but not enough to freak her out completely. Because there was always that possibility. Balance was the key. Subtlety, that was what Kesey would advise. Subtlety. Never his strong point, but he had to give it a go.

Lewis opened a third can of beer with a satisfying metallic ping and took a greedy gulp, still deep in thought, weighing up his limited options, considering all the angles as best he could. He reminded himself that Bronwen had a tendency to panic. Always had and probably always would. She'd never been one of life's copers, not even when things were going reasonably well. And her recent unexpected marital break-up only months before had left her fragile at best. Popping pills prescribed by the doctor, as if they were sweets. Or, at least, that's what his ex-wife had told him. The only reason he knew the details. Bronwen apparently hadn't seen the separation coming. Joe, the cheating bastard! He had been supposed to love her. To care for and protect her. To recognise her hidden beauty and be satisfied with that. But it didn't happen that way. Why the hell couldn't the prat keep his dick in his pants? Six years of marriage flushed down the drain. And for what? A quick late-night drunken shag with some cheap slapper who'd shouted her mouth off all over town. What a tragic waste. One thing he could agree with his own ex on. A rare event in itself.

Lewis reflected that he and Bronwen had never

been particularly close. Not even during her childhood. So maybe he'd let her down too. Not just Joe.
There was love, father–daughter, there was no denying
that, always had been. But they rarely spoke, not really,
not about things that truly mattered. If she had problems, she talked to her mum, that was the truth of it.
And, of course, he'd almost always been at work. His
number one priority. Hardly conducive to a happy
family life. The coppers curse. No wonder the missus
left. No wonder Bronwen had sided with her. His fault.
Maybe, in a small way, he could make up for it now.

Lewis drained his can, head back, Adam's apple
bobbing, then crushed it, dropped it to the floral
carpet at his feet, wiped his mouth with a shirtsleeve
and picked up his phone, finally ready to make the
call. A part of him thought that maybe he should
have called at Bronwen's terraced house rather than
ring. It had been a while. But now it was too late.
He'd rung, and she'd said hello.

'Hi, Bron, it's Dad; I thought I'd ring for a catch-
up.'

He could hear the surprise in her voice. 'You're
not ill again, are you?'

He felt his chest tighten, recalling the last time
he'd rung, months before, from a hospital bed. 'No,

not at all; I just wanted a chat, love,' he said, trying to sound convincing.

'Are you drunk?' she asked, the direction of the conversation just as challenging as he'd anticipated. He so wanted another beer – to taste the yeasty liquid, to take the edge off, to dull his senses, to swallow it down.

'That seems a strange question,' he said. 'Why would you ask me that? I haven't touched a drop.'

'It's been ages since you've called me,' she replied. 'You never ring to just chat. There must be something up. You wouldn't be on the phone otherwise. Is Gran okay? She hasn't had another one of her falls, has she?'

He picked up another can from a pack of six but didn't open it. 'Gran's fine,' he said. 'And I'm well. Still on the heart-friendly diet. Fitter than I've been for years. How about you?'

'Do you really want to know?'

He sighed, asking himself if conversations with Bronwen always had to be so hard. No wonder he didn't ring more often than he did. 'I asked, didn't I?' he said.

'But we never talk about this sort of stuff.'

'Then maybe it's about time we did.'

'Okay, if you're sure,' she said. 'You know what happened with Joe, don't you?'

'Of course I do. Mum told me all about it. You know that. I asked you if there was anything you needed in a text.'

'He told me he's so very sorry. That he wishes he could turn the clock back. That it would never have happened if he hadn't been drunk.'

'Oh, God, please don't tell me you're thinking of forgiving the prat?'

There was a brief pause. 'I miss him, Dad. We were together from the age of sixteen. We grew up together. And we have so much in common. I hate being on my own.'

Lewis was surprised at how much his daughter was opening up, and he thought that maybe it was her medication. Or was it that he was ready to listen for once?

'Men like Joe don't change, love,' he said with feeling. 'I've seen it too many times before. He cheated, and he got caught. And if you take him back, he'll do it again one day. He'll just be more careful next time.'

'People change,' she quickly replied.

'Do they? Really? I'm not so sure. He's shown

you what he is. Believe it the first time. Or you'll just get hurt again.'

'Give me a second, Dad. I need to take a tablet.'

'Are you still on those things?'

There were a few seconds of silence. 'There, that's better... I'm not taking as many as I was. I'm slowly cutting down. But it's not something you can do quickly. A friend at work tried and had all sorts of withdrawal symptoms. It's best to do it slowly.'

'You're doing the right thing, love. Very sensible.'

'I think so, thanks.'

Lewis asked himself if the time was right to talk of Shady. It had to be done sometime and couldn't be avoided for much longer. That was why he'd called, after all. And would it really make even the slightest difference how he timed it or what words he used? Bronwen wasn't stupid. She'd soon work out the true reason for his call, however he played it. So why delay? No point at all. Best get it over with. Be the good dad. Make up for the past.

'There is one thing I wanted to mention before we finish chatting, love...'

'Oh, here we go. I knew there had to be something.'

He asked himself if he was really so very pre-dictable, then decided it seemed he was. She'd read him so easily, using her female intuition. But there was no going back now.

'Did you see all that stuff on the Welsh news about a bloke called Mark Shady?' he asked. 'He was charged with rape but got off in court. It was my case. The system stinks! He's got a pizza place here in town, the Shady Shack.'

'Yeah, I know him. Well, I don't really *know* him, not personally. But I've seen him about. And me and Joe ate at the restaurant a couple of times. We both love Italian food. And the prices are pretty reasonable. Why do you ask?'

How much to say? How to word it? He had to say something. Another beer was calling, but he resisted.

'I just want to let you know the man's bad news. Like I said, I dealt with the case. And he's dangerous. The jury got it badly wrong. Avoid the restaurant. Stay well clear of him. You need to avoid Shady at all costs.'

Bronwen sounded hesitant when she responded a second or two later. 'He actually sent me a friend request a couple of hours ago.'

Lewis tensed, forming his hands into tight fists as was his custom. 'What, on Facebook?' he asked, opening the can in his hand as the pressure built up.

'Yeah, I get quite a few, mainly from men. I think most women do. But that one surprised me.'

Lewis took a slurp of beer. 'Did you accept it?'

'No, of course not, not after all that stuff on the news. He's a good-looking guy, but I'm not that desperate!'

'Good girl, that's good. You did right. If I were you, I'd block the bastard.'

'Already have.'

'Glad to hear it. You're a star.'

He listened carefully, trying to read her thoughts as she paused once more. Oh, shit, had she started crying? Yeah, that had to be the sound of sniffles. She probably had.

'What on earth's this really about, Dad?' she asked. 'You're starting to scare me. Mark Shady can't be the only sex offender in the area. So why warn me about him but not the others? You must have your reasons.'

Lewis thought back to his time standing face to face with Shady in the police car park and the dangers the man posed. Mental images flashed in his mind as if in real-time, and he felt more conflicted than ever. What the hell to say?

'I've been thinking a lot about the case, that's all. And Shady's the sort of bloke who seems all right when you first meet him. Like you say, he's good-looking. And he's got a few quid in the bank. He drives a flash car.'

She was quick to reply. 'You know I'm not impressed by that sort of stuff. So why would any of that matter to me?'

Lewis felt under increasing pressure to choose his words with care. 'Well, you've always liked pizza, even as a kid. So I thought maybe you'd go to his place sometime. And you did say you and Joe did. So I wasn't wrong.'

'Oh, come off it, Dad. Are you trying to claim that Shady contacting me on the very same day you rang to express your concerns is a total coincidence? That seems a bit unlikely at best, don't you think?'

'Maybe I should come round to the house,' he said, trying to buy time to think.

'If there's something I need to know, tell me now!' she snapped back, tears seemingly changing to anger.

Lewis lowered his head, accepting only partial defeat. He wasn't ready to share the full facts despite the effects of the alcohol oiling the conversational wheels. 'Shady doesn't like me,' he said. 'In fact, I think he hates my guts. I tried to put him away. And for him, that's personal. And I don't want his feelings for me to affect you in any way.'

'Affect me, how?'

Lewis stood, walked across the room and swigged a mouthful of blended Scotch from a half-empty bottle he'd left on the sideboard for easy access. 'I'm probably worrying about nothing, love. Just stay well clear of Shady. That's all I'm saying. And if he contacts you again in any way, I need to know.'

There was an urgency to her response. 'Do you think he might?'

'Well, it's always possible. He's done it once. Maybe he'll do it again.'

'Perhaps I should go to stay at Mum's place for a couple of weeks. I've got some leave due.'

His relief was almost palpable. If that was the best that came from the conversation, it was a win. 'That's not a bad idea, love. And you're always welcome here. I hope you know that. To you, the door's always open.'

She sounded hesitant when she spoke again. 'Are you certain there's nothing you're not telling me? It still all seems strange to me.'

Even now, Lewis wondered if he'd said too much or, perhaps, not enough. Emotions and family confused him. And for once, there were shades of grey where there was usually only black and white. Either way, he really wasn't sure.

'You're going to be fine, love,' he finally said, desperately wanting to be correct, trying to convince both her and himself. 'Just let me know if you hear from the bastard again. And if you do, I'll sort him out. You can trust your old dad. That's a promise.'

'I'll give Mum a ring.'

'Yeah, you do that.'

'Night, Dad.'

'Night, love. Look after yourself.'

Lewis reached for the whisky again after ending his call, filling a glass tumbler to the halfway point rather than drink from the bottle. He took a sip and then picked up his laptop from where it was charging, thoughts of Shady again on his mind.

Lewis placed his glass on the coffee table next to an unread paperback borrowed from Carmarthen Library, slumped heavily into his favourite armchair close to the gas fire, and opened his computer. He perused the various social media sites with surprisingly fast-moving fingers and was pleased to see that Shady's posts about Anna and himself were no longer there. A small victory, he thought, highly likely due to Laura Kesey's actions. Something to thank her for.

He relaxed slightly for the first time that evening, the tension slowly melting away as the fire warmed him. But then he saw it, and it changed everything. A Facebook message request from Shady stared him in the face. A message that couldn't be ignored. A message that reached out to drag him in. He took another swig of the strong spirit, then opened the message to see a photo of Bronwen sitting alone in a local café. And there was a short poem too. Just as there had been for him. A mocking little ditty that seemed wholly insidious despite its poetic wording. *Shady, you bastard! How dare you? Upping the ante. How fucking well dare you?*

A cold shudder along the detective's spine turned to red rage as he read the short rhyme for the second time, his blood pressure soaring:

> *Bronwen Lewis*
> *Trouble and strife*
> *One day soon*
> *I'll make her my wife*

12

Mark Shady was startled awake by the sudden, crashing sound of smashing glass at 4.15 a.m. on Sunday. He opened his eyes wide in the semi-darkness of his master bedroom, his heart pounding and muscles tense as adrenalin surged through his system.

Shady lay there for a second or two, listening intently, taking deep breaths, sucking in the air, blowing it out and struggling to relax his shaking limbs as he had so many times before. Then, when he'd finally built up sufficient resolve, he threw back his quilt despite a deep foreboding that threatened to overwhelm him. He thought back to his troubled childhood – the night-time terrors, the horrors of it all – as he sat on the edge of the memory foam mattress and told himself he was a man now. A lion, not a mouse. That the dark events of his formative years were in the past. But forgetting was never that easy. Not in the dark, not when alone. The memories often surrounded him, without mercy, as they did now, one flashback after another invading his mind. Only the domination of others drove them away. Then he was the alpha, the man in charge.

Shady pictured himself cowering in the corner of a brightly lit room as a seven-year-old child, pale and thin, his knees pulled to his chest and his tormentor looming over him.

He shook his head violently, driving the image from his mind. Then he jumped from the bed, flicked on a bedside lamp with a trembling finger, and urgently pulled on a pair of white underpants he'd discarded on the carpeted floor hours earlier, stumbling and almost falling in the process.

Shady's eyes darted from one part of the bedroom to another, bouncing off the walls, his gaze finally settling on the closed door, that barrier between him and the world beyond. He felt so very tempted to leave that door closed. To hide from whatever fears lay beyond it. But he urged himself on, driven by his male ego, feeling obliged to act. He

asked himself what the hell was going on as he
stared at the door. That smashing glass. He hadn't
dreamt it. It wasn't some nightmare construct of his
subconscious mind. It was real. All too real. Had
someone broken into the restaurant? Were they
there to rob him? Or maybe to hurt him? Perhaps
the same bastard who'd damaged his car. Just like
Porky Lewis had predicted.

Shady's mind continued to race, fight or flight,
searching for options. His phone. He could summon
help, dial 999. But where the hell was his phone?
Downstairs! Oh, for fuck's sake. So stupid! He really
should be more careful. He'd left it on the bar after
re-reading the stinking text from that skank Carly.
Dumping him! The bitch. How dare she? First, that
abomination and now this. No wonder he wanted to
scream.

He walked across the bedroom floor one tenta-
tive step at a time, placed a trembling hand on the
door handle, and slowly opened it, again urging
himself on, knowing deep down his actions were
driven more by fear than bravery. He told himself he
had to go down there, whatever the unseen threat.
That he had no other choice. Because there were
secrets on his phone. Photos, and a diary of events
no one else could see. Photos taken with a hidden

camera, all stored in a file labelled 'fun times', and carefully hidden under layers of security. Evidence the idiot police hadn't found, more fool them. He treasured that record of his private life, the girls who'd cowered as he once had, whimpering, with tears and snot running down their stupid faces. So he had to get down there. He had to get that phone. But what if someone was waiting for him in the dark? Waiting to harm him. Waiting to pounce. What then?

Shady silently acknowledged the awful reality as he stood shaking on the first-floor landing. He was scared, close to shitting himself. He'd never been more terrified in his life. Not when his mother beat him as a young child. Not when she'd yelled in his face, the smell of alcohol on her breath. Not even when one of her many male friends did what they did as she looked on, failing to protect him in a drug-addled haze. And deep down inside, he was still that scared little boy. Yes, he could talk the talk, even intimidate, when the circumstances were right. But he couldn't back it up, not really, not physically, not where men were concerned. Now, women, that was different; he was stronger than them. But males, no. And there might be a man waiting for him downstairs in the dark. A big man, a powerful man. Hidden and ready to attack.

Shady stood still, statue-like, for a few seconds more as his thought process continued. He leaned over the stairwell, allowing the wooden banister to support his weight as he listened carefully for any sounds from the restaurant below. But all was silent. And his hopes were momentarily raised. He told himself that whoever had smashed the glass might be gone. That maybe it was just some inadequate drunken fool who liked to break things for the pleasure it gave them. And that, in the best-case scenario, the mindless vandal hadn't come inside the building at all.

Shady's nagging anxieties briefly subsided as a result of his insistent self-assurance. But all too soon, his fearful apprehension returned, making his gut twist as his thoughts leapt in another direction, screaming caution. *Hold on*, he thought, hearing the words as if yelled in his head. *Be careful; the silence could be a trap*. Maybe the threat was still there. Shit! Yes! What if that was true? The pig said he had a lot of enemies. Not far from the truth. Misguided idiots who didn't recognise his greatness. Perhaps some potential attacker was luring him in by being still and quiet. There was always that possibility.

For the briefest of moments, as the hairs rose on his arms and neck, Shady considered retreating back to his bedroom to close the door against the world. To lock out the dangers. Maybe even pushing a wardrobe against the door until dawn's faint morning light drove his fears away. But he reminded himself his mobile was down there, over a grand's worth, and with all the secrets it held. And so he urged himself on once more. If they were still there, he had to appear confident. Tense his muscles, snarl and shout. Put on a show. Like a wild animal. The beast he sometimes revealed to pathetic, fearful girls as they pleaded and begged. But it wasn't nearly so easy when you were alone in the dark.

Shady began slowly descending the staircase, treading cautiously to avoid any creaking that might alert a waiting attacker. He was close to weeping as he reached the small hallway and the heavy security door that led from his private quarters to the restaurant itself. And once again he stopped, so tempted to run away. But the fear of losing the phone proved a powerful motivation. It was the potential loss of the photos that concerned him most. The majority taken himself of one pathetic female or another, and others downloaded from the dark web. Photos that fascinated him, dominating his masturbatory fantasies ever more with each day that passed. Images of death, destruction, and decay he told himself ordinary, less enlightened people would never comprehend with their rigid, straight-jacket morality. Because he was better than them, different, unique, and superior. He truly understood the attraction death could hold. The alluring sexuality of a female body, still and lifeless, accepting of his every whim and desire when they'd finally breathed their last breath. That was total domination, total and utter control.

He reminded himself that his inspired understanding was evolving like never before as he gradually embraced his dark side. There was so much to look forward to. So much to excite. And so he had no other choice. Scared or not, he had to get that phone. At least in part, a glorious, life-affirming future depended on his success.

Shady slowly opened the security door an inch or two at a time and entered the restaurant, just his head at first, craning his neck, then his entire body, to see numerous shards of broken glass all over the floor, along with half a red house brick that told its own story. And then, as he pressed himself against a wall, protecting his back, he raised his eyes towards the shattered pane to see someone standing outside in the darkness of the night. A hooded figure wearing a long dark coat. A masked person holding what looked like a wine bottle with a white rag in the top. An individual focused on him and only him, as if they'd been standing there the entire time, awaiting his arrival. And then, as Shady stared at the person, unable to recognise them despite his best efforts, they lit the rag with a lighter, drew their right arm back and hurled the bottle into the restaurant towards him. The bottle smashed on the floor tiles about ten feet in front of Shady, then exploded into yellow flames, an instantaneous fireball filling the space, burning his face, feet, and semi-naked body, making him scream.

Shady darted through the restaurant towards the rear exit, shaking, hyperventilating, his pulse racing, and his heart pounding in his chest as the heat intensified beyond anything he'd experienced. He moved with speed despite the soles of his feet being burnt and raw, keen to get out of there, desperate to save his life. He thought he heard the sound of laughter as he grabbed his phone off the bar mid-step. But as he glanced back with a rapid turn of his head, he saw the mystery figure was gone, the street now empty. Within seconds, he was falling headlong into the walled concrete courtyard at the back of the building, where he wept as he rang the emergency services, urgently summoning help.

Shady crawled away to the far side of the yard, panting hard and acutely aware he'd both soiled and wet himself as he lay there crying on the ground. And at that moment, one of the lowest of his life, as he curled up in the foetal position, searching for comfort, his many painful burns and grazed knees demanding attention, he swore silent revenge on whoever had humiliated and hurt him in such a way. He told himself it was the biggest mistake of their sad life as the smell of black smoke and excrement filled the air. Because one day soon, he'd find out who they were. And then they'd pay. He'd destroy them. Tear their life apart. Make them suffer like they'd never suffered before. When they were helpless. When they couldn't fight back. He'd make them wish they'd never heard the name Mark Shady, let alone dared petrol-bomb his business. Yes, they'd pay.

As he lay there writhing, Shady continued consoling himself with thoughts of revenge. Not just on the arsonist but on Carly too, as her image came to mind. He could see her face as if she was there mocking him in the light of the flames, finding satisfaction in his suffering. And in some strange way, his resulting hatred gave him strength. Now, he told himself, there were two people to punish. So he had to survive. He had to stay strong. Loathing gave him purpose. No one hurt Mark Shady and got away with it. A raging storm was coming their way – a dark, irresistible tide.

13

When his phone rang, Lewis had just removed his warm padded coat, hanging it on the back of his office chair. He shook his head and swore. Someone wanted him already. Demanding his attention so soon after he'd been called in. It was an entirely predictable start to his working day. Oh, the joy of Sunday mornings.

He held the handset to his face with a despondent look. 'DS Lewis, CID,' he said, less than enthusiastically.

'Morning, Ray, it's Laura. Fancy a cuppa?'

He settled in his seat, scratching his nose with his free hand when it began to itch. 'What, now?'

'Yeah, I need a word.'

'I'm surprised you're even in on a weekend.'

'Needs must, things that couldn't wait.'

His thoughts turned to the possibility of a second breakfast. A lovely fry-up piled high on his plate with plenty of sauce. He could almost taste the greasy fare as saliva formed in his mouth. 'Canteen?' he asked, more in hope than expectation.

'No, not this morning; I'll see you in my office in five minutes. I've got to be in Llanelli by ten.'

Lewis was ever so slightly out of breath when he opened Kesey's office door, despite their rooms only being a short distance apart in the same corridor. He smiled thankfully when she handed him a mug of coffee filled to the brim.

'You look tired, Ray,' she said in her Brummie accent, her words not surprising him at all. He grimaced as he sat, thinking Kesey had a frustrating tendency to mother him despite her comparative youth. It could be a pain in the arse, but at least it showed she cared.

'Long night,' he said, hoping that would satisfy her. 'The old back's playing up again – an unwelcome legacy of my rugby-playing days. Most props are the same. And the winter weather never helps. I only got a couple of hours of sleep.'

He was half expecting another lecture on his

need to lose some weight. But to his relief, it seemed Kesey had other things in mind.

'Did you enjoy the party?' she asked with a smile.

'I did, thanks,' he replied after a gulp of coffee, thinking back to a surprisingly pleasant evening.

'And you stayed off the booze,' she continued. 'Well done. I'm proud of you.'

He looked back at her, thinking he hadn't had a choice. Not when driving. But he'd somehow managed to enjoy himself none the less.

'Bet Jan was pleased,' he said with a grin.

'She was, and she loved the chocolates.'

I should bloody well hope so at that price, he thought. *Thirteen quid for a small box.*

'Glad to hear it,' he said with feigned enthusiasm. 'I was hoping she'd like them.'

'I'm assuming you've heard?' Kesey said, her demeanour suddenly changing, her smile disappearing as quickly as it had appeared. And he knew immediately that small talk was over. The actual reason for their meeting was about to be revealed.

'Heard what?' he asked, glad to change the subject and put the focus on something other than himself.

'You really don't know?'

He looked back at her with a blank expression, shaking his head before she continued.

'I was called out in the early hours after the party. Fortunately, I'd only had the one glass of wine. I just can't stand the hangovers these days. Not since having a child.'

Get to the point, woman, he thought. She was definitely building up to something. 'What happened?' he asked, keen to know more.

Kesey leaned forward in her chair, elbows on her desk as she supported her head with her palms below her chin.

'Shady's place went up in flames. The restaurant, the flat, the lot. And it looks like it's arson. The fire people think someone used some kind of accelerant to get the blaze going. We'll have a full report in a couple of days once all the lab tests are done. But the guy in charge at the scene seemed pretty certain what he was talking about. He's been in the job a long time. Said he had a talent for reading fires. And he was certain it had been started deliberately. Something to do with the fire evolving rapidly with high temperatures and particular burn patterns, which tell a story. Interesting, not something I'd heard before. It all made sense once he explained it. I've asked him to rush the report through.'

Lewis's eyes narrowed. It seemed like good news. Karma, a bit of natural justice with Shady on the receiving end for once. But there was always a need for suspicion where that scumbag was concerned.

'An insurance job?' Lewis asked, thinking maybe Shady was after a payout. Perhaps the restaurant hadn't been doing as well as it appeared.

Kesey shook her head.

'No, I don't think so. Shady was asleep alone upstairs. He got out, but with burns. And he'd inhaled a lot of smoke. Like I said, I saw the place. It's in one hell of a state. He was lucky to escape with his life.'

Lewis gave a little laugh followed by a caustic smile. 'More's the pity,' he said. 'Where's the bastard now?'

'On the burns ward at Morriston Hospital. I had a quick word with his consultant, a Dr Singh, before ringing you. The injuries are serious but not severe. There'll be no skin grafts, nothing like that. But Shady's going to be in a lot of pain until things start to heal. They'll give him something for that – topical applications for his skin, antibiotics for any infection – and then, in a few days, all being well, he'll be discharged. I suspect they need the bed.'

'Close but no cigar,' Lewis said with feeling. 'If it

is arson, whoever lit that fire would have done the world a massive favour if Shady had died.'

Kesey looked her sergeant in the eye, and he suspected he knew exactly where the conversation was going. There was another lecture coming. One he could almost predict word for word. And her tone would change as if she was pronouncing some universal truth; it always did. 'I'm very well aware of your thoughts on men like Shady, Ray. But we can't condone vigilante action, whoever the victim is. You know that as well as I do. Because if we did, where would it all end? We need to investigate the arson with due diligence, as in any other case. I've already had the chief super on the phone worried about the inevitable press coverage. Shady's got some influential friends. And he knows how to work the press.'

Lewis looked at his watch. 'What, Halliday? On the phone already? What a great start to your day. Does the twat ever get off your back?'

'You know what he's like, Ray. He's usually in by seven, even when he could be at home. He doesn't even take his leave. And he reads everything, all the incident reports, and doesn't miss a thing. It sometimes seems he knows what I've been doing better than I do.'

Lewis thought for a second or two, pondering

her earlier choice of words. Kesey rarely said anything without good reason. That wasn't her style.
'You said "we", that *we* need to investigate the case
as we would any other. What's that meant to mean,
exactly? Who's the *we* that we're talking about? Because I'm guessing it's not you.'

Unusually for the DI, she looked slightly sheep-
ish. 'That's, er, why I asked to see you rather than do
it on the phone.'

'Oh, here we go.'

She glared at him, and he knew she was about to
use his name again to drive home a point. No
change there. A familiar pattern. She often used it
more than the norm. 'You know we're short of staff,
Ray. That's no secret. I've got people on leave, others
on sick and on courses. And arson needs someone
with experience. It's a serious offence. Halliday
stressed that. He made it crystal clear. And with the
way things are, that means you. I need you to head
up the investigation for however long it takes. Make
it your number one priority. And by all means, use
one of the DCs to do the leg work if that helps.
Maybe that lad on secondment, Pete Gavin. He
hasn't got much on. With a bit of luck, Shady will
know something or will have seen something, and
you'll have it all tied up before you know it.'

Lewis leaned his head back with a moan, thinking he constantly drew the short straw. But then he felt that the case provided an opportunity. The chance to see Shady at his most vulnerable. To put some pressure on him at his weakest. First, the car was vandalised and now this, a fire, potentially deadly. It was likely the scumbag was scared shit-less. And being the senior investigating officer would give him some control. That had to be a good thing.

'I'm assuming Shady dialled 999?' Lewis asked with a pretend look of boredom masking his growing enthusiasm.

'Yeah, of course,' Kesey replied, seemingly glad he was cooperating.

'What time?' he asked.

'Twenty minutes past four.'

Lewis nodded. 'Okay, useful to know.'

'I listened to the recording of the call,' she said. 'It wouldn't be a bad idea for you to do the same. Shady sounded in one hell of a state, yelling that the place was going up in flames, saying that someone tried to kill him, in a total panic. And he could be right. Maybe someone did try to kill him. As of now, we're looking at arson. But it could become at-tempted murder when we know more. We need to follow the evidence. See where it takes us. I can always ask Halliday to allocate more resources if necessary. My overtime budget's not looking great.'

Lewis liked the sound of Shady panicking; it raised his spirits, and he smiled. If the scrote was suffering both physically and mentally, then good, there was some justice in that. Shady deserved no less. Perhaps it would give him an idea of the trauma his victims experienced. Not that psychos ever cared about anyone else. No one but themselves.

'Any number of people would like to see the bastard dead,' said Lewis, cutting short his thread of thoughts. 'And who can blame them? I'll take a look at the restaurant building and then pop down to Morriston to give Shady the good news. I'm sure he's going to love me being the SIO. It should cheer him right up. I can't wait.'

Kesey laughed, seemingly amused as he'd intended. But a more severe expression quickly followed. Something else that didn't surprise him. She was almost as predictable as night and day.

'I don't want you giving Shady a hard time, Ray. And especially not on the ward. Not when staff and other patients are watching and listening. Be careful what you say. Remember, he's the victim this time, not a suspect. And we need to treat him accordingly. He's a member of the public like everyone else.'

Lewis blew out air. 'Yeah, yeah, I know. You'll be telling me he's a taxpayer next.'

Kesey shook her head with a sigh. 'Make sure you keep me updated,' she said insistently, ignoring his comments, as she often did. 'And I want to read Shady's statement once it's done. Halliday's all over this. I need to know what's happening.'

Lewis struggled to his feet with a groan, placing his empty mug on her desk next to a thick sheaf of papers. 'I bet he is,' he said. 'And a statement you shall have. Anything your little heart desires, ma'am. Your wish is my command.'

'You can stop taking the piss.'

Lewis looked back on approaching the door.

'I might call at that big Tesco near Swansea while I'm out. Is there anything you want me to pick up? I plan on buying some real sugar to replace those horrendous sweeteners you're so keen on.'

She smiled. 'A packet of chocolate biscuits would be nice. Digestives; you've eaten most of mine.'

'Dark chocolate or milk?' he asked with a small curtsey.

She picked up a blue cardboard file. 'Make it

dark; you might not scoff so many of them. And drive carefully. There's ice on the roads.'

'One last question,' he said, his hand on the door handle as he ignored her words of caution. 'We do definitely know Carly Flowers wasn't in the flat at the time of the fire, don't we? Daisy said she's been up in London – something to do with her course. But I'm not certain when she's expected back.'

'There was just Shady. He was alone, like I said. You can stop worrying. No one else was there.'

His entire body relaxed as he prepared to go. 'Well, thank fuck for that,' he said. 'Dark choccy bics it is. And I mustn't forget that sugar. Time I was on my way.'

14

Despite Kesey's earlier description, Lewis was surprised by the degree of destruction he witnessed when he parked his CID car as close as possible to Shady's blackened restaurant home later that morning. As he exited the vehicle, standing stiffly in the chilly lane, staring into the fire-ravaged building, Lewis noted the entire ground floor had been completely gutted, the tables, chairs, and wooden bar all burnt to an unrecognisable blackened cinder. All the internal walls and flooring were badly smoke- and fire-damaged, and the water damage from extinguishing the inferno was extensive too. The restaurant really was a complete wreck. Getting the place straight would take a great deal of money, time, and effort.

As he stood there, silently cursing the cold, looking to left and right, the ghost of a smile played on the detective's lips as he considered the implications. It would probably take months to sort the place out, if it ever opened again. Any inconvenience to Shady had to be a good thing. Something to celebrate. Here was hoping the scrote didn't have the correct insurance cover. *That*, Lewis said to himself, *would cheer me right up*. A bright spark in a dark world of woe.

The DS lowered himself back into his car as a winter drizzle began to fall, seemingly coming from every direction at the behest of a swirling east wind that made him shiver. He switched on the engine and turned up the heater to maximum but didn't engage the gears, leaving the vehicle in neutral. One job at a time, he said to himself. It was a case of priorities. Time to give Daisy another ring. Keep him updated and put him in the picture. An old friend deserved that much. Or maybe he already knew. Even had something to do with the fire. No, surely not, though nothing was beyond the bounds of possibility.

Lewis took his phone from a jacket pocket and

dialled Flowers's mobile number. He only had to wait a matter of seconds before receiving an answer.

'Hi, Daisy, it's Ray. Got five minutes?'

'Yeah, of course, no problem at all. I'm just at home with the missus. Typical Sunday.'

Lewis massaged his chin. 'She's back from London?'

'Yeah, sorry, I meant to let you know,' Flowers replied. 'She is, and it's good news. Things are looking up. Carly seemed a bit more receptive to our concerns. Or, at least, she was willing to listen to her mum's point of view. And then, yesterday afternoon, she rang to say she'd just dumped Shady by text. She didn't use those words, not exactly. She just said she'd ended the relationship for personal reasons. Not because of anything her mum or I had said, but because she thought he was getting too serious. She wants to go off travelling in the summer with a girl-friend on the same course. Greek island hopping. They planned it together in London. And, of course, Shady hated the idea when she told him. Tried putting her under all sorts of pressure not to go. Said she was being selfish. That if she really loved him, she wouldn't go, that sort of thing. And that was it. Carly decided he wasn't the man for her.'

'You must be well chuffed.'

'It's a massive relief, to be honest. I couldn't be happier. If she wants to go off for a few weeks in the summer, I'll happily help fund the trip. Anything to keep her away from Shady is a big plus for me. I'll do whatever it takes.'

Lewis paused for a beat, weighing up the information in his analytical mind, taking it all in. Suspicion went with the job.

'Carly sent the text yesterday afternoon, yes? Saturday?'

'Yeah, that's right, but what's it matter?'

'Someone torched Shady's place in the early hours of this morning.'

'What, a fire?'

'I'm there now. The whole place went up. Shady got out alive, but only just. We're looking at a major investigation. Arson, maybe even attempted murder. I should know more once I've taken a statement and we get the forensic reports back.'

Flowers was quick to respond, his tone darkening. 'It wasn't me, if that's what you're thinking. I haven't been anywhere near Carmarthen. Not for weeks.'

Lewis forced an unconvincing chuckle. 'Not a bad break, though. For you, I mean. If he had you recorded like he claimed, that's likely gone. That has to be a weight off.'

There was an agitated tone to Flowers's voice when he fired out his reply. 'That fire had fuck all to do with me! I want to make that crystal clear. And I resent you even suggesting it. I thought you knew me better than that.'

'Come on, Daisy, take it easy. Never crossed my mind for a second, mate,' Lewis said as he lowered the heating a notch or two.

'I should fucking well hope not.'

Lewis hesitated for a beat, still wondering if Flowers knew more than he was letting on. 'There is one other thing that comes to mind.'

'What's that?' Flowers snapped back, still seemingly irritated by the direction of the conversation.

'Shady's not going to like being dumped. Not one little bit. He's the sort of bloke who holds a grudge and takes rejection personally – a lot of his kind do. You're all right for a day or two at least. The bastard's lying in a hospital bed in Morriston. But he'll be out soon enough. And he may well have revenge on his mind. You'll need to tell your Carly to watch her back.'

15

Lewis was lamenting the nagging pain in his arthritic joints as he drove south down the M4 towards Morriston, a short distance from the seaside city of Swansea with its sweeping bay. The approximately twenty-five-mile journey passed slowly due to the various traffic enforcement cameras, Lewis reluctantly sticking close to the speed limit because he felt he had to. And he wasn't in the best of moods when he finally drove into the 750-bed teaching hospital's busy car park about half an hour later, struggling to find a parking space for about ten minutes, before finally switching off the engine and pulling up the handbrake.

Lewis lit a large Havana cigar brought back by a

long-serving colleague from a holiday in Cuba and smoked it in the car, greedily sucking in the toxic grey fumes and intermittently coughing and wheezing before eventually stubbing it out, telling himself it was time to get down to business. And that maybe Kesey was right for once. Perhaps he should give up smoking. Breathing was sometimes tricky. Something he had to accept. His chest seemed to be getting worse almost by the day. Or it could be the stress of the job. That could be it. Not the fags at all.

When the detective reached the main hospital building he asked a pretty dark-haired nurse for directions to the burns ward. And that one brief, simple, and informative conversation beat him down a little further, leaving him even more dejected than he'd felt in the car. As the young woman walked away with a sway of her hips, he was left feeling old, worn out, and jaded by her evident youth and vitality. He was reminded of his mortality. The grim reaper watching his every step. Time passed so very quickly. One minute, he ruminated, you were a bright young thing starting your career full of hope and expectation, just like the nurse with her bright eyes and glowing skin. And the next, well, retirement dawned, and all your youthful idealism was gone. It wasn't the first time such things had come to mind. And he knew it wouldn't be the last. It seemed ageing surprised everyone as it crept up, sinking in its claws, him included. He had to accept he was getting old. Even if that same young and idealistic copper he'd once been was still somewhere deep inside.

Lewis pushed his melancholy thoughts from his mind as he strode on looking for a lift, keen to avoid the stairs and making a conscious decision to focus back on work, a task he sometimes thought was the only thing that kept him sane. Because policing gave him purpose. It wasn't only the salary, although that came in useful; he was contributing, doing something worthwhile for society, and locking a few miserable scumbags up when things went his way. And that made life worth living. So he'd keep doing it for however long he had left.

Lewis spotted Shady as soon as he entered the busy burns ward. And he was pleased to see that the other man really did look in a terrible state as he lay propped up on several white pillows, attached to various monitors, intermittently snoring with his eyes tightly closed.

As he slowly approached the bed, Lewis recalled a much-loved episode of the classic British comedy show *Only Fools and Horses* in which one of the characters had lain under a sunbed for far too long, with the inevitable results. And like Rodney Trotter, Shady's face looked red raw, his eyebrows virtually gone, and the usually immaculate hair, of which he had seemed so very proud, cut short, revealing a blistered scalp.

The detective resisted the impulse to laugh as he pulled up a chair, reaching out to shake Shady awake before sitting. Lewis noted that Shady was all about image, that he must find his new reality tough to take, and there was some satisfaction in that.

'Oh, for fuck's sake. What the hell are you doing here?' Shady blurted out as soon as he opened his eyes, blinking away the sleep.

'Lovely to see you as well, Mark, my boy. I would have brought you some grapes, but I ate them on the way. You really do look like shit.'

'Is that supposed to be funny?'

Lewis grinned. 'Not as funny as your face. What a state. More a cesspit than Brad Pitt. Not so handsome now.'

Shady bared his teeth, nostrils flared, focusing on Lewis with cold, hard, and flinty eyes.

'Just fuck off and leave me alone, or I'm calling a nurse.'

'A nurse? What, to hold your hand or tuck you in? Or maybe to read you a bedtime story. Is that the best you've got?'

'Get the fuck out!'

Lewis lowered his tone as a middle-aged male nurse with a shiny bald head that caught the light glared in his direction. The detective adopted a more relaxed persona, sitting back in his chair. 'Oh, come on now, Shady, don't be like that. I'm just doing my job, that's all. Someone burnt your place down. And they did a cracking job of it too. It's my job to find out who.'

Shady made a face. 'Are you telling me *you're* investigating the attack? You, of all people. Is that your idea of a joke? Because it doesn't seem very funny to me.'

Lewis forced a laugh followed by a sardonic smile that came more easily. He wanted to leave, to tell Shady precisely what he thought of him, to pin a medal on the arsonist's chest. 'Do you want the fire looked into or not? Some things you can't control. It's me or nobody. Make your choice.'

Shady didn't reply.

Lewis craned his head towards Shady, speaking directly into his right ear, lowering his tone so as not to be overheard. 'Look, you piece of shit. There's a thousand places I'd rather be. I don't like the situation any more than you do. So if you want the arson investigated, if you want to make it official, answer a few questions and make a statement. You know the routine. The quicker I'm out of here, the happier we'll both be. So let's get it over with, shall we?'

Shady shook his head while mumbling obscenities. 'Is there no chance of someone else doing this? I don't care who. Just not you.'

Lewis noted that the younger man appeared very different from their previous encounters. He seemed less full of himself and not nearly as self-confident. Shady was trying to convey his usual self-assurance. Trying to be the big man, the dominator, but failing miserably. All the swagger was gone. The detective knew that didn't make Shady any less dangerous – not to the vulnerable when he was discharged and back on the streets. But it pleased him nonetheless. He answered Shady's question with only one word. 'No.'

Shady responded while holding the detective's gaze, Lewis thought not wanting to seem squeezed or lose face more than he already had. 'Okay, have it your way, let's play your game,' Shady said. 'There's only so much time I can spend chatting up the nurses. None of 'em are up to much – not on my level. What do you want to know?'

Lewis took a yellow plastic biro and police-issue pocketbook from the inside pocket of his jacket. He thought the situation as ridiculous as Shady seemed to, but he told himself needs must. Best go through the motions. It would feel so much better to ram the pen up one of Shady's singed nostrils until he squealed. That would feel so good, so satisfying. If only such things were possible.

'I want you to talk me through everything that happened that night leading up to the fire. Give me as much detail as possible. Don't leave anything out. Sometimes even the most seemingly insignificant details can be important.'

Shady outlined events from when he was woken by the sound of crashing glass to when he called the emergency services as Lewis listened with interest. The detective felt no compunction to ever catch the arsonist – not on a personal level. Every cell of his being would have preferred not to investigate at all. But he was resigned to doing his job as best he could because that was the nature of policing. Like it or not, he was under orders. That was the way the system worked.

'Okay, so you're telling me you actually saw whoever threw the petrol bomb through your smashed window?'

'Are you deaf or something? That's what I said no more than a few seconds ago.'

Lewis pondered that the investigation might end almost as soon as it started.

'And did you recognise this person from your legion of enemies?'

Shady shook his head, clearly agitated as Lewis had intended, grimacing with the effort of it all. 'No, I fucking well didn't. But he will pay big time when I find out who he was. Look at the state of me. And my business has gone up in flames. No one gets away with that. I don't care who they are.'

Lewis chose to ignore Shady's bravado, knowing nothing he said would make any difference, and felt more amused than anything else. He poised his pen above the next blank page of his pocketbook, marked with a large paperclip for convenience.

'So you're telling me you've got no idea at all who carried out the attack? There's not a single suspect who comes to mind. No one who stands out amongst all the men it could have been.'

'I said so, didn't I?'

Lewis crossed one heavy leg over the other.

'Okay, right, if we're going to do this, we'll do it

properly. Let's get a description down on paper. How tall was the attacker?'

Shady seemed temporarily distracted as a shapely blonde-haired nurse of about thirty walked past carrying a bedpan. He focused on her bum as it moved rhythmically under her uniform. He blinked repeatedly, then looked back at Lewis, licking his dry lips with a darting tongue.

'I think he was probably about five foot seven or eight. Maybe a bit taller. It all happened so very quickly. One second I saw him standing there in the darkness, and then the next the place burst into flames. It was like an explosion, and then he was gone. Lucky for him, he got away. If I'd got my hands on him, I'd have torn him to fucking pieces. He wouldn't have stood a chance. Not against a man like me.'

Lewis smirked, thinking there was that contrived machismo again. But it seemed a lot less convincing than before. Shady was a small and pathetic individual in so many ways, like a playground bully looking to boost his fragile self-esteem. Lewis had never been more certain of anything in his life.

'What about the attacker's build?' he asked, almost on autopilot, following a protocol he'd used more times than he could count.

Shady took a deep breath through his nose and closed his eyes briefly as if thinking back to the events of the early hours was getting to him.

'He was wearing a big, full-length coat that came right down to his knees, and he had a hood up. I think he was a beefy bloke, but it was hard to tell. I can't be a hundred per cent certain.'

'What about his face?'

'Well, he was masked. So, it was impossible to tell.'

'No beard or glasses visible?'

'Not that I could see.'

Lewis made a scribbled note of the response, deciding to move on.

'What colour was the coat?'

Shady gave a puzzled expression.

'Dark, I think. Yeah, dark. Black, dark grey, or maybe navy blue. It was hard to tell. I was focused on the petrol bomb in his hand. I only saw the bastard for seconds at most. And then the entire room was on fire.'

Lewis nodded less than enthusiastically, glad to be approaching the end of an interview he wished had never happened at all. He thought Shady's information was as useful as a chocolate teapot. Which didn't concern him at all. It wasn't a significant loss if he failed to catch the arsonist. He could still say he'd done his job.

'Anything else you can tell me before I head off?'

'That's it. I've told you everything. Let me know if you find anything out. And I'll need something for the insurance. I want to get the work started on the restaurant. I've got no money coming in and no flat. I can make a claim from here.'

'I'll just get the statement written. You can read it, date it, sign it as a true record, and we're done.'

Shady nodded and said, 'Okay.'

Once finished, Lewis stood, fastening his jacket and waiting for a white-coated male doctor, who was chatting to a nursing sister with red hair who did nothing but smile, to stroll past. The detective leaned in towards Shady as he had earlier, again whispering just inches from his ear. And then he said what he had been planning to say all along – the things that conveyed his true feelings. Stuff he needed to get off his chest.

'I'll do my job because that's what I'm paid for. I'll investigate the arson as I would any other case. I can guarantee you that. Even if the description you gave is a pile of steaming shit. But don't ever go thinking I've forgotten who or what you are. When you're out of here, you go anywhere near my daughter, Carly Flowers, or any other girl, and you'll have more than a petrol bomb to worry about. That fire showed you just how much in danger you are. Hurt any woman again, and I'll fucking end you. Even if I finish my career in the process. Because it would be worth it. I'll put you in the ground.'

16

Lewis entered the well-appointed West Wales Police Headquarters lounge bar just after six that evening, smiling at Tanya, the familiar barmaid, as he approached the serving counter. He ordered a pint of best bitter, three packets of his favourite salt and vinegar crisps, and two Cheddar cheese and onion rolls, reluctantly rejecting the idea of a third roll in the interests of his heart-healthy diet.

'Nice to see you again, Ray. It's been a while.'

He nodded and then checked his watch.

'Yeah, I'm more of a rugby club man these days. I'm meeting Laura Kesey for a quick one before heading home. Her idea, not mine. No idea why.'

'People can surprise us sometimes.'

He nodded his agreement, momentarily focusing on the middle-aged barmaid's ample cleavage as she prepared his order, self-consciously tearing his gaze away as she handed him his fifty-pence change.

'You can keep it, love, or put it in the charity box – whichever suits you best.'

She slotted the coin into a blue plastic container collecting donations for the local air ambulance, then ran a hand through her dyed black hair, pushing it away from her face.

'I'm not in the best of moods to be honest, Ray. I got a speeding fine in the post yesterday morning, a hundred quid for doing thirty-four in a thirty near Llansteffan. It was early morning, and there was no other traffic about. It seems so unfair. You can't make it go away for me, can you?'

Lewis shook his head forlornly, then took a slurp of beer, savouring the yeasty taste before swallowing. 'I wish I could, love. It's all on computer these days – more than my job is worth. I've got six points on my licence myself.'

The barmaid grinned, heavily made-up blue eyes twinkling under the bright fluorescent lights. 'And there was me hoping you'd be my knight in shining armour.'

Lewis laughed, thinking her surprisingly chatty. Like she wanted to talk.

'The old armour's a bit rusty these days, love,' he said. 'It creaks when I move.'

She smiled, revealing slightly yellowed teeth with an apparent gap between the front two. 'Yeah, I know the feeling. None of us are getting any younger.'

He opened his first packet of crisps, still standing at the bar rather than sitting. 'Is it always this quiet?' he asked, speaking with his mouth full.

'Yeah, usually till about seven. It gets a bit busier after that.'

'Have a drink on me if you fancy one,' he said, taking a large bite of roll and chewing.

'I'll have a coffee, if that's all right? I don't usually drink while working. Not with all you coppers about. I like to keep a clear head.'

He handed her a five-pound note taken from a trouser pocket. 'Course it is, love. Have whatever you want. Makes no difference to me.'

She poured the black coffee, added a small carton of cream, and then returned to their conversation. There were no other people in the room. 'It's my birthday, the big five-oh.'

Lewis drained his glass to the halfway point,

thinking she looked her age, despite the makeup. She appeared worn out by life, just like him. But for all that, there was still an attraction.

'Don't worry about it. You're just a girl,' he said. 'I've got a few years on you. I wish I was fifty again. Those days are long gone.'

She gave a nervous little laugh. 'My sister was supposed to be taking me for a curry in town on Thursday evening to celebrate. At that nice place in King Street. The Ginger. I was really looking forward to it. I love a vindaloo. But she's laid up with a broken ankle after a fall off a ladder, poor thing. You don't fancy it, do you?'

Lewis tilted his head back, then emptied his glass, wondering if she was joking, just messing about. It had been a long time since he'd been on a date – a very long time. Years. To his surprise, he found himself hoping she meant it. He chose his words carefully, not wanting to make a fool of himself if she retracted what seemed a genuine offer, letting him down. He sometimes thought he'd never date again, that those days were gone. 'Well, if it's your special birthday, and your sister can't make it, I'd be happy to step in,' he said. 'But the meal would be on me, my treat, if you're up for it. What do you say?'

He was half expecting Tanya to suddenly make some excuse not to go. But instead, she gave him a beaming smile, fluttering her long, mascara-laden eyelashes as Kesey entered the bar. 'That'll be lovely, Ray. I'll meet you at the restaurant at eight. There's already a table booked. I don't think my sister cancelled. You know how popular it is.'

Lewis nodded enthusiastically, glanced sheepishly in Kesey's direction as she approached the bar, then quickly gathered together his remaining snacks before heading to a nearby table.

Kesey ordered a pot of tea and joined Lewis after asking Tanya to bring her hot drink over once it was ready. She looked down at the crisps and rolls on the low table before Lewis and shook her head. He was half expecting another lecture on the benefits of healthy eating, but for once, it didn't come. 'Do you want a drink, Ray? I didn't realise you haven't got one.'

'I'm all right, thanks. I've had the one pint, and I'm driving.'

'What about a tea or coffee?'

He shook his head. 'No, I'm good, ta. When I get home, I'll have a few cans in front of the telly. It'll help me sleep.'

Kesey frowned, which came as no surprise to

Lewis at all. He looked up and smiled as Tanya brought Kesey's tea to the table on a green plastic tray. The barmaid turned her head, looking back and winking as she walked away.

'Don't forget our date, Raymond. I'm looking forward to it. There's a curry with my name on it.'

Lewis swallowed hard without reply, acutely aware that Kesey was stifling a laugh. He decided on a strong, sweet coffee after all, ordering at the bar and taking a gulp before returning to his seat with cup in hand.

'Okay, let's get it over with,' he said. 'I'm sure there's some comment you want to make. I was hoping you wouldn't find out.'

Kesey grinned. 'A date, eh? With the lovely Tanya. I didn't think you had it in you. Quite the Casanova.'

Lewis felt a flush creep across his cheeks, making him feel like a fool – a man his age blushing like a schoolgirl. 'It's her birthday,' he mumbled. 'Her sister can't make it. So I stepped in. It's just a meal. Not a romantic thing. You can stop taking the piss.'

'Yeah, yeah, I believe you. A thousand wouldn't. You'll be on *Love Island* next. I can picture it. You on the beach in your Speedos.'

He frowned hard, ears turning red. 'Are you finished?'

'No, I'm pleased for you, Ray. It's about time you got back in the saddle. You deserve a bit of female attention. It'll be good for you. And Tanya's a lovely person. I've always liked her. You could do a lot worse.'

'Yeah, yeah, I know,' he replied. 'I do quite fancy her if you must know. Fingers crossed it all goes well.'

'I hope you're planning to dress up nice and smart. And have a proper shave. She'll like that. Make a good impression for once.'

Lewis ignored Kesey's comments, keen to change the subject – anything to take the focus off himself. He couldn't figure out why he was finding the conversation quite so embarrassing, but for whatever reason, he was. 'I saw Shady at the hospital,' he said, looking the DI in the eye. 'He's looking in a right state. Although, like you said, I can't see him being in for long.'

Kesey sipped her tea. 'Did he have anything helpful to tell you?'

Lewis screwed up his face. 'Toss all, really. He saw his attacker. But the description he gave was less than useless. Nothing that helps. Could be almost anyone. Complete waste of time.'

'I had a word with Pete, who's been reviewing the CCTV footage.'

'Well, yeah, I know. Who do you think told him to do it?'

She gave him a look that said a thousand words, none good. 'Do you want to know what he told me or not?'

Lewis opened his third packet of crisps and began munching. 'I'm all ears.'

'Dylan – Anna's brother – was in Carmarthen a short time before the fire, or at least his car was. The recording's not clear enough to identify the driver with any certainty, but the car was driven up Lammas Street just after ten. And there were two people in the front seats.'

Lewis raised his eyebrows. 'What? Ten o'clock? The fire was close to four. That's about a six-hour gap. Hardly the best evidence in the world.'

From Kesey's expression, he could see she didn't appreciate his dismissive response. But some things needed saying. 'I'm not saying the CCTV makes Dylan an obvious suspect, Ray. And he hasn't got any kind of record; I checked. But he's got to be worth looking at after everything that's happened. He's a person of interest, at the very least. Surely you agree with that.'

Lewis was very much hoping Dylan wasn't the guilty one. And if he was, that there wouldn't be enough to convict him. 'I'll have a chat with him in the morning at his parents' place. See what he's got to say for himself. I won't bring him to the station unless he says something implicating himself. I want to keep it as low-key as possible. The family has had enough upset without us making things worse.'

Kesey nodded. 'Makes sense.'

Lewis decided it was time to leave when Tanya waved from behind the bar. By then, other officers had started arriving – not many, but enough – and the last thing he wanted was rumours. Staying low-key was a priority after Shady's recent social media hilarity. He looked at Kesey with a sigh. 'So, are you going to tell me what happened about that promotion you were promised? I thought you'd have been a DCI long before now.'

Kesey gave a sour expression, placing her empty cup back on its saucer before standing. 'I'd better be on my way, Ray. Jan's making a lasagne for seven.'

Lewis nodded. 'I'll walk out with you,' he said.

'Aren't you going to say goodbye to Tanya?'

He stood stiffly, stretched, then gave Tanya a quick smile and called out, 'Bye.' The last thing he wanted was gossip. But it seemed the right thing to do.

Kesey talked as she walked, her car keys in one hand. 'Keep me fully up to date with the case, yeah? Halliday wants regular reports on this one. And you know what he's like. He does love to be critical.'

Lewis gave a little curtsey, meant to make her laugh. 'I'll let you know how it goes with Dylan as soon as I've seen him.'

17

Lewis listened to an opera compilation as he drove towards the Edwards family's smallholding just after nine the following morning, something he hadn't done for a while. He had no idea of the meaning of the various Italian arias. But he found himself enjoying the soaring solo singers and chorus nonetheless. He thought back to an impressive Welsh National Opera performance of Bizet's *Carmen* he'd attended with his ex-wife in Cardiff as an anniversary treat before she'd left, the years melting away, then pushed the thoughts from his mind as his eyes moistened. *Sometimes*, he said to himself, *memories do me no good at all*. The past was gone. Never to be repeated. There was only the now.

And she was never coming back. So maybe forgetting was best.

Lewis switched off the music a mile or two from Brechfa as the winter sun broke through the dark clouds, illuminating the Cothi Valley in a soft white light that seemed to make the green fields glow. God's creation at its very best. He might have appreciated the vista for a little longer in other circumstances. But he was suddenly focused back on work: the pending interview with Dylan and whatever it would bring.

Lewis thought it unlikely Anna's brother was the arsonist, suspecting he'd have used his fists rather than a petrol bomb. He'd met Dylan during the rape investigation, and arson just didn't seem his style. But the detective reminded himself it was a possibility he shouldn't ignore. Experience had taught him to rule little out without excellent reason. Keep an open mind and follow the evidence; that was best. And then, maybe, he'd find the truth.

To his satisfaction, Lewis spotted Dylan Edwards as soon as he approached the house, pulling up the unmarked police car and switching off the engine. Dylan had come out of a stone outbuilding pushing a rusty metal wheelbarrow filled to the top with what looked like horse manure. Dylan stopped, let go of the barrow's handles, raised himself to his full height, and glared at Lewis as he exited the car, never looking away.

Lewis stood his ground as the younger man quickly approached him, Dylan's big hands repeatedly forming into tight fists. The detective half expected Dylan to punch him, but the younger man stopped a short distance from where Lewis stood, bracing himself, looking directly into his eyes.

His anger was evident when Dylan spoke in a robust Carmarthenshire accent. He wasn't shouting, but his voice was raised in pitch and tone, again putting the detective on his guard. Lewis had been assaulted several times over the years. He didn't want it to happen again.

'What the hell are you doing here again so soon?' Dylan asked, thrusting a finger towards the detective's chest as he took another step towards him. 'Anna's out with her mother, if it's her you want to see.'

Lewis resisted the temptation to look away. He was a big man who could move with surprising speed when required. And he knew how to throw a punch with force and accuracy. But he accepted he was no physical match for a skilled, well-muscled young boxer if he chose to attack, even with his significant weight advantage. 'It's not Anna I need to speak to,' he said. 'It's you.'

Dylan jerked his head back, sucking in a quick breath, his eyes widened, showing the whites.

'Me? What the hell for? Don't you think you've wasted enough of my family's time?'

Lewis noticed a purple vein on the right side of Dylan's neck was bulging and wondered if the boxer had used steroids to build those muscles. These days it seemed that many young men did, despite the negative consequences. 'I'm investigating the alleged arson of Mark Shady's restaurant and flat early yesterday morning.'

Dylan let out a snorting laugh. 'Yeah, I saw that on the Welsh news. I can't say I'm sorry. I wish it had been worse. But it had toss all to do with me.'

'Your car was seen in Lammas Street at about ten, a few hours before the fire. It was caught on camera. Were you in the driver's seat?'

Dylan was silent for a second or two, shifting his weight from one foot to the other as if contemplating his reply. 'So I was in Carmarthen Saturday night. Big deal. So what? It's not illegal. A lot of people were.'

Lewis tilted his head back, looking up in frustration. 'I've got to ask. It's just routine. Someone torched Shady's place, and I need to rule you out. You've got more reason than most to hate the bastard. I wouldn't blame you if you did do it, but I've got a job to do. So answer my questions, and then I'm out of here.'

Dylan's eyes darted from one part of the yard to another. 'Do I need a lawyer?'

'You're not under arrest. You're helping me with my enquiries, that's all. We can do it here or at the station. It's up to you.'

Dylan looked to the darkening sky as it began to rain. 'Okay, you're wasting my time and yours, but let's get it over with. I'm the only one here. We can talk in the house. And then I never want to see your face again.'

Lewis followed Dylan into the same room where he'd interviewed Anna only days before, sitting in the same seat. The wood burner wasn't lit this time, and the air was cold. A black cat slept curled up on the sofa, seemingly oblivious to their arrival.

'What time did you go into town that night?' Lewis asked, keen to move things along.

Dylan blinked rapidly as he undid the top button of his shirt. 'About seven, but what the hell's the relevance of that?'

'Were you alone?'

Dylan remained silent for a beat. When he replied, he seemed reticent, breaking eye contact. 'Well, no, I was on a date as it happens.'

Lewis noted Dylan's reply, wondering why he seemed so apprehensive. It didn't necessarily mean he was guilty of anything. People were often nervous when talking to the police, even if they were innocent.

'Where did you go?' Lewis asked, using a method he'd used before. He thought a casual, almost chatty approach may make Dylan more ready to talk.

'The Warren in Mansel Street.'

'Ah, yeah, I know it. Nice?'

'Great food, nice atmosphere, but what's that got to do with anything? I've told you I had nothing to do with the fire. Isn't that enough?'

'What time did you get to the restaurant?'

'About eight.'

'And what time did you leave?'

'About ten.'

'And then you drove through town?'

Dylan nodded, painting a picture. 'Yeah, we were parked by the old Wilko's in the town centre. I drove out of there, up Blue Street and then Lammas Street.'

'Okay, that fits. Where did you go from there?'

Dylan responded slowly after a hard, pro-
nounced swallow. 'To her place in Laugharne. I was
there all night. Didn't leave until gone seven the following morning.'

Lewis pondered why Dylan hadn't said that in
the first place. If he had an alibi, why not use it?
Why the delay? 'The name? What's the woman's
name?' he asked, wondering what was coming next.

Dylan gave a pained look. 'I, er... can't tell you.'

'What the hell are you talking about? You went
for a meal with the woman. You're saying you spent
the night with her. Surely you must know her
name.'

'She's married. Has been for a while; her husband was away. Something to do with work.'

Lewis thought that if Dylan was lying, he was
pretty good at it. His emotions seemed genuine. But
he still needed to know more. 'Okay, I understand. I
can see where you're coming from. But we're talking
about serious offences. Arson and quite possibly
attempted murder. Both of which carry long prison
sentences. If you're telling me the truth, there's only
one way to prove it. Give me a name, and I'll do all I
can to talk to the lady concerned without the hus-

band finding out. Have we got a deal? That's the best I can offer.'

Dylan appeared to be sweating despite the winter chill. 'He's not a nice bloke,' he said with emotion. 'A bit of a bully. She wants a divorce. It's crucial he doesn't find out. It's not a casual thing. She matters to me. Do you give me your word?'

Lewis reached out to shake Dylan's hand. 'I do.'

'Her name's Rhian Rees. She works for the council in County Hall Carmarthen, in the planning department as an admin assistant. Her husband checks her mobile. It might be an idea to contact her at the office.'

Lewis nodded twice. 'And when I do, she's going to tell me exactly what you have, is she? She's going to confirm your story?'

Dylan rose to his feet. 'Why wouldn't she? It's the truth – nothing but the truth. A big part of me wishes I had burnt Shady's place down – with him in it. But I can't take the credit. That was someone else. It wasn't me.'

18

As Lewis drove off, Dylan watched from the lounge window, half hidden behind the dusty Venetian blinds. Once satisfied the detective wasn't coming back, he took his mobile from his jeans pocket with trembling fingers and dialled County Hall, the number recorded in his contacts. He listened with growing impatience to the usual recorded message, opting for Welsh, his first language, rather than English, and tapping a foot against the floor until a female receptionist finally answered the call. He asked for Rhian and only had to wait a few brief seconds before hearing her familiar voice.

'Hi, Rhian, it's Dylan. Are you alone?'

'Yes, I'm in my office. But why do you ask?'

He took a deep breath. 'It's nothing we can't deal with. But please just listen carefully to what I've got to say.'

He could hear the apprehension in her speech when she replied. 'What is it? You're worrying me now. My husband hasn't found out about us, has he?'

'No, no, it's nothing like that,' he said, keen to put her at ease, or at least as far as was possible in the circumstances. 'I've had the police here at the farm. The same man who investigated my sister's rape. His name's Ray Lewis, a detective sergeant. He's just left. You may well hear from him very soon.'

'What on earth are you talking about? Why would I hear from him? I don't understand.'

Dylan looked down as the old cat approached him, rubbing herself against his leg and purring. 'He's investigating the arson at Mark Shady's place. It happened a few hours after we left The Warren. My car was caught on camera as we drove through Carmarthen.'

There was an urgency to Rhian's tone, a jerkiness, hesitation. 'Oh my God, d-do the police think you did it? Do they think you caused the fire?'

Dylan pushed the cat away with his foot. 'No, no,

it's just routine, that's all. The police just want to rule me out. It's nothing to worry about. You can relax.'

There were two seconds of silence before Rhian spoke again. 'You didn't do it, did you?' she asked. 'I know how much you hate Shady, and I'd rather know the truth. If you did do it, you can tell me. We agreed on no secrets, remember? It wouldn't change anything between us. I wouldn't love you any less. If he'd raped my sister, I'd hate him as much as you do. Maybe even more.'

Dylan rushed his reply. 'The fire was nothing to do with me. I swear to it. But I had to tell the copper I stayed at your place that night. I said Gary was away with work. It was the only way I could think of getting an alibi. And I need you to stick to the same story if Lewis asks. The last thing I need is the police sticking their nose in for God only knows how long. I had enough of them with Anna's case. They get a lot of things wrong. I don't need them focused on me.'

'Why didn't you just tell the police you went night fishing after dropping me off at my car? That's what you did, isn't it? In Ferryside. That's what you told me.'

Dylan felt his jaw tense. 'I couldn't tell him that because no one saw me. It was pitch dark, and as far as I knew, I was the only one on the beach. If I'd told DS Lewis the truth, he'd only have my word for it. I'd still be a suspect. It seemed much easier to say I was with you.'

He listened, thinking Rhian might be crying. 'You are... you are telling me everything, aren't you, Dylan?'

'Of course I am. I swear to it on my life.'

'I really wish you hadn't given the police my name.'

'So do I, but I didn't have a choice. You must be able to see that. It was that or I might have been arrested. Can you imagine how much that would upset Anna and my parents after everything that happened? You will back me up, won't you? I don't think Anna could stand the stress of it all if you didn't. She's close to a breakdown as it is.'

The sound of a sigh. 'I'll tell the police exactly what you want me to tell them. But don't think I'm happy about it. Gary lies constantly. It's one of the things I can't stand about him. And I hate doing the same.'

Dylan broke into a slow smile.

'I love you, Rhian.'

'I love you, too. My boss has just opened the door. I'd better go.'

19

Lewis arranged to speak to Rhian that lunchtime, meeting her in Carmarthen Park at one o'clock and interviewing her sitting on a park bench near the rugby pitch rather than making it formal. He was fully aware that Dylan might well have prewarned her of his enquiries. But as he awaited her arrival on this cold winter afternoon, Lewis told himself there were some things he couldn't control. Anyway, he still thought Dylan was an unlikely suspect. He was dotting the i's and crossing the t's like a good detective should. Going through the motions more than anything else. He could simply have asked all his questions on the phone. But he wanted to see Rhian's face, the look in her eyes, and study her body language because such things often told their own story. He thought himself good at reading people after so many years on the job. His skills were honed. He could usually see through liars, even good ones. In one way or another, their deceptions seeped out.

Lewis sat on the bench a few minutes before his appointment, wrapped in his warm padded coat and eating two fast-cooling sausage rolls bought from Greggs about twenty minutes before. He was just finishing off the second of the two, stuffing it into his mouth with greedy enthusiasm and salivating, when he glanced to his right towards the park's main entrance to see a young, slim, red-haired woman, who he recognised from her social media photos, walking towards him. He thought Rhian looked nervous as she strode in his direction, possibly trying to exude an air of relaxed confidence she didn't feel. She had that look about her. As if she wasn't looking forward to their meeting one little bit. And who could blame her for that?

Lewis stood, nodding in greeting as the young woman approached, now just a few feet away. He reached out his hand to shake hers but withdrew it when she didn't reciprocate. She was the first to speak.

'DS Lewis?'

He forced a smile, then wiped pastry flakes from his mouth with a sleeve. 'That's right, love. Thanks very much for coming. It's nice to meet you. We can talk sitting on the bench or take a stroll – whatever suits you best.'

She sat, looking at the ground, arms tightly crossed as if hugging herself, forming a barrier. 'If we could make this quick, that would really help. I need to get back to work.'

'Just a few questions. It shouldn't take us too long.'

She kept her focus on the ground at her feet. 'I don't think I can add much to what I told you on the phone. Me and Dylan left the restaurant and then went to my home near Laugharne. It's in a quiet spot away from other houses, so I was confident no one would see us together. I haven't told my husband about Dylan yet. Gary's not an easy man. He's got a temper. I'm trying to build up the courage to make the break.'

There was something about her story that, for Lewis, didn't ring true. It was an instinctive thing more than anything else. A gut feeling he often relied on, much to Kesey's consternation. But in such circumstances, he was usually correct. It was almost as if Rhian had rehearsed her version of events, like an actor learning their lines.

'You do realise this is a criminal investigation, don't you, love? Everything you tell me will form part of the official record. You don't want to waste police time or pervert the course of justice. That would only get you into trouble. Everything you tell me must be true. If there's something you're not telling me, now's your chance.'

Rhian responded quickly, turning to meet his gaze for the first time since sitting. 'I have told you the truth!'

Lewis still wasn't entirely persuaded but knew there was little else he could do to challenge her. She was a witness, not a suspect. There was only so much pressure he could exert. He played one final card. 'So, in that case, you'll be willing to make a formal written statement confirming what you've told me, will you?'

She looked away again and hesitated. 'Yes, I guess so, if that's really necessary. I've decided to tell my husband I want a divorce this coming Saturday when his mother's visiting. He's less likely to kick off with her there.'

Lewis frowned hard. 'Your husband hasn't ever been violent towards you, has he?'

'No, Gary's controlling and verbally abusive, but he never hits out. I've sometimes thought he was about to, but he's never crossed that line.'

Lewis stood, thinking that maybe she'd told him the truth after all. Or at least a part of it. 'Well, you know what to do if he ever does. Dial 999.'

She seemed distracted, avoiding his gaze. 'When do you want me to make the statement?'

Lewis put his hands into his coat pockets as the chill began to bite. 'Oh, I think I've got enough for now. If that changes, I'll give you another ring at work. Good luck with Saturday. And you know where we are if you need us.'

20

Kesey looked up from her seemingly endless piles of paperwork with a tired smile as Lewis entered her office shortly after two that afternoon. She was fed up with the monotony of the red-tape drudgery that sometimes seemed to dominate her role, and was glad of the interruption.

'Coffee?' she asked with a smile, hoping he'd make it, which he did.

'I'll have a couple of those nice biscuits I like if you've got any left,' he said. 'I didn't have time for a proper lunch. Busy, busy. Just a quick snack on the go. I'll fade away to nothing if I don't eat something soon.'

Oh, yeah, that'll be the day, thought Kesey, taking

a packet of chocolate digestives from a desk drawer as he bent down stiffly, switching on the stainless-steel kettle with a groan.

Kesey smiled again, with more enthusiasm this time, as he handed her a full mug. She waited for him to sit before speaking, thinking he looked as if he needed the rest.

'How did it go with Dylan?' she asked, gently blowing her hot drink before taking a sip.

Lewis took two biscuits from the packet. 'Yeah, I had a good chat with the lad. He's got a sound alibi. I never really thought he was a likely suspect, and that confirmed it. He was with his girlfriend all night.'

'Have you talked to her?' she asked, now more serious.

Lewis nodded once while chewing. 'Yeah, nice girl, works in County Hall, planning department. She backed up everything Dylan told me. I'd say they're both telling the truth. That's my gut instinct, anyway. It rarely lets me down. She's married, and to a right tosser by the sound of it. Best handle it on the quiet.'

Kesey's face took on a sour expression. 'Oh, here we go again.'

'What are you talking about?'

'Those gut instincts of yours aren't always nearly as reliable as you seem to think they are.'

'I beg to differ.'

'What about the Martin case?'

'Oh, come on. Give me a break. That was a one-off. Every copper gets it wrong now and again. I'm not infallible. No one is.'

Kesey sighed, frustrated with his response. 'You are taking the arson seriously, aren't you, Ray?'

'Of course I am. I don't know why you're even asking.'

'Did you take written statements?'

He shook his head. 'I don't think we need them. Not at this stage. Not unless something else comes up. I can always talk to them again if need be. She could be lying; they both could, and the alibi could be crap. There's always that possibility, however remote. But I don't think so. My gut's not ringing any alarm bells. If it was, I'd have dealt with things differently.'

Kesey drummed the fingers of one hand on her desk, rat-tat-tat, wondering what it would take to convince Lewis to follow the evidence methodically and rely solely on that. 'I've been thinking,' she began. 'I know this is a bit left field. But you don't think your mate Flowers could be worth talking to, do you?'

Lewis swallowed the last of his second biscuit, pulling his head back before speaking. 'What the hell are you talking about now?'

'I've just been thinking about that whole business with his daughter. He must hate Shady with a vengeance. Do we need to consider him a suspect? Or, at the very least, rule him out.'

Lewis shifted in his seat. 'Oh, come off it, Laura. Shady's got any number of enemies, loads of them, me included. If Daisy is a suspect, he's a very long way down the list. And that's if he's on the list at all.'

Kesey grinned, thinking that, for once, her sergeant might get her point. 'You didn't do it, did you, Ray? Did you throw that petrol bomb? One last hurrah before retirement beckons. Something to remember in your golden years when you're down the rugby club with your friends. A tale to tell. The perfect crime.'

He screwed up his face. 'What the hell's up with you today? Have you been on the wacky baccy or something? I hope you're taking the piss. First Daisy and then me. This is bordering on the ridiculous.'

Kesey held her hands out wide, eyes narrowed. 'And what if I said that was my gut instinct? There's no evidence to support any of it, of course. But that never seems to bother you a great deal.'

Lewis took a third biscuit before she put the packet away. 'Ah, okay, very clever. It's another one of your lectures, and you've made your point.'

'Have I, Ray? Have I really? Are you actually going to take my comments on board this time?'

'Of course I am. Goes without saying.'

She strongly suspected he'd do nothing of the kind. It was a recurring theme. And she sometimes wondered why she kept trying.

'I hope so,' she said. 'I know you've been in the job a long time. But things have changed. Standing orders are there for a reason. I don't want to hear about your gut feelings again.'

'Anything else?' he asked, looking bored, a smear of chocolate on his chin.

'There is, as it happens. So you can stay there if you're thinking of escaping. And don't even think about asking me about my promotion again.'

He checked his watch. 'Okay, I'm listening.'

'Have you seen Shady's Facebook page?'

Lewis frowned hard. 'Oh, for fuck's sake, not to-day. What's the bastard done now?'

She hesitated, holding her mug in both hands. 'You're not going to like this. But you need to know.

He's made a big announcement. Says he's coming out of hospital sometime tomorrow. And he'll be staying at the Ivy Bush Hotel here in town. His insurance company is paying for it, apparently. Until his flat is habitable again. And he made some sarky comments about us not finding the culprit for the fire. I think that's probably intended to wind you up. He reposted that photo of you outside Boots.'

Lewis spoke through gritted teeth. 'I'll take a look when I get back to my office.'

'Yeah, and better let Flowers know. In case Shady targets Carly with revenge in mind now he's back on the streets. You know what I'm saying. It could happen. It's a potential risk we can't ignore.'

Lewis nodded. 'I don't think Shady will be attracting a new girlfriend anytime soon, not with that burnt face. That's one thing to be glad of. Although you're right, it could increase his focus on Carly. He got dumped. I can't imagine him letting that go. I'll give Daisy the heads-up as soon as we're finished here. Anything else before I make a move?'

Kesey swallowed a mouthful of coffee and grinned, glad to raise the mood.

'I saw the lovely Tanya earlier today in reception. She seemed full of the joys. And she asked about you. For some reason, she seems to really like you.

Beats me why. That's one mystery I'm never going to solve.'

'Must be my film star good looks and sparkling personality.'

Kesey laughed. 'Oh, yeah, that must be it.'

'Right, I'd better make a move. Places to go, people to see.'

'Remember to ring Flowers,' she said, back in business mode.

Lewis gave another little curtsey with one hand on the door handle. 'Will do, ma'am. Anything you say. I'm here to serve.'

21

Shady did a lot of thinking in his hospital bed once the worst of the pain was controlled by the busy burn ward's doctors and nurses. He sometimes fixated on the blonde staff nurse to pass the time, a woman he thought was in her late twenties or early thirties, a few years too old for him in an ideal world. But, he told himself, needs must if his boredom was to be alleviated. There was little else on offer. Nothing younger, no one more attractive or beguiling. So, too old or not, she'd have to do.

He pictured the nurse naked each time she walked past, his hands around her throat, squeezing tighter and tighter, a pleading look in her frightened eyes as she approached her pending demise. Then each and every time as his cock filled with blood, swelling to its full size, standing to attention under the metal frame protecting his body from the bed-clothes, he imagined killing her while he mastur-bated faster and faster until he ejaculated with a quiet groan of delight.

But, despite the sexual entertainment value his fantasies of the blonde nurse provided, Shady thought more about his life. He dwelt on such things, often late into the night when other patients slept in the semi-darkness and relative quiet of the hospital ward. He thought about his life experience up to that point and how much better it could be-come if he genuinely embraced what he considered his almost infinite potential. And the more he con-sidered such things, the more determined he be-came to maximise his physical and emotional pleasure to the nth degree once he had the opportu-nity. Because there were no limits to what he could achieve. He was shrouded in greatness. More so than almost any other man.

As he lay there for hour after hour, drifting in and out of fitful sleep, caught in a world somewhere between dreams and reality, Shady repeatedly re-lived the arson attack as if in real-time, acutely aware of how close he'd come to death. And the more he thought about it, the more he began to believe that the frightening events of those early hours weren't such a bad thing after all. He asked himself if the universe and whatever unseen power controlled creation were somehow acting in unison to deliver him a glorious destiny he was intended for all along. A wonderful future building on what he'd already achieved. A life focused on his own needs and desires without concerning himself with his needy, whimpering victims or with the misguided, interfering law. Men like Piggy Lewis and Flowers, who wouldn't know a good time if it blew them. Men who'd never understand the attraction of death. Fantasy was one thing, but making that fantasy a reality... now, that would be quite another. Seeing the light of life fade in some pathetic girl's eyes would be the ultimate turn-on. Wow, he would come so hard. So very hard. An explosive orgasmic release like never before.

Yes, yes, yes, Shady said to himself with utter conviction while gently kneading his genitals under the bedclothes; that must be it! It all made absolute sense now. It seemed so very obvious. It was a light-bulb moment, when everything became clear in his mind for the very first time. His best times were ahead. He thought and believed it, all doubt fading away to nothing as his mind raced. He was evolving into the consummate killer he was always meant to be. Death and human destruction were his life's purposes. The reason for his existence, for his birth. Why the hell hadn't he seen it before? The painful burns, even the destruction of his cherished restaurant and lovely home, were an unfortunate necessity. Things that had to happen. A wake-up call of sorts. All part of an evolutionary journey started in his ghastly childhood at the hands of his skank mother. And now the attack was the culmination of that process. Reminding him that his development was reaching its dramatic conclusion. And of the urgent need to fully embrace his dark side, to live out his deepest desires before it was too late. He could have died. It could have been all over. He could be lying in a morgue. Because nothing lasted forever. Not in this world. Life passed all too quickly, even for extraordinary men like him. And so he had to make the most of whatever time he had left on this earth before it was too late. There was so much to do. So much to achieve. So much to enjoy as he explored the extremes of human behaviour. And he really shouldn't miss out, not on a thing. That would be a travesty. An actual miscarriage of justice. Only men like him could ever understand that. Just men like him.

Shady silenced his busy mind. He stared with unblinking eyes, giggling to himself, as a middle-aged male nurse with an all-too-obvious twitch approached with a friendly smile to check the medical chart hanging on the metal frame at the end of the bed.

'Looks like you're doing very well, Mark,' the man said in a cheery voice. 'Well done, you're making excellent progress. The doctors will be doing their rounds in an hour or two. Hopefully, you'll have some good news about an early discharge. We never like to keep patients for longer than we have to. You may be out of here sooner than you thought.'

Shady looked intensely into the nurse's creased face, wondering if the man had read his dark thoughts as he went about his work. But he quickly dismissed the idea as crazy, likely stemming from the pain medication still in his bloodstream rather than rational thinking. Others couldn't read his mind, could they? No, of course not. *Get a grip, Mark, for fuck's sake, get a grip.*

Shady nodded once, forced a reluctant smile that hurt his face, and said, 'I've already been told.

It's my last night.' Then left it at that. The conversation was the last thing he wanted. And particularly with a male. There was no joy in that; never was.

Shady quickly returned his thoughts to killing as the nurse hurried away, asking himself who would be the ideal first victim of his new plans as he relaxed back on his pillows, closing his eyes tight. A vulnerable stranger, perhaps: a homeless stray or druggy snatched off the streets or lured in with promises he wouldn't keep. Or maybe a simpering girl he knew well. A girl who'd let him down and deserved to die a horrible death for her rejection. Someone whose past behaviour warranted punishment of the worst possible kind. There'd be justice in that. Yes, Carly Flowers! The ungrateful, unfaithful bitch. She'd be the first to die. And maybe he'd even film her death for posterity. Send it to her parents so they could say a proper goodbye. That was only fair. And then, perhaps, Ray Lewis's piggy daughter would come next. Not because of anything she'd done. But because of him. If the pig lost his flabby pink daughter, that would be his fault. Only his! He'd have brought it on himself.

Shady laughed out loud as he pictured the scene, bright, bright and loud. All that fatty pork, he said to himself. Now, that would provide some fun.

He could imagine roasting her on a spit. The bitch would scream like a demented banshee. *Listen, Mark, listen!* He could almost hear her.

22

Shady sat in the far corner of a dimly lit Carmarthen pub as Carly Flowers, a student friend of hers named Hannah, whom he'd met once before, and a third girl of similar age whom he didn't recognise, gathered around a low table and chatted over what looked like a shared, strikingly blue bottle of Welsh sparkling spring water. He could tell that, even in the relatively quiet room, the three girls were oblivious to his presence, as if he was a non-person, a ghost, just as he wanted it and precisely as he'd planned before following them from Carly's student digs at the other end of town. He told himself his feelings of intense loathing were entirely justified as he glared in their direction, then quickly looked away, washing down yet another strong painkiller with a swill of French brandy he considered medicine.

As Shady approached the bar, ordering a second neat brandy and paying with a ten-pound note, he reminded himself of the extensive efforts Carly's unreasonable behaviour and rejection had forced him to go to in his search for righteous revenge. Getting out and about in town at all was difficult enough, given his still-painful injuries. There was only so much the tablets could achieve, however many he took. And now he was in danger of running out of his medication just when he needed it most.

And then there was the disguise he'd been forced to buy. The shoulder-length brown wig made from something closely resembling human hair, the matching beard he'd ever so carefully stuck to his face despite the discomfort it caused, the charity shop, non-prescription, tinted glasses that hid his eyes, and the ridiculously unstylish hippy clothes of the type he'd never usually even consider wearing. *Carly should try donning that lot when her skin is charred and stinging.* The total and utter bitch! She had no idea what she'd put him through or of the punishment coming her way. And whatever happened to her, she deserved no less. No suffering would ever be enough for a girl who'd let him down so badly. Any reasonable person would understand that, and they'd sympathise with all he'd experienced and congratulate him on his endeavours. Because he was in the right, acting as judge, jury, and executioner, and Carly, the she-devil, was in the wrong. It all seemed so glaringly obvious as Shady glanced across at Carly, who smiled then laughed, focused on her girlfriends rather than him. The girl was evil personified. It was as clear as day.

Shady took another swig of the strong spirit, his mind still racing as his anger intensified, making him shake. Maybe it was Carly who lit the fire. It could have been her in that long dark coat with a petrol bomb in hand. Or it could have been her obnoxious git of a father. Yeah, that all made sense. She might even have encouraged the pig. It was probably him. That snorting, grubby little fucker who liked to stick his snout in. Guilty as charged.

Shady sat back at his table for a few minutes longer, confident of not being recognised and urgently taking another tablet from its brown plastic bottle, which was excessive even for him. He looked across again at Carly, who now had her back to him, asking himself if the time was right to act on the next stage of his plan. He had hoped she'd be drunk, senses dampened by alcohol, making things easier. But it seemed she couldn't even get that right. Yet another way she'd let him down at the worst possible time. So like her, he thought, so very typical. The obnoxious cow hadn't even visited him in the hospital. Not even once had she come to his bedside. She really was the scum of the earth.

Shady tilted his head back, lifted his glass to his mouth, and drained it, grimacing slightly as the potent liquid aggravated his throat. He carefully rubbed at his chin with the flats of his fingers, the false beard itching intensely. Again, blaming Carly for the discomfort, he urged himself on, hating her more than ever. The quicker she was dead, the better, he said to himself. There'd be no annoying him then, no letting him down. She'd just lie there, still, legs wide apart, enabling him to indulge his deepest desires and not saying a single word. The first worthwhile thing she'd have done in her useless life. He'd shut the bitch up once and for all. And he'd get away with it. That mattered. He'd never get caught. Not by the pigs. Because he was better than them, cleverer and more insightful. He'd leave them floundering in his wake and clutching at shadows. That would be fun. He could look forward to that.

Shady put his empty glass down, blowing out three short, sharp breaths and urging himself on, searching for the courage to act, to live out his dreams, to manifest the ultimate pleasure, making fantasy real. *Come on, Mark*, he said in his head, *it's now or never. You can do it, man. If not you, then who? Reach for greatness.* He'd got hold of the sedative in a clear liquid form. Just as required. That was a triumph. So why not use it? The bitch was there, just a few short feet away, ready and waiting like a sacrificial lamb. So why not get it done? She might wander off soon, escape. There was no time to lose.

Shady sucked in one last deep breath through his mouth, scratched his right cheek with a broken nail, stood on trembling legs, and walked slowly and deliberately towards the three seated girls, a small glass vial of the clear, fast-acting sedative liquid clutched tightly in one sweaty hand. As he approached their table, forcing himself on, one step, two steps, three, he mimicked what he liked to think was a convincing trip and stumble, one of several potential actions he'd repeatedly practised for over an hour the previous afternoon. Shady let out a small yelp as he fell, knocking the empty blue bottle and three partially full glasses to the tiled floor and then quickly standing, full of feigned apologies and adopting a strong Northern Irish accent very different to his own.

'I'm so very sorry, girls. Stupid of me. Let me replace those drinks for you. I insist. What are you going to have?'

'Are you okay?' Carly asked him as a barman approached carrying a broom and an orange plastic bucket.

'I'm just fine,' Shady replied, holding his nerve, determined to avoid her gaze as he turned away, head bowed low, the long wig hair falling forward and masking his face. 'But I'll be a lot better after I buy you three lovely ladies a drink. Now, what are you going to have? A proper bevvy, or more of that Welsh water you seem to like?'

'There's really no need,' Carly replied, the other girls nodding their agreement as the barman walked away.

Shady cleared his throat, still avoiding eye contact, focusing on the floor, fearing all his best-laid plans might melt away. *Take a drink, you bitch. Cooperate, agree!* What to say? What the hell to say?

'No, I insist. Have a drink with me, please,' he said, glancing up, wanting to hit out as he broke the brief silence. Desperate to smash Carly in the face, knocking off a smile that seemed to mock him. 'Just another water, if you must. It would make me feel so much better. I feel such a fool.'

His relief was almost palpable when the three girls finally agreed, Carly again taking the lead; he thought it was more about shutting him up and alleviating her embarrassment than anything else. Selfish bitch!

Shady stood at the bar, gave his order, and again paid in cash, not wanting to leave any technological record of his presence that could come back to haunt him. This time he told the barman to keep the change. He glanced to the left and right with quick, jerky movements of his head, ensuring no one was watching as he poured chilled spring water into three fresh glasses, declining the offer of ice. He leaned forward, both hands in front of him below the bar's counter, hurriedly unscrewing the vial's small, black plastic top and pouring the clear, flavourless liquid into a glass he was careful to keep separate from the other two. His whole body trembled as he walked back across the room to hand that one crucial glass to Carly and a second glass to Hannah, both girls accepting their drinks with a smile.

As Shady handed the third girl her water, he could have cheered when Carly took a sip, wetting her full lips before swallowing. Shady studied the slight movement of her slender white throat and told himself everything was finally going his way, just as he'd pictured the night before. And at that moment, as Carly took a second sip, all doubt left him, and his confidence soared. It was a high of a type he'd only ever previously experienced when carrying out an assault. When he'd felt all-powerful, a king amongst men. He asked himself what he'd been worrying about as he backed away with a fixed grin under that bushy beard, repositioning himself, sitting at the opposite side of the room to where he'd been earlier so he could easily continue studying Carly's reaction to the drug. He could have punched the air in triumph as she laughed at some joke and drank about 20 per cent of her water in one swallow. And now he knew he was winning, his self-belief soaring to even greater heights, his pride almost bursting from his chest as his cock began to swell. Soon, he assured himself, the bitch would be his to do with whatever the fuck he wanted. No more than he deserved after all his efforts, and what she deserved too. He just had to make it happen – no more, no less.

Shady watched the seconds tick by on his high-end Swiss sports watch, time passing slowly as he waited for the drug's desired effects to kick in. His swelling confidence threatened to slip away again as time dragged. But then, after about three minutes that had seemed like endless hours, he clearly saw what he believed were the first welcome results of the sedative. Carly yawned a big yawn, head back with a hand raised to her mouth. And then she closed her eyes, screwing up her face. It was working, he said to himself; it was definitely working! What a triumph. Halfway to success. Now all he had to do was stick to his plan.

23

Carly tried to blink the sleep away as Hannah reached across the pub table, gripping her wrist.

'Are you okay, Carly? You nearly drifted off.'

Carly tried to focus on her friend's familiar face, but the entire room became an impressionist blur of misty, cloudy colours that made little sense. It took all the concentration Carly could muster to reply, forcing out the words as if in a dream.

'I... I'm not feeling at all well. Can you... can you please help me get to the toilet? I've... I've got a bad stomach. I think I'm going to puke.'

Hannah quickly stood, taking Carly's arm and assisting her across the room towards the women's toilet, where Carly fell to her knees, gripping the white porcelain bowl with both arms and repeatedly throwing up, her body heaving until there was nothing left but green acidic bile. She heard Hannah's voice somewhere behind her as she spat into the bowl, warm tears flowing from her eyes. It was as if her entire body had rebelled against her.

'Do you think I need to call for an ambulance, Carly?' Hannah asked. 'One minute you were fine, and now look at you. You seem really ill. We've only been drinking water. You're scaring me. I can't believe how pale you are. You can only just keep your eyes open.'

Carly shook her head, focused on the now, then placed her hands on the edges of the toilet bowl, helping herself unsteadily to her feet. She'd never felt more exhausted. Never more in need of sleep as she leaned against the wall. She rehearsed her reply before forcing the words from her mouth as the small space began to spin.

'Please, just... just call a cab. I want to get back to the digs.'

'Are you sure?' Hannah asked with evident concern.

Carly nodded, which hurt her head, a jolt of pain making her wince. She'd never been so confused, her decline so rapid. Her head had never ached more.

'Yeah, a cab, please, just a cab. I need to get to my bed. Can you help me reach the sink? I want to wash out my mouth.'

Hannah flushed the toilet, then lowered the seat.

'The sink looks a bit manky. I'm going to fetch you some fresh water from the bar. You sit down there and please don't try to get up again until I'm back. I'll be as fast as I can. And then we'll give your hands a quick wash, and I'll call that taxi. Promise me you're not going to move. I don't want you falling over.'

Carly nodded again, ever so carefully this time, her sight still blurred.

'Please, hurry.'

'Are you sure you don't want an ambulance?'

'Certain,' Carly replied. 'I just need to sleep.'

'Okay, if you say so.'

When Hannah returned less than a minute later, Carly had her eyes closed. When shaken awake, she opened one eye and then the other, gratefully accepting the water with a heavy hand. She yawned again as she stood, approached the sink, and swilled the cold liquid around her mouth for a few seconds before spitting.

'That's it, good girl,' Hannah said, standing beside Carly on her left at touching distance. 'Give me the glass once you're finished. That's it, now clean your hands. Do you want me to contact your mum or dad for you? You still look terrible. It might not be such a bad idea.'

Carly had never wanted her mother more. She longed to have a hug, or *cwtch*, as her mum had called it in her lyrical Welsh many times during her childhood. And Carly was sorely tempted to tell Hannah yes. But even in her exhausted state, she feared her parents' involvement wouldn't go well – not after everything that had happened with Mark. There'd been such bad arguments, so much disagreement. And she'd said things she wished she never had – things her parents didn't deserve. Because she loved them really, deep down, where it mattered, and they loved her. Even if they sometimes seemed to think she was still a little girl.

'No thanks,' Carly finally replied, her voice hesitant. 'My dad would only assume I'm drunk or took some drug. I think it's his job. He's always suspicious about something. That's what he was like with Mark. I don't think he'd believe a word I said.'

Hannah frowned hard. 'Okay, take my arm, let's get you back to the bar. There's just me and you now. Paloma has headed off. That new boy she's dating sent her a text.' She laughed and then added, 'She must be keen. She couldn't get out of here fast enough.'

Carly took deep breaths as she slumped in her seat, fighting the impulse to sleep, which seemed to increase with each passing second.

'I can't believe how bad I'm feeling,' she said through tears. She knew her friend was trying to lighten the mood, raising her spirits with talk of ordinary things, which she appreciated. But focusing on anything other than how she felt proved an impossibility.

'I think it must be that bacon I ate for breakfast,' she said, concentrating. 'I should have chucked it in the bin. I knew it was about three weeks out of date. I've been so stupid.'

Hannah made a face. 'Can food poisoning make you sleepy?'

'I think it must do.'

'Well, if it was the bacon, throwing up might have helped.'

'I hope so.'

Hannah looked at her phone when it suddenly pinged, holding the screen a few inches from her face. 'Right, great, the cab will be here in two minutes. Come on, up you get. Let's get your coat on, and we can wait outside. The cold air might do you some good.'

Carly nodded ever so carefully, not wanting to aggravate her headache, which was still pounding, pain and compression coming in waves like the booming beat of a drum. She held a hand to her face. 'Thanks so much for looking after me, Han; you've been an absolute star. Sorry to ruin our night out.'

'Don't be silly, not a problem. I know you'd do the same for me. It's what friends do.'

Hannah raised a hand and waved as the two girls stood arm-in-arm on the wide pavement, which was starting to frost over as the night-time temperature fell below zero.

'Look, it's that guy who fell against our table,' she said with a grin. 'He's sitting in that old blue van parked outside the butcher's shop. He seemed nice enough. And so shy. Always looking away. I felt quite sorry for him. Did you see how red his skin was? I think he must have his problems.'

Carly swayed as her friend spoke, hoping the conversation might help her stay awake and that the cab wouldn't be too much longer. 'It's strange,' she said, shivering with cold. 'He reminds me of someone, but I can't think who. It's all a bit of a blur. I'm not wearing my contacts. Everything looks like an impressionist painting.'

'Ah, here we go,' Hannah replied with another smile. 'That's our cab, the white Toyota.'

Carly raised her tired eyes, looking heavenward. 'Well, thank God for that. I'm really struggling.'

'Not much longer now. You'll be back at the digs before you know it. And then we'll get you up to bed.'

'I cannot wait,' Carly replied, climbing awkwardly into the back seat as Hannah opened the car door. 'The nausea seems to have worn off. But I'm still crazy tired. It's not like anything I've ever experienced before. And my head, it's awful.'

Hannah sat close to Carly, holding her hand. 'Try and stay awake until we get there. You know it's not far. A good night's sleep will make you feel much better in the morning. Just you wait and see.'

24

Shady congratulated himself on his purchase as he followed the taxicab in his recently acquired Volkswagen van, careful to stay a few vehicles behind so as not to raise suspicion. Cunning subterfuge, he told himself with a grin, was everything. Taking his time, not rushing, and getting everything just right really mattered. And so far, he'd done it all so very well. Close to perfection. Yes, with aplomb, another reflection of his creative genius. All essential elements of an inspired plan that could only lead to ultimate success.

He chuckled at how very different he looked from the norm as he travelled through the west Wales market town on full alert, keeping his eyes on the Toyota, never looking away. And the van, too. Such a contrast to his Merc. A very different vehicle for a very different purpose. Carly would find that out soon enough. The cow! The look on her stupid face would be hilarious.

He'd bought the rusty old vehicle from a private seller for cash only three days after leaving hospital, travelling to the fading industrial town of Llanelli by train, wearing his disguise and giving a false name before driving off in triumph. And now, as he changed from second to third gear, pressing in the clutch, he assured himself it was money well spent. Just fifteen hundred quid to remain anonymous, confuse the pigs, and stay safe – all part of his plan. And soon it would all pay off. He was sure of it. He'd get his hands on the disloyal bitch. His reward. The glorious culmination of his scheme. What more could he possibly have done to make fantasy a reality? What could possibly go wrong?

Shady pictured the light fading from Carly's dying eyes, making his spirits soar as he drove on, pleased to see the cab was travelling in the direction of her student digs, a large four-bedroom terraced house he'd visited once before on the evening of his recent acquittal. He steered slowly past as the cab pulled up in the dimly lit street and then watched in a rear mirror as Hannah helped Carly from the Toyota's back seat.

He was so very tempted to act quickly. To abduct Carly at the earliest opportunity and be on his way with his captive. But as he parked two streets away in a quiet spot under a faulty street lamp, Shady reminded himself of the need for continued caution. It would be best to wait until the early hours, take another tablet or two, and sit there until the time was precisely correct. Patience was everything. Stick to the plan, with no deviation, whatever the temptation. Carly, Hannah, and any other potentially interfering girls who might be there had to be asleep. And the sedative needed time to take its full effect, even if she had consumed almost five times the recommended maximum adult dose. So he had to wait. Another inconvenience Carly would pay for. Her fault, all her fault. The more he thought about it, the more it seemed almost everything was.

Shady switched on the radio, Classic FM, took a tablet from its plastic bottle, swallowed it, then closed his eyes and tried to relax, enabling the painkilling drug to fulfil its role to the best effect. He'd decided to wait until 1 a.m., something he found more challenging than anticipated.

And he was stiff, cold, and aching when the time to act finally came.

He looked through the windscreen to see it was snowing, white flakes sticking to the ground in the pale light of a half-moon shrouded in cloud. He prayed it would stop soon. But if anything, as he looked up at the dark sky, it was falling heavier. He checked the time on his watch for the third time in less than five minutes, having left his phone switched off in the interests of security. It was, he concluded, time to make a move because the last thing he needed was hazardous driving conditions. The one potential incumbrance he hadn't considered. *Come on, Mark.* This was it – no time for delay. The waiting was over. It was time to be on his way.

Shady cursed loudly and crudely as he turned the old van's ignition key, his frustration escalating by the second until the engine finally spluttered into reluctant life on the fourth attempt. He realised he was sweating profusely despite the winter chill as he lowered the handbrake, engaged first gear, and drove off towards Carly's abode. This was the moment he'd been waiting for. The time had finally come – the culmination of all that had gone before. Everything had been leading to this. And soon there'd be no need for half-measures. He was a different creature now. A new sentient being. And he'd indulge his deepest desires without limit or hesitation.

Shady was pleased to see the rented student digs in total darkness as he pulled up at the back of the house, where a painted metal gate led to a small walled yard and the back door, an access point he was sure was his best option. He slipped on the snowy ground when exiting the van but somehow held his footing, preventing a fall. He closed the driver's door quietly with only a slight click, then carefully made his way through the gate and towards a terracotta flowerpot next to a small brick outbuilding, under which he knew the girls sometimes left a spare key. His heart sank when he lifted the heavy pot with trembling hands to see no key was there. He looked a second time, hoping he may have missed it, but with the same negative result. Something else to blame Carly for. Another inconvenience requiring punishment. The bitch! The girl really was a curse. Even worse than he'd ever thought before. Maybe, in some strange way, she'd even caused the snow.

Shady looked for an open ground-floor window with darting eyes, left to right and back again, very close to tears of frustration when his efforts failed.

He could have screamed as he approached the double-glazed back door, fully expecting it to be locked but telling himself it was worth a try – one last possibility to rescue his plan.

He'd never felt more dejected, never as low, but his heart suddenly soared as he placed his hand on the freezing metal door handle and turned it, the door opening with a slight creak, which made him jump. Once again, it seemed all was well with the world at that very moment. He could have danced a happy jig. All he had to do was trust. And then everything would be fine. Why did he ever doubt it? The universe was on his side.

Shady stood in the small, white-tiled kitchen, listening intently for any sound of movement, and he was both relieved and delighted that all was silent. It seemed the girls were asleep and lost in their dreams. He switched on a small handheld torch he'd bought for the purpose, pointed the surprisingly bright beam towards the floor, and made his way to the hallway, where the aged staircase led to a landing, communal bathroom, and the four bedrooms, Carly's included. He began slowly ascending the stairs, treading as lightly as possible and avoiding the third step, which he knew from experience creaked under his weight. He was pleased to see all bedroom doors were closed when he reached the landing, sure in the knowledge that such things significantly reduced the possibility of his getting caught at the worst possible time.

As he slowly approached Carly's bedroom door, one cautious step at a time, Shady assured himself that, as expected, things were now going his way. He, indeed, was a prince amongst men. A grade-A hunter at the very top of his game. A living god with the power of life and death held in his hands. Now all he had to do was get the ungrateful cow out of the house and into the van. *You can do it, Mark. Come on, count to five, ignore the pain, get it done.*

Shady took a slow breath as he opened Carly's bedroom door a few inches and peeped in with the aid of his torch to see her stretched out, fast asleep and snoring, fully clothed on top of her yellow quilt. He could quite easily have thrown the door wide open and raped her there and then as his rage intensified, building inside him, swelling in his chest. The desire to rain down blow after powerful blow until she was bruised, bloody, and dying was almost too great to ignore as his cock became erect. But he urgently reminded himself of the need for continued patience as he opened the door wider, entering the room. There'd be so much more fun to be had once he had her captive, alone, and helpless. He could take his time without fear of being caught. And the bitch could scream then as much as she wanted because there would be no one there to hear. He had to bide his time and look forward to that.

Shady resisted the impulse to laugh as he approached the bed to see a line of drool running from one corner of Carly's mouth. He fully expected her to remain wholly insensible as he gripped her jumper with both hands, planning to lift her from the bed and over one shoulder. But as he pulled her slight body towards him, Carly let out a sudden groan, then opened her eyes and her mouth wide as if to shout out, a look of confused terror on her face.

But Shady moved with speed and grace, far too fast for Carly in her drug-addled state, shoving her back onto the single mattress, then using all his weight and strength to force an open hand over her mouth, silencing any sound before it materialised.

He was surprised, irritated, and amused in equal measures by how hard Carly struggled to free herself. But he knew her limited strength was no match for him as he continued to press the palm of his right hand down hard over her mouth, then pinched her nose tightly shut with the fingers and thumb of his left.

Carly continued to fight for life as he held her there for what felt like an age. But her struggles became gradually weaker and more intermittent as the seconds passed, and then they stopped entirely as Shady ejaculated without the need to touch himself. He thought Carly was dead at first as he looked down at her face, panting slightly with the effort of it all. But then he saw the slight movement of her chest as her shallow breathing caused it to rise and fall just enough to be seen. And at that moment, he realised she was unconscious rather than gone. Another triumph in his eyes. Now, he told himself, he'd have the opportunity to relive what had been a truly glorious experience all over again. Make her suffer more. But all that was for later. Less thought, more action. There was only so long until she came round. He needed to get out of there. He had to be quick.

Shady lifted Carly's unconscious body from the bed, placing her over one shoulder with what he considered unsurprising ease, just as he'd originally planned. He was suddenly enraged to discover she'd lost control of her bladder, warm urine soaking into his clothes as he supported her weight. But he told himself he had no choice but to ignore her lack of consideration, at least for a time. And as he made his way back onto the landing without the need for his torch, his eyes now adapted to the gloom, his anger turned to joy, his ultimate victory now in clear view as he descended the stairs one step at a time. Had one of the other girls suddenly appeared, sticking their noses in where they didn't belong, he had planned to throw Carly to the floor and attack. But such things weren't necessary as the student house retained its silence.

Shady made his way as quickly as he thought advisable across the hall and towards the kitchen, where the back door was still partially open, allowing in the cold. He was relieved to see the snow had stopped falling as he carried Carly into the yard and to the gate, avoiding the worst of the ice. The sky was clearing, the moon shining bright. One final act of the supreme creator in his favour, he told himself. That seemed likely. Or maybe the great Mark Shady was controlling the weather by thought alone. It seemed so much more than a fortunate co-incidence. Yes, that must be it. He had more power than he'd ever imagined.

Shady smiled widely as he slid open the van's side door, throwing Carly into the back. She let out a single gasp of air as she hit the metal floor, but no more than that. Shady reached out to shake her, reassuring himself she remained unconscious thanks to the potent combination of sedation and asphyxiation, before hurriedly closing and locking the door. He glanced all around him, satisfied there were no snooping curtain twitchers in any nearby houses, climbed into the driver's seat, and started the engine, which this time fired at the first turn of the key. He sang a happy song as he drove towards a remote, somewhat dilapidated Pembrokeshire stone cottage sometimes used by his mother as an off-grid home, but which was now empty. An hour or so, and he'd be there – alone with his captive, away from prying eyes, with no one to interfere while he lived out his dreams.

25

When Carly first woke in total, black, inky darkness, she thought she must be dreaming, a nightmare constructed by her subconscious mind, creating a bleak and frightening fantasy that seemed far too real. But all too soon, as she lay there shivering on the cold metal floor, her gut twisting and her heart pounding, she realised she was awake. She lay there, holding herself, her arms wrapped around her belly, tense muscles rigid, and let out a loud primal scream that filled the space with vibrating sound. It was real! Oh, God, where was she? Where the hell was she? Was that the noise of an engine? What the fuck was going on?

One urgent thought after another bombarded

Carly's troubled mind as she thought back to the evening before, desperately trying to make sense of it all. She rasped for breath, eyes bulging but seeing nothing and unable to blink. She frantically searched for her phone with trembling fingers, remembering feeling ill at the pub. She repeatedly patted at her damp jeans pockets, but nothing. No mobile. She recalled leaving the pub by taxi as she raised herself into a seated position, reaching out all around her in a further unsuccessful attempt to locate her phone. Then, arriving back at the digs, where Hannah helped her to bed. And then, oh God, and then, yes, she'd seen the silhouette of a man in the semi-darkness of her bedroom sometime during the night. She had, hadn't she? He was real, wasn't he? Oh, God, yes! It wasn't a nightmare. A man had loomed over her. A man who'd pinned her to the bed with a hot, sweaty hand pressed down hard on her face when she'd struggled to fight free. And then nothing, nothing at all until now. She must have lost consciousness. The nightmare was real.

Carly began sobbing now, her chest heaving, tears flowing freely. She was lost in a sea of despair, still thinking, searching for answers, and more scared by the second as reality dawned. Wherever she was, wherever she'd been taken, it had to be down to the man. He'd abducted her, made her his captive. That must be it. The only explanation that made any sense at all. But what now? If the mystery man was capable of such things, what else might he do? Would he rape her? Or even kill her? Did he have murder in mind? *Please, God, help. Mum, Dad, please come to find me.* She screamed out again. 'Help, I'm in here! Please, somebody, help!'

Carly continued yelling until her throat was sore and her voice hoarse. But it seemed no one heard, however loud she shouted. She repeatedly told herself she needed a single-minded focus on escape as she moaned and whimpered, her knees raised to her chest. It became a mantra as she began repeatedly banging on the metal.

Carly reflected that she must be in some kind of vehicle as she tired, clinging to hope and reaching for an inner strength she didn't know she had. Yes, a vehicle. That explained the noise, the movement, the cold metal, and nothing else made sense. And if it was a vehicle, a van, or maybe a small lorry, surely there had to be a way out, didn't there? Yes, of course there was. *Search, girl, search; there must be a door handle. Find it.* All she had to do was find and open it. Throw herself out, run if she could, and wave down a passing car. She had to get away. However dangerous, however risky, anything was better than staying captive. There was no other way.

Carly cried as she ran her hands over every inch of the metal cabin again and again until her nails were broken and her fingertips raw. Whatever surface the vehicle was on now seemed a lot bumpier than before, as if there were stones on the road, many potholes, or perhaps both, sometimes causing her to stumble to the right or left. And she was close to giving up all hope of escape when she finally found what might be a handle. But as she pulled and shoved it in every conceivable direction, full of new optimism but without any sign of success, the vehicle suddenly slowed, then stopped, the engine now switched off. And all she could hear was the sound of her sobs.

Carly lowered her trembling hands, retreated from the handle, quickly scuttling away on her bum in the darkness as far as possible, then pressed herself against the metal, her head and shoulders dropped low in a hopeless attempt to make herself smaller. What now? *Please, God, help.* Her dad had warned her about such awful things. About dangerous men. Cruel predators who only wanted one thing, thinking only of themselves. He'd told her to be careful. Not to be too quick to trust. And she had been cautious, hadn't she? What could she possibly have done differently? Nothing, absolutely nothing. *Oh God, help, please help.* What would happen next?

Carly stared with narrowed eyes, the moon's winter light appearing unusually bright as a man with long hair, tinted glasses, and a beard slid open a metal door. And at that second, as her eyes repeatedly blinked like a faulty bulb, she knew she'd seen him before. It was him, wasn't it? The guy from the pub. The one who'd seemed so nice. The one who'd reminded her of somebody she couldn't identify. Had he drugged her? Put something in her water? Is that what had happened before he'd invaded her room?

Carly briefly considered pushing past the man and running as fast as her bare feet could carry her. But here he was, standing so very close, blocking her escape. And he looked young, fit and strong. So persuasion may be best. Try to befriend him. Try to use reason. Or plead, make an emotional appeal.

'Okay, we're here,' the man suddenly barked in that Northern Irish accent, the sounds shorter and less round than the Welsh. 'Get the fuck out. And don't even think about trying to get away. I'd break your fucking legs. You're mine now. My property.

Like a pet. The quicker you get that into your head, the better for both of us.'

Carly cringed, her skin clammy.

'I... I haven't done anything to y-you,' she stuttered, avoiding eye contact. 'Where are we? Why... why are you doing this? Please let me go. I won't tell a-anyone what's happened, I promise. And, and anyway, I've got no idea who you are. I haven't even seen you clearly, not in the pub and not here. I haven't got my c-contacts in. Honestly, it's true. They make my eyes sore. And I hate my glasses.'

'Out!' he shouted, just the one word.

But Carly still didn't move, knowing her pleading had fallen on deaf ears. She had to try again. 'I'm begging you,' she said, forcing herself to smile. 'I'll do anything you want me to. Anything! Don't hurt me. Please let me go.'

The man laughed, reached in, grabbed her left wrist, and then dragged her out of the van, where she fell to the frozen ground. He drew his right leg back and kicked her once, hard in the stomach, making her gasp.

'Do you think I can't see through your bullshit? You don't get to influence what happens here. I'm in charge. I'm the boss now. And nothing you can do or say is going to change that. Not for a second. I gave you an order, and I don't like to repeat myself. Now get the fuck up and move towards the cottage.' He stamped down on her right ankle. 'Up, get the fuck up. Are you stupid or something? Up! You do what you're told when you're told. Follow orders and you live; defy me and you die. And you won't die easy. I can guarantee you that. Is there any part of that you don't understand?'

Carly choked back tears as she struggled to her feet, stumbling and falling twice as he shoved her towards a small detached stone building with a dark, bowed roof with missing slates. She could see no other buildings in the vicinity as she limped on, struggling for breath; no dwellings or farms, so calling out for assistance seemed a lost cause. And she knew such things would only enrage him further. So, for a time, she decided silence was best. The pain in her ankle was even worse than her aching gut as he pushed open an old wooden front door with peeling black paint. She wondered if a bone was broken. Or if the ankle was simply severely bruised.

Carly's weakened legs buckled under her when the long-haired man punched her to the filthy concrete floor before taking a small torch from a pocket. She peeped up, coughing blood from her mouth as he lit two tall candles with matches taken from a nearby shelf. In the warm light of the flickering flames, she could see a sparsely furnished kitchen with an old wooden Welsh dresser, a dirty white sink, and an ancient black range cooker, all covered in cobwebs. It was as if she'd gone back in time, as if nothing in that room had changed since the Victorian era. And the room's only window had metal bars on it. Oh, God, no! Like a cell, she thought; just like a cell. That wasn't good at all.

The man switched off his torch before picking up a third candle and lighting it. He reached down with his free hand and grabbed her by her long hair, dragging her across the concrete to a second, adjoining room, which was empty of any furniture.

As in the case of the kitchen, the only window was barred. He continued dragging Carly to the far side of the room, where an old, blackened cast-iron coal-burning stove was secured to the wall. She could see in the candlelight that two coiled lengths of blue rope were positioned next to the fire. And a set of shiny steel handcuffs, the sight of which made her wince. She asked herself if she should say something as he released her hair. Should she plead for mercy? Or maybe tell him her father was a police officer? But each option seemed equally fraught with danger. And in the end, after a few seconds of conflicted thought, she said nothing at all.

He knocked her with his knee. 'Take your clothes off.'

Carly glanced up at him, brow furrowed, pulse racing, then quickly looked away. 'What?'

'You've pissed yourself, you dirty cow. You stink. And you're making a mess all over my nice floor. Take your clothes off. And you'll do it quickly if you don't want a hammering.' He laughed humourlessly, head back. 'I haven't got time for this shit. You should have realised by now I'm not a patient man.'

Carly resisted the strong impulse to vomit as she followed his orders, believing she had to. She wanted to live, to survive. And it seemed that to do what she was told until she could finally find a means of escape was her only viable option. Because, as she slowly removed her clothes, she was in no doubt the man was capable of killing her. He seemed not only evil but insane, a maniac, totally mad.

Carly removed her jumper first, then her T-shirt, followed by her blue jeans, which were still wet and cold. She left both her bra and knickers on, hoping but already doubting he'd be satisfied with that.

When he licked his lips, first the top, then the bottom, she knew her instinctive fears were correct.

'And the rest,' he yelled in that Northern Irish accent, wild tangled hair around his face, his eyes sparkling behind his tinted lenses as he bent easily at the waist to shout directly into her ear as she tried to pull away. 'Get the fucking things off. There's no place for modesty. Not here, not for you. I gave you an order. So you do it. It's that simple.'

Once she was naked, the man secured the steel handcuffs tightly around Carly's thin wrists and behind her back. She pulled her knees to her chest, trying to cover herself as she wept. The handcuffs were followed by a knotted nylon rope, which dug into both her ankles when he leaned back, seemingly pulling on it with all his weight. And then, as Carly cowered and whimpered, he left the room without another word, returning a minute later with a green plastic bucket held in one hand. She flinched again, shivering as he stood over her, pouring ice-cold water over her head and body. She opened her mouth to speak, teeth chattering, but then closed it again when she couldn't find the words. It seemed nothing was beyond her jailer. No level of depravity. He had no mercy in him, no kindness at all.

'There you go, you dirty bitch,' the man said, laughing, jumping from one foot to the other. 'That's got rid of the worst of your filth. I'll leave the bucket here for you out of the kindness of my heart. It'll serve as your ensuite facility. Not quite five-star, but the best a little skank like you deserves. And then we'll give you a proper wash down in the morning with hot water and scented soap. I can boil some well water on a nice roaring bonfire. I want you nice and clean for what comes next. You can look forward to that. Now would be a good time to thank me for my generosity. I wouldn't take it for granted if I were you.'

Carly desperately tried not to wonder what further horrors he had in mind for the morning, focusing on the now because that was as much as she could cope with. Survive for one minute, then the next, she told herself. And then, maybe, just maybe, he'd see reason and have a change of heart. 'Thank you,' she muttered, forcing the words from her swollen mouth.

'There, that's better. Now you're getting the idea. Show me the respect I deserve and things will go better for you.'

Carly wondered if she could reason with him after all. Had she seen a spark of humanity? Or was she deluded, kidding herself, seeing what she wanted to see? She really wasn't sure. 'I'm begging you, please,' she began between sobs, already doubting the wisdom of her words. 'I'm absolutely freezing. Could I have a blanket or quilt? Or at least a towel. I could dry myself if you took the cuffs off. There's ice on the window. On the inside... I've never been so cold.'

The man turned away, leaving the room for the second time without a response. A couple of minutes later, he returned with four more candles, which he lit, placing one in each corner of the room. Once the task was complete, he sauntered towards Carly, who was asking herself what terrors were coming next.

'There, that's much better. Now you can see me properly,' he said, his tone gleeful as his accent gradually morphed from Northern Irish to Welsh. 'Even with those dodgy eyes of yours. There'll be no bedclothes and nothing to dry yourself with. Not tonight. And probably not tomorrow, either. But I have got a little surprise for you. Something I'm certain you'll find almost as entertaining as I will. Are you ready? I thought I'd keep the disguise on until now, you know, just for fun, before the big reveal.'

Carly could tell he could hardly contain his excitement as she watched him in stunned, frightened silence. A few feet before her, the man began rhythmically swaying to the right and left, then spun in a tight circle on one leg, loudly performing the sixties hit 'The Stripper' as he danced.

The man took off his long brown wig first, then his tinted glasses, and finally his bushy beard to reveal the face of a person she knew well. Shady looked different to when she'd last seen him. He had a red and inflamed face, no eyebrows, and very little hair on his head. Just tufts here and there. But it was definitely him. Of that, she had no doubt, even if he was slightly out of focus.

'Mark?' she said with an incredulous stare, her bloody mouth falling open. 'But why? What on earth have you done?'

She could see the bulge in his pants as he stopped dancing to saunter towards her.

'Welcome to your new home, Miss Flowers. Nice, eh? I hope it's to your satisfaction. I went to some effort to prepare for your arrival. So I hope you'll make the most of it now you're here.'

She noticed his eyes were different, wild, showing the whites. Even in the dim light there was an unmistakable madness about them, a serpent-like coldness, as if he'd lost his mind. But the fact he wasn't some unknown stranger still gave her hope. She quickly decided to talk about *him*. Something he'd always appreciated during their short time together. Something he truly enjoyed above almost all else. Maybe then, she told herself, if she pleased him, he'd set her free.

'I was so sorry to hear about the fire.'

He tilted his head to one side at a slight angle, eyes narrowed almost to slits. 'Were you? Is that so?'

She wondered what he was likely to believe. How far should she push it? *Say something.* This was her chance. She had to say something. She was reminded of all her parents' warnings, of the alleged rapes and her denial. Was she really that naïve? How had she not seen the man for what he was?

'Yes, of course I was sorry,' Carly said with manufactured conviction, closely watching his every reaction, carefully considering each word. 'I was so distraught when I saw the report on the Welsh news. I still care about you, Mark. I couldn't stop crying.'

'You cried for me, really? I did hear you right, didn't I?'

She nodded enthusiastically, thinking if she continued speaking with emotion, he might be more likely to believe her. 'Yes, yes, for you, only for *you*,' she said, stressing the final word. 'I still can't believe someone would do such an awful thing.'

He took a single step towards her. 'So, you don't think I deserved the attack? Is that what you're saying?'

She screwed up her face. 'Deserved it? Why on earth would you? I very much hope whoever did it is caught and goes to prison for a very long time. They should throw away the key.'

He took another step. 'And you claim you still care about me? I have got that right, haven't I? I didn't mishear?'

She gave another nod, thinking she might be making progress, but she wasn't entirely sure. 'Yes, yes, Mark, I never stopped loving you. Not for a single second. Ending it was the worst mistake I ever made. I've never regretted anything more. We were meant to be together, you and me. We were made for each other. It's meant to be.'

He stood above her now, looking down as he had in her student bedroom just hours before, his hand clutching her long hair, roughly pulling it up from the scalp. 'So all along, you claim you've loved me?'

Carly spoke through her tears. 'Yes, Mark, absolutely. I still do.'

He paused, and she thought it was probably for effect. His way of upping the tension. 'But not enough to visit me in my hospital bed.'

Carly flinched. Oh, God, no, what to say now? It had to be convincing. 'I... I didn't know where you were. Had I known, I'd have been there, I promise. I'd have come straight away.'

He tugged at her hair with more force now, lifting her from the floor and making her yelp. 'Oh, Carly, is that really the best you can do? You could have asked your piggy father where I was. He could have found out easily enough. It's not as if there are many burns wards in our area. But you couldn't be bothered. I wasn't important. You'd moved on. Cast me away like a piece of rubbish. Like shit on your shoe.'

Carly swallowed hard, tears running down her face. 'Please, Mark, I'm begging you, if you ever had feelings for me, please let me go. I know I've done wrong. But I don't deserve this. We could be a loving couple again, like before. I'll forgive you. And you could forgive me. I should never have sent you that text. I was just being silly.'

'What, me and you back together?'

'Yes, Mark, yes. Why not?'

'And you wouldn't tell your piggy father what I've done to you?'

'No, not a word.'

He was silent for a second or two as if considering her proposition. 'Oh, I don't think so, my little darling,' he finally said with a contemptuous mocking sneer. 'Things have gone a little too far for that.'

'Please, I'm begging you. It's not too late for us. Tell me what you want. That's all you have to do, just say.'

He paused again, then grinned. 'I wrote you a little poem. Do you want to hear it?'

She'd thought his rhymes childish since he'd first shared one with her while on remand. But she was never going to admit that. Not now. Not to him. 'I'd love to hear it.'

'And you won't laugh at me?'

Carly shook her head, thinking that maybe she was getting through to him. That perhaps she'd soon be free. 'No, of course not, no. I love your poems.'

He beamed then gave a little bow as if performing on a West End stage.

'It's only short. Not one of my best. But I think it encapsulates all it needs to say.'

Carly was shaking almost too much to speak. But once again, she forced out the words, certain the fire and all it entailed had driven him mad. 'I'm... I'm listening,' she said, as if she had a choice.

'Right, here goes: Carly Flowers, not so nice, one day soon, she'll pay the price. Carly Flowers, scream or cry, one thing's sure, she's going to die.'

He paused, still focused on her, never looking away. 'That's it. A mere ditty. Short but sweet. What do you think?'

'Tell me you just want to frighten me. You don't mean it, Mark, do you?' she replied, cowering.

He glared at her. 'I asked you your opinion. You do appreciate my poetry skills, don't you? And think carefully before you reply. It could be the last thing you ever say.'

All she could do was play his game. 'Well, yes, I... I think you're very talented.'

He smiled. 'Then surely a round of applause is warranted. You can give a little cheer instead if clapping's difficult, what with the cuffs and all. I wouldn't want to be unreasonable. Not after everything we've shared together. So come on, cheer away.'

She dropped her chin to her chest. 'Please,

Mark, I'm hurting; you're really scaring me. Please set me free.'

He drew his hand back and slapped her hard, reddening her cheek. 'If I tell you to do something, you do it immediately, with no deviations or any of your pathetic excuses. I thought we'd already established that. Now, tell me you understand.'

Carly remained focused on her feet as she gave a little cheer.

Shady smiled again. 'There you go, that's much better. What's not to like? Do what you're told the first time and you won't get thumped.'

'Yes, Mark. Thank you.'

He took a quick step towards her, then kneed her, fracturing her nose, a white bone breaking the skin. 'And stop your fucking snivelling, you inconsiderate bitch. Can't you see I'm tired? It's been a long night. I need to get some rest.'

'Sorry,' she spluttered, dark drops of blood falling to her chest.

'Good, that's very good,' he began while touching his genitals through his trousers. 'But disturb me even once before morning and it'll be the last thing you ever do. So say no more. I'll snuff those candles out and be off to my bed.'

26

Carly didn't sleep even for a moment after her captor left the room that had become a cell. She sat there bleeding, hunched up on the unforgiving concrete, shivering in the darkness, and struggling to breathe until dawn's grey winter light finally illuminated her new world. And as her entire body shook and her teeth chattered, her plight now felt infinitely more challenging than on her arrival. Time passed slowly, ever so slowly. And there were dark and emotional moments when she would have welcomed death as the only means of relief. She even prayed for it. Asking God to take her. But there were brief moments of hope, too. Carly repeatedly told herself she had much to live for. And that nothing lasted forever. One way or another, her trauma would end.

As she drifted somewhere between wakefulness and insensibility, Carly recalled her mother once telling her a childhood illness she'd suffered would soon pass. Her mum had been so very kind, supportive, and gentle. And Carly clung to the memory, giving her mental strength when she needed it most.

She gave her captivity a great deal of thought as she awaited Shady's inevitable return, trying to develop a positive escape strategy despite her pain and fear. But nothing that came to mind offered any great hope. Not unless her captor had a sudden change of heart. Which seemed far from likely. Or her dad came to the rescue. Surely Dad was looking for her. Surely he'd realised by now she needed his urgent help. If only she'd listened to him. If only! But what could she have done differently? Nothing. That was the truth of it. Mark hid his true nature so very well. Hid it from her. And all his victims. Poor Anna. She was called a liar after everything she'd gone through. Humiliated for all to see. Mocked and ridiculed for no good reason at all.

Carly silently swore she'd contact Anna Edwards to offer sympathy and support if she was ever set free. They had so much in common. More than she could ever have imagined. Conned and abused by a manipulative man. A rat disguised as a prince. A nasty, selfish, sadistic bastard! Yes, Mark wore the mask well.

Carly began crying again, wailing as the searing pain in her face escalated exponentially as her entire body tensed. She pictured herself with her hands pressed together as if in prayer and tried to manifest a new reality. *Please, Dad, come to find me.* Perhaps he was already on his way. *Please, God, please, let it be so.*

Carly had never felt lower as she squatted over the plastic bucket, finally accepting the urgent need to evacuate her bowel. Some things, she told herself, couldn't be avoided forever, and that time had come. She silently swore she'd fully appreciate all the little things life offered if she ever got out of there. That she'd never take anything for granted ever again. Not a warm bed, not a shower, and certainly not a toilet, if only she got the chance.

She was climbing off the bucket, careful not to knock it over, and thinking things couldn't get any worse when she heard the sound of happy male singing coming from another room. And as she mournfully anticipated her jailor's inevitable reappearance, she realised she'd been horribly wrong. Things could get worse. Because it seemed evident that Mark was enjoying himself. There was a gleeful tone to his voice. Her nightmare was his joy. *Oh, God, no, please, no.* It seemed as simple as that.

Shady was naked when he appeared minutes later with what looked like a dog bowl in one hand. He walked towards her with a disgusted look on his reddened face. He sniffed the fetid air, making his revulsion obvious.

'Fuck me, girl, what have you been eating? Poo! And look at the state of you. What a mess.'

Carly curled up in a ball. 'Let me go, please. I think my nose is broken. I need to go to hospital. I've lost a lot of blood. You used to say you loved me. Please have mercy. I've said I'm sorry. Surely I've suffered enough.'

Shady placed the steel bowl containing what looked like dog food on the floor next to her, then picked up the bucket without saying a single word. He returned all too quickly with a wide grin on his face. The bucket looked full now, soapy water slopping from the top as he strode towards her.

'What, not hungry?' he asked. 'And after all the trouble I went to opening the can. You really are an ungrateful bitch.'

Carly avoided his accusing gaze. 'Water... please can I have some water? My throat's so parched.'

Shady shook his head with a sneer. 'Who the hell do you think you are with all your demands? Shut the fuck up. Time for a wash,' he said, shoving her onto her side. He took a yellow sponge from the bucket and began roughly scrubbing her down, pushing her one way and then the other to facilitate the process. He left the room again and returned with a refilled bucket a short time later, hurling what was now cold water over her and washing away the soap.

'Right, that's you a bit more presentable,' he said, standing back to study her, obviously amused and slightly aroused. 'Not exactly a beauty queen. But I suppose you'll have to do. You're here now. There's just you and me until I capture the next one. And I'm feeling horny. So it's not like I've got a choice.'

Carly hoped his words were more intended to scare her than real. All part of his sadistic games. But something told her she was wrong. She tried to push her dark thoughts from her mind, focusing on survival.

'Can I please have a drink, Mark? Please, for old time's sake, do that much for me. I need some water. It's not too much to ask.'

He left the room again, then returned carrying a brown pottery mug, which he held to her mouth. Carly choked and spluttered as he forced her head back, pouring the cold liquid down her throat.

'Be careful what you wish for. Now, sleep, Carly, sleep,' he said, standing back and studying her, his head tilted to the left. 'It will all be over soon. It shouldn't take too long. Give in to it. It'll be better that way.'

'What have you done?'

Shady touched his penis, which was again starting to swell.

'I've tired of our time together. You're too much trouble, what with your endless chatter, loud breathing, and the mess you make. I like you quiet and still. There are no demands that way, no inter-ruptions. And you'll never leave me again. Not of your own volition. That's a plus. It's time to bring it to an end.'

Within a short time, Carly realised she'd been drugged. The room quickly became a blur, as had the pub. Although it all seemed to be happening so much faster this time. She fought to stay conscious but with no chance of success. The room went black seconds later as she thought of her parents. And then nothing, nothing at all.

27

Lewis didn't hear from Mike Flowers again until the evening of his second date with Tanya, ten days after the first. The birthday celebrations at the King Street curry house had gone surprisingly well, with no awkward silences, as copious amounts of chilled Cobra Indian beer oiled the conversational wheels very nicely. The tasty, spicy food was excellent, the company convivial, and Tanya even kissed him goodnight at the end of the evening before getting into her taxicab. It wasn't a sexual kiss, more an affectionate peck on the cheek rather than passion. But still, it was a gesture Lewis thought a triumph after so long off the dating scene. He'd got back on the horse, to use a familiar metaphor. Something he'd thought he might never do. And it felt good, as if he was a younger man again. In some strange way, for a time, the years had melted away.

Lewis had thought about that kiss often after that first heady evening. The touch of Tanya's warm red lips on his rough skin had been both pleasant and surprising. And he found himself wanting more. He reminded himself that he'd even bought a packet of Viagra online – something he'd never done before – more in hope than expectation. Just in case he got lucky. A bit of chemical assistance if he needed it. A confidence builder. Because he wasn't getting any younger despite his thoughts of youth; getting up three or four times a night to pee told him that. Sex seemed little more than a distant memory. If it ever happened again, he might need all the help he could get.

Lewis had been surprised to find himself feeling both nervous and excited as he'd prepared for date number two, this time a visit to the local cinema to watch a comedy film he didn't particularly want to see. He drank a can of strong German lager as he watched the seconds tick by, just the one can to take the edge off and to calm his jangling nerves as he dressed and shaved. And he really did want to look his best, to make a good impression and maybe get another kiss... or even more.

Lewis splashed cheap musky aftershave, he thought a manly scent, on his face as he looked in the bathroom mirror, asking himself what any woman would see in him. She seemed so out of his league. The sort of woman who could have someone so much better than him. Maybe it was his warm personality she liked. That Welsh charm. He chuckled to himself, pushing his self-deprecating thoughts from his mind. Yeah, his cheeky charm, that must be it. Just like he'd told Kesey.

Lewis checked his appearance one final time in the full-length mirror on the back of his wardrobe door, ran a hand through his short, thinning hair to no good effect, and told himself that, like it or not, his appearance would have to do. There was only so much he could achieve, however hard he tried. And time was getting on. The last thing he wanted was to be late. One of his pet hates. It was time to go.

Lewis drove through Carmarthen listening to Radio Wales, parked his hatchback in the large mul-tistorey car park close to his destination, and met Tanya in the cinema's brightly lit foyer as arranged. She was dressed more casually than on their first date, but he still thought her attractive in her slightly flared blue jeans and tight red jumper. Far too good for him with his beer belly, heavily lined face, and big balding head. And he was determined to treat her like a queen. To hold on to her for as long as he could. So she wouldn't run off like his wife had, attracted by another man, while he worked every hour God sent. But it would be different this time. Tanya understood the demands of his job. Let the good times roll.

The two were chatting in the short queue, waiting to buy tickets, which Lewis had planned to pay for, when his mobile rang in his jacket pocket, making Tanya jump. Lewis glanced at the phone's cracked screen and sighed heavily. 'Sorry, love, I'm going to have to take this. Looks like it's a work thing.'

Tanya nodded her understanding with a gap-toothed smile.

Lewis strode to a quiet corner, phone in hand, before answering the call. He knew his frustration was betrayed by his tone. 'What is it, Daisy? I'm a bit busy right now.'

'Carly's missing.'

'What are you talking about?'

'She's missing, she's fucking missing! I don't know how I can make it any clearer than that.'

Lewis allowed a wall to support his weight, sucking in the warm air, feeling the need for nicotine. 'Right, take your time, let's get this straight. When did you last see or hear from her?'

'Half six in the evening two days ago. Her mother talked to her by text. And since then, not a thing. She's not answering her mobile, her Whats-App, nothing. And she hasn't even posted on social media. Fuck all. That's not like her. She's always posting something. She's obsessed with that stuff.'

Lewis glanced across at Tanya, who was now at the front of the queue with her purse in hand. He held his hands wide, catching her eye and indicating his frustration, keen to join her as soon as possible.

'It's only a couple of days, Daisy. Carly's a university student, not a young kid. And you said yourself she can be a bit independent and headstrong when the mood takes her. Maybe you're worrying about nothing.'

Flowers rushed his response.

'That's the way I saw it at first. But the missus thought differently. I called at Carly's student digs before ringing you and spoke to Hannah Graham, one of Carly's friends, one of the girls she's planning to go travelling with in the summer. It seems the two of them drifted apart for a while thanks to Shady. You know what he's like. But they've reconnected again now. Carly, Hannah, and a Spanish girl they know went for a night out in Carmarthen later on the same evening we last heard from Carly. They were in a bar in town when Carly said she was feeling like crap with a headache, dizziness, and nausea. Hannah called a cab, and she and Carly returned to their digs at about half-ten. The other girl, Paloma, stayed in town. She met up with some boy she knew.'

'Maybe Carly had too much to drink.' Lewis shrugged as he spoke. 'Sounds that way to me. We've all been there. She wouldn't be the first student to get pissed on a night out.'

There was the sound of a heavy sigh before Flowers replied. 'I wish it was that simple. But Hannah insisted not. They're all on some sort of health kick, no alcohol. It's a charity-sponsored thing arranged by the students' union – a month of abstinence. Apparently, the three of them just got together for a gossip and to share ideas for the summer trip. Where to go, how long for, that sort of thing. And it was soft drinks all evening. Just bottles of spring water. They were intending going to some club for a dance at some point had things worked out differently. But, of course, that never happened.'

'Carly could have some kind of winter bug or something. There's a few doing the rounds. One of my DCs was off work for a couple of days.'

'I don't think so,' Flowers replied. 'Hannah said one minute Carly was fine, and then suddenly she wasn't. I've got a horrible feeling she might have been spiked. I dealt with a similar case a few months back. Some bastard injected a girl in a club. And then, hours later, he assaulted her. She couldn't remember a thing.'

Lewis made a face, less than convinced as the seconds ticked by. 'Okay, it's possible, I can't deny that. But you said the two girls got a taxi back to their digs. So, if she was drugged, which she may well not have been, what's the relevance to her going missing? It doesn't make a lot of sense.'

Flowers was fast to respond, rushing his words as if he couldn't express himself as quickly as he'd like. 'Hannah said when they got back to the digs she helped Carly get to bed. Carly was too out of it to even undress. Just laid down on top of her quilt and went straight to sleep.

'Hannah took Carly's shoes and socks off for her and left her there. She got up early the following day to go for a run, noticed Carly's bedroom door was open and looked in to see how she was doing after the night before. But Carly wasn't there. Hannah looked around the house calling Carly's name but there was no sign of her anywhere. And the back door was partially open, just a few inches, as if someone had either gone out or come in that way. She said they sometimes forget to lock it. It's a low-crime area. But that still seems stupid to me. I really wish Hannah had contacted me then. She must have known I'm in the job. But she said she just assumed Carly was fine again and had gotten up early to go out somewhere, so she thought no more about it. Carly had told Hannah she planned to visit her mum for a catch-up. So I guess it's understandable.'

'Perhaps Carly did go out when she was feeling better. She might have left the back door open herself. It could be that simple. She could turn up any minute and ask you what you were worrying about. Like I said, she's not a kid.'

'I don't think so, Ray. I really don't think so. Something's not right.'

Lewis tapped a foot against the floor as Tanya waved to him, paper tickets in hand. And then he asked a question that had been playing on his mind.

'You don't think there is any chance that Carly and Shady have been back in contact again, do you? It's all a bit of a coincidence her going off the radar so soon after the scumbag comes out of hospital. He could have played the sympathy card. You know, made her feel sorry for him. He'd use anything to his advantage if he thought it would work. That could explain why she hasn't been in touch. Or, if she was drugged, in the worst-case scenario, it could have been him. He's certainly capable of it. Wouldn't think twice.'

'I can't say it hasn't crossed my mind,' Flowers replied in anguished tones, as if close to tears. 'I'm seriously worried, Ray, absolutely shitting myself. Where the hell is she? She's still my little girl.'

Lewis began ambling back towards where Tanya was waiting with an apologetic look on his face. 'Have you reported Carly missing? Formally, I mean. Made it official?'

'I needed to get things straight in my head. To make sure I wasn't overreacting. I wanted to speak to you first.'

Lewis tilted his head back, his gaze to the ceiling. He knew Flowers tended towards indecisiveness, but this seemed crazy even by his standards. 'I'd get it done now straight away if I were you, mate.

And maybe call at the Ivy Bush Hotel with a recent photo of Carly to see if any staff have seen her there. Shady's staying there while his place is being fixed up. Someone will likely have seen them together if she is back in contact with him. At least then you'll have an idea what's going on.'

'The wife's in a right state. Crying her eyes out. I'd rather not leave her on her own. Can you visit the hotel for me? It's only a couple of minutes from your place.'

Lewis pressed his lips together. 'Wish I could, mate. But tonight's not going to be possible. This one's down to you. Unless you want the local uniform to do it. I could make a quick call. Get it sorted.'

Lewis could hear the disappointment in the other man's voice. 'I'll take the missus with me. I don't want to leave it to uniform. She can wait in the car.'

Lewis made a silent gesture to Tanya, indicating he was nearly done.

'Sounds like a plan,' he said, looking to end the conversation. 'And get Carly notified as a missing person. The quicker, the better. Do it now.'

'Will do.'

'I'll give you a ring in the morning, Daisy. To see how things are.'

'Thanks, I'd appreciate that.'

Lewis joined Tanya, his mobile now back in his jacket pocket. He wanted to focus on his date and all she could offer. But now his gut instinct was ringing alarm bells. Something he could never ignore. He shuddered as they walked hand in hand towards screen number two, recalling very similar circumstances, a case years before that had ended with a funeral. Carly was in danger, grave danger. The more he considered it, the more that message seemed loud and clear. He'd never been more sure of anything in his life.

28

Flowers drove the twenty-six miles from his sea-view terrace Tenby home to the three-star Ivy Bush Royal Hotel in Carmarthen's Spilman Street with his wife crying constantly in the French saloon car's rear seat. And the sound of her sobbing seemed to dominate his every thought. He'd tried his very best to soothe her. He'd said what he thought were all the right things, prioritising his wife's needs and putting her first despite his own nagging anxieties that wouldn't let up. But as their journey continued, Flowers quickly concluded that nothing he was likely to say would go any way to alleviating her angst. She wanted her daughter. To know she was safe and sound and to hold her close. And nothing else would do. Nothing else came even close to second-best.

As he pressed his foot down hard on the accelerator pedal, speeding along the A477 in the direction of Carmarthen, Flowers reassured himself he was doing all he could. Carly had been officially reported as missing. A recent colour photo and a detailed description had been quickly circulated to all officers in the force. And now he was about to visit the hotel to make his enquiries, just as Ray had advised. He was being a good father, and a good copper too. Life didn't always greet you with roses. He really couldn't do any more. He had to be satisfied with that.

As he drove up Carmarthen's Castle Hill and past County Hall with its Welsh, European, and Ukrainian flags flying high on their white poles, he told himself he wanted his daughter safe too, just like his missus did. He, too, could have wept until he was rung out and dry. But what did tears achieve? Less emotion, more action. That was what was needed. He had to get on with what he was there to do.

Flowers slowed the saloon, waited for two oncoming vehicles to pass on by, and then turned right into the hotel's busy car park, keenly anticipating what was to come. If Carly was with Shady, he was determined to find her because nothing was as important as family. Not his career, not his pension, nothing. Carly was everything. Recent events had brought that into sharp and unrelenting focus. Nothing mattered more.

'Okay, we're here,' he said, trying to exude an air of positivity as he switched off the diesel engine, wishing his wife would stop sniffling as it was feeding his anxiety. 'Are you going to come on in, or wait for me here in the car?' he added, speaking a little louder this time, careful not to sound angry, impatient, or irritated. Because he all too easily could have. He knew that full well.

She dabbed at her eyes with a paper tissue and sniffed as he turned in his seat to face her. 'Do you mind if I stay here? Look at the state of me. I'll only get in the way. It's better for you to go in by yourself. I know you'll do everything you can. I'm relying on you. And our Carly is, too.'

A big part of him was relieved his wife was staying where she was. Some things were better done alone. 'Are you sure?' he asked, hoping the answer was yes.

She repeatedly nodded without the need for words as he prepared to exit the car.

'I'll be back as soon as I can,' he said in a final attempt to raise her spirits even for a moment. 'Hopefully, with good news.' He patted a trouser pocket. 'Give me a ring on my mobile if you need me. I won't be far away.'

Flowers pushed open the hotel's glass door and quickly made his way to the comfortable, well-appointed lounge with its impressive stained-glass window dominating the far end. He'd been to the hotel before, attending a multi-agency course. And he liked the place. He'd had a good time and enjoyed himself. But this time felt so very different. He was acutely aware that his hands were shaking as if frozen as a young waitress passed by, delivering a tray of tea and biscuits to two elderly, grey-haired women seated at a nearby table.

He took his police warrant card from his jacket pocket out of habit, opened the black leather folder, and held the silver badge of authority in plain sight, gaining the waitress's attention as she walked back in his direction, the tray now empty.

'I'd like a word, please. My name's Flowers, Detective Constable Flowers, West Wales Police. I need to speak to whoever is in charge – and it's important – if you could get them for me.'

The young woman's concern was obvious as she

met his gaze. 'Yes, of course, I'll fetch the duty manager. He'll be with you very shortly, sir.'

'Thanks, it's appreciated; one more thing before you go.'

Flowers showed the waitress a relatively recent photo of Carly on his mobile. An image taken at a family birthday celebration only a few months before Shady had cast a dark shadow over their lives. Carly looked so happy in the photo, smiling brightly and carefree. So much had changed in such a short time.

He waited as the waitress studied the image closely, holding the phone a few inches from her face. And he was grateful she was taking her time.

'The girl in the photo is my daughter, Carly; she's missing. I have excellent reason to think she may have been here, possibly with a guest, a Mr Mark Shady. She could even be staying here with him. Have you seen her?'

His disappointment was almost palpable when the waitress shook her head and said, 'Sorry, no,' before handing back his mobile.

Flowers wasn't ready to give up that easily. So he asked again, desperately hoping for a different response, as if asking the same question twice would somehow change things.

'Take another look, please,' he said. 'Her hair is a little longer now. It comes right down to her shoulders. Although she sometimes ties it back. Have a really good look. I need to find her urgently.'

The waitress took the phone from his hand, studied the image closely with narrowed eyes, but then shook her head again, as she had the first time.

'I'm really sorry, I haven't seen her. I'd say if I had, honestly, I would. She's gorgeous. I'd remember. And I haven't seen Mark either. Not for weeks. I know him. Not that well. But I know who he is. I've eaten in his pizza restaurant a few times. And he's usually there, chatting with customers. It's terrible what's happened to the place, the fire; someone told me it was arson. I didn't actually know he was staying here, but I've been off most of this week.'

Flowers took back his mobile for a second time, glancing down at the photo of his daughter for a beat before returning the phone to his pocket.

'If you could fetch the manager now,' he said, accepting temporary defeat, tears welling in his eyes, blinking them away.

The waitress raised a hand and pointed.

'He's in his office. It will only take me a second. And I'll tell him it's urgent.'

Less than two minutes later, Flowers turned to

see a tall, slim, olive-skinned young man wearing a stylish dark grey lounge suit walking towards him with an evident youthful confidence.

'Detective Flowers?'

Flowers nodded, not bothering with his warrant card this time.

'How can I help you?' the manager asked in what sounded like an Italian accent.

'Is there somewhere we can speak privately?'

This time, it was the manager's turn to nod. 'If you follow me, we can talk in my office.'

Flowers followed the younger man into a small, brightly lit room dominated by a work desk. He closed the door behind him and sat in one of two padded seats. He showed the manager the photo of Carly, as he had the waitress, hoping for a very different result.

'I'm looking for this girl,' Flowers began, his voice threatening to break. 'Her name's Carly, my daughter, Carly Flowers, a student at Trinity. She's been missing for two days, and I have good reason to believe she may have been here.'

The hotel manager studied the image closely for a few seconds, having taken a pair of reading glasses from an inside jacket pocket. He looked at the photo again, the spectacles perched on the tip of his nose.

'I've seen her in town,' he said, temporarily raising the detective's spirits, 'but not recently. I last saw her, what? Three or maybe four weeks ago. Sorry I can't be more helpful.'

'Are you certain you haven't seen her since then?'

'Yes, I'm sorry, I'm sure.'

Flowers swallowed hard, shoulders slumping at another blow.

'You've got a guest staying here – a Mark Shady. Until recently, he was in a relationship with Carly. They might have reconnected. Is he here for me to talk to?'

The manager looked uneasy, as if unsure how to reply.

'Is this an official police investigation?' he asked, his voice hesitant. 'Or is it a personal matter?'

'It's both,' Flowers quickly replied, hoping to overcome the other man's apparent reluctance to talk. 'And I really would appreciate your cooperation. We could arrange to speak at the police station if that suits you better. But one way or another, I need that information. I need to talk to Shady, and soon.'

'Mr Shady does have a room booked. It's paid for directly by his insurance company for however long it takes to repair his accommodation. That's what I understand to be the case. But he's not here. I can't help.'

Flowers leaned forward, making intense eye contact. 'Can you at least check his room for me? Surely that isn't too much to ask?'

The young man shook his head, a look of regret on his face. 'Mr Shady hasn't been here at all. I spoke to him on the phone when he booked the room. But he hasn't actually spent a single night at the hotel, not one. His bed hasn't been slept in at any point. I've tried contacting him to clarify his intentions but without success.'

Flowers stood on unsteady legs, fearing they might give way at any moment and thinking the situation was far more complex than he'd ever imagined. It seemed he was dealing with two missing people. Not just Carly but Shady too. And maybe if he found one, he'd find the other. But where? That was the big question. Where?

As Flowers walked back through the hotel towards his car, he silently swore that if Shady had harmed even one hair on Carly's head, he'd make the bastard pay. He was more than the mild-mannered copper most people thought he was. It was a role he played because it made life easier, suiting his purpose. But he reminded himself he was capable of violence when the situation demanded. He could hit out with the best of them. A few burns would be the least of Shady's worries.

Flowers actively calmed himself as he opened the car door, climbing into the driver's seat and tightly gripping the steering wheel with both hands, knuckles white. Tense muscles changed the contours of his face.

'Sorry, love,' he said. 'No news, red herring, waste of a trip. But we'll find her. Don't you worry about that. The whole force is looking for her. She'll be back with us soon. You wait and see.'

29

Following what Lewis considered a glorious night of unbridled passion, ably assisted by his little blue pills, the detective contacted Mike Flowers, as promised. Lewis would have liked to spend the entire day with Tanya, doing what lovers do. Perhaps a brisk walk in the park, followed by a nice pub lunch and a pint or two. But as always, as soon as his alarm sounded at 7 a.m., work was calling, a responsibility he could never find it in himself to ignore for very long. He made his call in his small, dated kitchen while Tanya showered.

'Morning, Daisy, any news?'

He heard what sounded like a long sigh, which didn't surprise Lewis at all.

'No sign of her. Not a thing.'

Lewis scratched his nose. 'What, no joy at the hotel?'

'That's the strange thing, Ray. Shady's got a room booked. It's all paid for, but he hasn't been there. His bed hasn't been slept in.'

'Not at all?'

'That's what I was told.'

'Okay, that's unexpected; it had to be worth a try. The bastard's got to be staying somewhere. I'll ask about in town. See if I can find anything out.'

'Thanks, it's appreciated. The more I think about it, the more I think Carly might be with him. Maybe her saying she'd finished with him was just a story to keep me and the missus happy. You know, to get us off her back, shut us up.'

Lewis heard the shower switch off and pictured Tanya towelling herself dry. He wondered if he could do without the blue pills the next time. Maybe, yes, now his confidence was rising.

'Do you think so?' Lewis asked, focusing back on his conversation as the mental image faded.

'Could be,' Flowers replied. 'Anything's possible.'

'Have you rung round the local hospitals, just in case she's been admitted or turned up in casualty?'

'Yeah,' Flowers said, sounding despondent, 'I made a few calls last night, but no joy.'

Lewis checked the kettle was full before switching it on.

'Okay, I'll make sure someone's checking CCTV when I get to the station. There are no cameras outside the town centre. But we might spot something helpful; fingers crossed. And I'll have a chat with Laura Kesey about a potential press release. It might be an idea to ask for the public's help. Someone must have seen the girl. She hasn't disappeared off the face of the earth.'

'I still can't believe all this is happening.'

Lewis attempted to sound much more optimistic than he felt when responding. 'We'll find her, mate,' he said, hoping they'd find her alive and well. 'Every copper's on the alert. You know what it's like when it's one of our own. There'll be no stone left unturned.'

There was a second's silence before Flowers spoke. 'Any progress finding out who threw that petrol bomb?'

Lewis dropped instant coffee granules into two mugs, adding several heaped teaspoons of white sugar to his own. 'I've got my theories,' he said, reaching for the milk. 'But the fire's not my highest priority, to be honest. Some crimes are better not solved. Fuck Shady! I'll go through the motions, but no more than that.'

'Bet Kesey doesn't see it that way.'

A small laugh. 'You got that right.'

'Give me a ring straight away if you hear any news of Carly, will you, mate?'

'Of course,' Lewis replied, keen to end the interaction as Tanya entered the kitchen with a friendly smile, her hair still damp. 'I'll be straight on the blower. Goes without saying.'

'And you'll ask about that press release asap?'

Lewis pecked Tanya on the cheek, her sweet floral perfume filling his nostrils. 'Like I said, yeah.'

'Sorry, I can't stop worrying. It's like a bad dream come true.'

Lewis poured boiling water into both mugs and stirred with a tarnished silver spoon inherited from his paternal grandmother years before. 'I've got to go, mate,' he said. 'Busy, busy, you know what it's like.'

'Okay, thanks, Ray. Thanks for everything you're doing.'

'Least I can do, Daisy.'

'Well, I'm grateful.'

Lewis ended the call and handed Tanya her coffee, thinking he should have bought cream.

'Who's Daisy?' she asked, a slight hint of concern in her voice.

'Mike Flowers,' he said with a frown. 'His daughter's missing.'

A look of recognition dawned. 'Is it serious?'

Lewis nodded twice. 'Yeah, I think so, probably. I've got a horrible feeling it might be.'

30

Shady released his vice-like grip from Carly's slender neck, slowly rose to his bare feet, and began weeping as he stared down at her recently deceased corpse. He cried not because she was dead. Not because he'd taken the life of a beautiful young woman who had once claimed she loved him. But because the act of murder was over. The killing, he ruminated as he stood there looking her naked body up and down, had so far exceeded his dark fantasies in every conceivable way. He'd never felt so powerful, never so utterly aroused as his erect cock stood proudly to attention, harder and bigger than ever before. Roleplay games, he pondered, wiping away his tears, were one thing, a bit of fun in themselves. No harm in that. But the reality of death, actually acting on his instincts, snuffing out a life, watching the light of life leave a victim's eyes... now, that was quite another. Undoubtedly, it was the most incredible experience of his life. The culmination of everything. He'd finally become what he was always intended to be. Yes, the great Mark Shady was continuing to evolve.

But now, as he looked down, studying Carly's lifeless face, he was again reminded it was over. No wonder he was weeping. No wonder a sadness had enveloped him like a dark cloud of depression. The heady high had already faded away as if it hadn't happened at all. So sad, so very sad. Most of all, Shady told himself as he took a backward step towards the kitchen door, he was desperate to do it all over again. So very desperate. And he had to make that happen. One way or another. It seemed he had no other choice. Murder was his reason for living now. And maybe, next time, he could make the process last a little longer. If he could control himself. If he could stand to wait. Shame he hadn't filmed it. Oh well, perhaps next time.

Shady left the killing room, deciding on an early lunch after a minute or two's further contemplative thought. And as he sat in the kitchen, eating a stale cheese and onion petrol station sandwich collected from the van, it suddenly hit him. The body! What the hell was he going to do with the body? A regrettable inconvenience he hadn't even considered until then. 'All Carly's fault,' he murmured, hissing his words as if someone were there to hear. 'So typical of the bitch.' What the hell, he pondered, should he do with her now?

As he finished his food, Shady quickly ruled out dismembering Carly's body where it lay. Not because the idea repulsed him. Quite the opposite, in fact. The possibility amused him, making him laugh. All that blood and gore had its undoubted attractions. But the likelihood of leaving forensic evidence for the piggy police to find should they ever come sniffing was a distinct disadvantage. He noted that pigs like Lewis and Flowers tended to stick their snouts in. They might get lucky. Actually do their job for once. And there were no prospective victims in prison. All male, not his thing at all. Getting caught, he reminded himself, had never been a part of the plan.

Shady dressed to combat the cold, then returned to his killing room, where he sat next to Carly's fast-cooling corpse, still considering the best method of disposal. Burial in some remote spot miles away from the cottage seemed a reasonable idea until he considered the frosty hardness of the ground. Too much work, far too much effort, he concluded. So maybe dumping the inconsiderate cow in a quiet wood, a local river, or the sea would suffice. Yes, that should be easy enough, especially in the early hours when it was dark and he wouldn't be seen. And then he could think about the next one. The fat detective's tubby daughter, maybe. As he'd thought before. Fatty Bronwen, with all her blubber, still seemed the logical choice. Yes, her, why not her? She had a throat worth squeezing.

Shady smiled, teeth gleaming, as he made his imaginings big and bright again. Yeah, target the Lewis family. Sergeant Piggy Lewis deserved no less. Now it was his turn to suffer. Call it karma. Real justice. He'd brought it on himself. But he needed to forget him for now. There were things to do.

Shady enjoyed spending time with Carly's lifeless body as the hours passed, forcing her stiffening legs apart, having decided to make the most of the opportunity while he still had her. And he found real satisfaction in that. All his death fantasies had become real. And that, he told himself, was something to be celebrated.

Shady decided to avoid sleep as night-time approached, fearful of not waking at an opportune time for the body's safe disposal. And it was a little after 2 a.m. when he finally began dragging Carly's corpse out of the old stone building and towards the van, surprised by the degree of physical effort required. He was panting hard by the time he finally lifted and threw her into the back of the vehicle. Something else he resented her for. And as he climbed into the driver's seat, he told himself Carly had deserved to die. That he had done nothing wrong. Any right-thinking individual would understand that and applaud his activities if they knew the full facts. They'd see him for the innovator he was.

Shady repeatedly relived the killing in his mind as he drove in the direction of Pendine, with its long seven-mile stretch of flat yellow sand once used for land speed records. He'd last been there on a school trip when he was just seven or eight, and he'd now decided the place offered the ideal opportunity for the disposal of an unwanted body if he drove some distance along the beach away from the village with its potentially prying eyes. The more he thought about it, the more convinced Shady became that leaving Carly's corpse beyond the tideline made perfect sense, enabling the cold grey sea to wash her and any evidence away while he made his timely escape. Minimum effort with maximum results, he thought with a snigger, congratulating himself on his prowess. Another reflection of his inspired genius. What was not to like? He truly was a hunter at the very top of his game.

Shady arrived at the coastal Carmarthenshire village at 2.40 a.m., having driven cautiously, again keen not to draw any unwelcome attention to the van. He was pleased but unsurprised not to see a single living person as he approached a concrete ramp leading to the sand and told himself things were going his way. He could see the rising tideline was about fifty metres away and fast coming in, another plus giving him cause for celebration. Once again, as he first smiled, then laughed, it seemed the universe was conspiring in his favour. Making his life easier. Supporting him in his quest. Sending him the message that all was good with his world.

Shady drove on for another ten minutes or so, keeping his speed low and careful to steer the vehicle on the hard, sea-washed sand rather than risk the softer, undulating area closer to the high dunes. He slowed to a stop once satisfied he'd travelled far enough for his purpose, switched off the headlights, thinking the moon offered sufficient illumination, then exited the vehicle and looked around him, turning in a slow circle three times until he was sure he was alone. And once again, as he shivered with cold, he reassured himself the location was just about perfect. He really couldn't have made a better choice.

Shady pulled Carly's stiff body from the van as a dog barked somewhere in the far-off distance, allowing her to fall to the wet sand and then dragging her by her feet towards the rising sea. He briefly considered lifting her over one shoulder when the task became a little onerous, but he quickly decided any lingering bodily fluids might soil his clothes. That would be so typical of the bitch. Anything to inconvenience him. All her fault, all her fault.

Shady released Carly's feet, resting for a second or two to catch his breath when he reached the tide-line. He briefly wondered if he should have parked closer to the sea as he stood there shivering at the water's edge. But he then decided he'd judged it perfectly. The last thing he needed was for the van to get stuck. He shuddered at the thought of being left without transport miles from home.

Shady reached down, grabbing Carly by her hair now and forcing his bleak thoughts from his mind. The sea was cold and shallow, getting deeper slowly, much more gradually than he'd anticipated. And for the first time, he asked himself if his choice of location was the best after all. He'd always been so cautious in the past, always so calculated. And now this. It seemed so much had changed. He strode into the rolling white-topped waves, determined to make the best of it, pulling Carly behind him until he was soaked to the waist. And then he stopped, telling himself he was deep enough as he pushed her body under, imagining the salty water washing his semen away.

Shady observed he should have weighed the corpse down as he turned and made his weary way back towards the beach. But it was too late for that now. Maybe, he pondered, the universe wasn't on his side after all. Or was all the discomfort and inconvenience simply a message that he had to make more advanced plans the next time? To focus on events after a killing, not merely the murder itself. Yes, yes, that must be it. It was a learning process he had to embrace.

Shady's thoughts again turned to Bronwen Lewis as he climbed back into the van's driver's seat, starting the engine on the third attempt and turning the heating to maximum as he drove back along the beach towards the road. How was he going to trap the bitch? How would he get her at his mercy? And what would he do to her when he did? Whatever those answers, she was going to die. How exciting would that be? How delicious?

Despite the wet and cold, he chuckled to himself as he approached the ramp, picturing Bronwen pink, trembling and naked in his killing room lair. Now, there was a body that would take some getting rid of. There'd be no lifting that mound of flesh. Not a chance. He'd have to chop her up, potential evidence or not. Buy the right tools, cut her up, bag her, and then throw her away somewhere safe. Somewhere far away, where she wouldn't be found. And then, maybe wash down the cottage with bleach. Loads of the stuff, splash it everywhere. Or burn the house down, like some bastard had his place. Perhaps that was another reason for the arson: to teach him, a learning exercise, giving him ideas when he needed them most. All part of his evolution. Yeah, that must be it.

As he engaged second gear, driving up the steep hill leading out of Pendine, Shady asked himself how long he should leave it before targeting Bronwen in a meaningful way. And he quickly concluded he should get on with it. Come up with an effective plan and act on it at the earliest opportunity. Why wait? Killing was such fun. Such a joy. And the piggy detective had it coming. If his daughter died, he deserved no less. So bring it on. The sooner, the better. Now all he had to do was work out the details.

When he reached the top of the hill and turned left towards Amroth, he composed a little ditty in his head, simply because it amused him.

> *Bronwen Lewis*
> *Maybe I'll phone, or perhaps I'll text*
> *But one thing is sure*
> *You'll be next*

31

Lewis was back in the police canteen, sitting alone at his favourite table and tucking into another fried breakfast, when his mobile rang at 8.05 a.m. He washed down a mouthful of black pudding with a slurp of sweet, milky tea before answering Kesey's call.

'Morning, Laura, what can I do for you, love?'

The detective inspector's voice had an evident urgent tone when she responded. 'I need you to get yourself down to Pendine. I'll meet you on the beach about three miles to the left of the slipway. And put a warm coat on. It's frigging freezing.'

Lewis looked down at the remains of his food, wondering how fast he could eat it.

'Pendine? What, now?' he asked, hoping there was no rush but thinking there probably was.

Kesey sounded a little impatient now, which came as no surprise. 'Yeah, straight away, we've got a body.'

Lewis shifted in his seat, sitting more upright. 'A body?'

'A local jogger found a naked young woman washed up on the sand about half an hour ago. Sorry, Ray, it's bad news. We'll have to get a formal identification, of course, once the body's at the morgue. But I'm pretty certain it's Carly Flowers. Slim, blonde hair, blue eyes. She looks a little different to her photograph for obvious reasons. But I don't think there's much room for doubt.'

Lewis felt a sinking feeling deep in the pit of his gut. He pushed his plate away. All of a sudden, he wasn't hungry at all. 'Oh, for fuck's sake. Poor Daisy and his missus. They're going to be devastated. Horrendous! Have they been told?'

'Not as yet. I've only just got here. I'd appreciate you giving them a ring.'

Lewis rose stiffly to his feet, quickly draining his tea before speaking. 'What, tell them on the phone? I'd rather do it face to face if I'm going to do it. They deserve that much. Carly's their only child. It's the worst news in the world.'

There was a second's silence. 'I need you here, Ray. There's bruising to her neck, ankles, and wrists. A broken nose. Multiple scratches on her upper legs. And what looks like a human bite mark on one shoulder. We're talking murder, so I'll give the duty inspector a ring in Haverfordwest. He can arrange for someone local to do the notification. Someone who knows Flowers well. Okay? Are you happy with that?'

Lewis put on his coat, patting the pockets to locate his car keys. He silently acknowledged that a part of him was relieved. Giving bad news was never easy, especially not to a friend. 'How long do you think she was in the water?'

'We'll know more after the post-mortem. But I don't think very long. A few hours at most. That's my bet.'

Lewis formed his hands into tight fists. 'We need to find Mark Shady.'

Kesey was quick to reply. 'Keep an open mind, Ray. He's a suspect, no more than that. Pendine is hardly the ideal place to dump a body if you want it to disappear. The water's too shallow. She was always going to end up on the beach. Shady's clever.

You've said that yourself. I don't think he'd be so stupid.'

'Unless he's cracking up,' Lewis protested, speaking with passion, keen to make his point. 'He might have lost it, got overconfident, and made a bad call. Maybe he thought an outgoing tide would take her body out to sea. Or he could have dumped her somewhere else along the coast in deeper water. The current could have taken her to Pendine. Or, perhaps, he wanted her found. Maybe that's all part of the buzz for him. Her loved ones knowing she's dead. He's one sadistic bastard. There are any number of possibilities we shouldn't rule out. Not without very good reason. So Shady's still very much in the frame for me.'

He heard what sounded like a sigh, Kesey slowly blowing out air. 'Okay, Ray, I get what you're saying. And maybe Shady killed her, or maybe he didn't. Follow the evidence. No gut instincts. Do you hear me? I don't want you jumping to conclusions. Not all sex offenders become killers. Not even those with necrophilia fantasies. You know that as well as I do.'

'Shady's Merc's still at the paint shop, I checked. And his insurance company haven't provided him with a replacement vehicle. Apparently, he hasn't requested one. That's suspicious in itself. If he has got a car from somewhere, we need to find out what it is. He took a load of cash out at a local bank on the day of his hospital discharge. And that's the last trace of him I can find.'

'Oh, shit.'

'Any tyre marks on the sand?'

'If there were, the sea's washed them away. Is there nothing useful on CCTV for the night Carly went missing? Something that could prove your theories one way or another?'

'Seems not. They've all been looked at. If Shady did abduct her, he avoided the main streets. And why wouldn't he? He knows the town well. It's not like there's many cameras he'd need to worry about.'

The sound of a cough. Then a sniff before Kesey spoke again.

'I'll be on the Welsh ITV evening news at six, to talk about Carly. We'll have her identification confirmed before then. Hopefully, someone will ring in to say they've seen something useful. I'm still convinced whoever killed her left her here. And he either drove or used a boat. I think a car more likely. It's the one beach in the area with such easy vehicle access.'

'Let's have a proper chat about it once I get there. I'll be with you in half an hour,' Lewis replied on leaving the headquarters building. 'You have to admit Shady's a person of interest at the very least.'

Another long sigh. 'We need to talk to him. See if he's got an alibi. Check his movements. I'll give you that. But you've got to remember the killer might be somebody else. I don't want you fixated on the one suspect. That's never a good idea.'

Lewis flashed a quickly vanishing smile, thinking her reply was a small win. He looked up at the grey sky as icy rain began to fall. 'You were right about the weather. Do you want me to bring you a coffee? I can call into Starbucks on my way if that helps? On my way through St Clears.'

He imagined her nodding enthusiastically. 'Oh, yeah, thanks, you know how I like it. And maybe get a couple more. The crime scene people are on the way. I'm sure they'd appreciate a brew.'

Lewis was wishing he hadn't offered at all. 'I'm not made of money, you know. We're not all on inspectors' salaries.'

Kesey laughed, seemingly amused as intended. 'And don't go thinking you can claim it on expenses. Halliday'd do his nut.'

Lewis unlocked the car doors with the click of a button. 'You mentioned bruising to Carly's neck. Reminds me of something Anna Edwards told me.

Shady liked to put his hands around her throat when he was shagging her. Do you think Carly was strangled?'

'Let's wait for the pathologist's report. That's best. Then we'll know for sure. And like I said, keep an open mind.'

Lewis started the engine before turning up the heating. 'Who's doing the post-mortem?'

'Minnie Rolands. I've already spoken to her.'

Lewis left the police headquarters car park, turning right towards Carmarthen and the A40. 'That's good; she's much better than the new bloke. Nothing is ever certain with him. And he's crap in court. One of the worst I've ever seen. Wilts under the pressure.'

A brief silence. 'Can you get me a sandwich with the coffee?' Kesey asked in her Brummie drone. 'Cheese and pickle, if they've got it. I didn't have time for breakfast.'

Lewis smiled as he approached a large round-about at the edge of town. 'Anything you say, ma'am. And would you like it delivered on a silver tray?'

'You can stop taking the piss.'

'Sorry, Laura, I know it's been a shit morning. Just trying to lighten the mood.'

'Got to go; the SOC photographer has just

turned up. I want plenty of photos before the body's taken to the morgue.'

'I'd be willing to bet this is all down to Shady. The vicious bastard! I'd bet my pension on it.'

'Open mind, remember, open mind,' Kesey said with feeling.

'Twenty quid says I'm right.'

'I really have got to go. See you when you get here. And don't forget that coffee.'

32

It wasn't Laura Kesey's first media interview. She'd undertaken several over the years since transferring to Wales from the West Midlands force. But despite a growing professional confidence, the prospect still felt onerous as 6 p.m. fast approached. Not because the interview in itself posed any prospective difficulties. She invariably had an excellent grasp of the cases under her command and could happily speak without written notes. But because so much hope was invested in the outcome. Carly's death had hit her hard. No doubt it had hit the force hard. Carly was the daughter of one of their own. And nothing was more important than catching her murderer. Not only in the interests of natural justice and officer morale. But for the fear that the killer might strike again at any moment. Until they were caught, there was always that risk. And the danger was real. Something the detective had learnt from painful experience. There was every chance another young woman might lose her life. And that was real pressure that weighed heavily on the senior detective's shoulders. It was a burden of rank.

Kesey watched a recording of her interview as soon as she arrived home a little after seven the same evening, sitting on the sofa with her loving partner, Jan, to take it all in while their young son played computer games in his bedroom. And overall, Kesey was pleased. She thought she'd performed well with no sign of nerves. A clear colour photo of Carly in happier times was shown on the screen, and Kesey had the opportunity to say when Carly was last seen alive and when and where she was found dead. Kesey hadn't gone into any details regarding Carly's many injuries, keen to keep them in reserve, but she did say a murder investigation was now underway with her as the lead officer. And finally, when prompted by the TV journalist, she asked for the public's help.

'If anyone saw or heard from Carly Flowers on or after the third of February, please contact the police immediately. We must know. So please don't delay. And if anyone saw a vehicle of any description on Pendine beach in the last seventy-two hours, please do likewise. You can contact your local police station or ask for me, DI Laura Kesey, or DS Raymond Lewis at police headquarters in Carmarthen. Either way, we'll be very happy to hear from you. The beach has been closed to motor vehicles for several years. So if you did see one on the sand, that would be unusual in itself.'

As the recorded interview ended, Kesey turned to Jan, hoping for positive feedback. A pat on the back was always welcome, particularly from the person who mattered most.

'What did you think? Any good?' she asked with a thin smile.

Jan stood and headed for the kitchen door, speaking without looking back.

'Your tea's ready. Chicken curry with rice. I kept it warm for you. Hope that's okay. I ate mine earlier. I got tired of waiting.'

Kesey rushed after her partner. 'What's on earth's up? Have I done something to upset you?'

Jan opened the gas cooker's door. 'It's nothing. I'm just being silly, that's all. There's a bottle of white wine in the fridge if you fancy it. Chardonnay.

It came with the Tesco order. I could do with a glass.'

Kesey filled two wine glasses to the halfway point, then sat at the kitchen table. 'What's up?' she asked. 'I know there's something.'

Jan wiped away a tear. 'I said it's nothing.'

Kesey made a face. 'Come on, please tell me. If you're feeling unwell again, you need to say. I'd much rather know. I know COVID hit you hard.'

Jan placed Kesey's full plate on the table next to a bottle of sweet mango sauce. 'It's nothing like that.'

Kesey's posture slumped, her relief evident. Jan's health issues had taken a toll on both of them and, to some extent, on their relationship. The detective sometimes felt she was walking on an emotional tightrope. 'Then what is it?' she asked, feeling the tension.

Jan glared at her in a way she rarely did. 'Another major investigation. With you as the SIO. I hardly ever see you, Laura. You're either at work or off teaching karate at the leisure centre. And now you're going to be working every hour God sends looking for a killer, with all the dangers that are involved. And I'll be stuck here in the house worrying about you. I wish you had a very different job.

Something safe. Things are going to be even worse than usual.'

Kesey picked up her knife and fork, keen to eat but delaying her first mouthful. 'We've talked about this. You knew what my job entailed before you married me. I made it crystal clear.'

Jan sipped her wine, wetting her lips. 'Well, will you at least cut down on the karate classes? Maybe teach one class a week instead of two? Just until this big investigation is over.'

Kesey nodded. 'Okay, fair enough, if it keeps you happy.'

Jan sat opposite her. 'It does, and thank you.'

'Not a problem.'

Jan's expression suddenly darkened. 'It just dawned on me. I've seen the dead girl somewhere before. Her face is familiar. But I can't think where from.'

Kesey spoke while eating. 'You must have seen her about. She was a student here in town.'

Janet nodded. 'That must be it. Such an attractive girl. How awful. Any idea who killed her?'

Kesey paused between mouthfuls, making a face. 'Ray's got his theories. All down to his gut feelings as usual. No change there.'

'And you don't agree?'

'It's just that he tends to become fixated rather than keeping an open mind. But try telling him that. It's hard to dislodge an idea once he gets it stuck in his head. My cross to bear, as my gran used to say. He'd use all my limited resources to find his suspect if it was up to him. Forgetting about everything else.'

Jan gave a pensive look. 'Laura—'

'Yeah?'

'I've been looking at villas online. How do you fancy me booking a place in Lanzarote for half term? We loved it there the last time – all that sun, sea, and sangria. There's a gorgeous two-bedroom place available in Arrieta with a pool. And it's easy flying from Cardiff.'

'Lovely idea,' Kesey replied, and meaning it. 'But let's delay booking until I know what's happening with the case. It would be a shame to cancel and then lose money.'

Jan looked crestfallen. 'But we will definitely go as soon as you can, yes? It would do us all some good.'

Kesey recalled the sight of Carly's naked corpse stranded on the cold, wet sand. The mental image hung in her mind for a few seconds before she pushed it away.

'We'll book when I catch the killer. When he's locked up in custody.'

'Do you promise?'

'Of course I do. I'm as keen as you are. Lanzarote, here we come. Can't wait.'

Jan lifted her wine glass to her mouth. 'Ray might be right, you know. He is a good copper. You've said that yourself.'

Kesey nodded. 'I'm not saying he's wrong. Just that he could be, that's all. The obvious suspect isn't always the guilty one. But let's talk about something else. I'm tired. It's already been a long day.'

'Okay.'

'Thanks for the food, Jan. It's delicious, as always. I don't know what I'd do without you.'

'I love you. Sorry to complain.'

Kesey smiled. 'Nothing to apologise for. I love you too. Now, how about another glass of wine?'

33

Lewis was checking various social media sites for any new signs of Shady when his office phone rang at 9.10 a.m. the following day. He picked up the receiver on the third insistent ring, holding it to his face.

'CID.'

'Morning, Sarge, it's Ben on reception. I've got an Anna Edwards here asking to speak with you. What do you want me to tell her?'

Lewis continued perusing Shady's Facebook page, which hadn't been updated since his hospital stay. It seemed there were no signs of the scrote anywhere. In the detective's opinion, no doubt deliberate.

'Put her in whichever interview room's free and offer her a brew. Try to put her at her ease. She's been through a lot of shit. I'll be down in five minutes.'

Lewis entered interview room three to see Anna seated and waiting, her face concerned. A cup of coffee was on the desk next to her. The detective remained standing. 'Morning, love,' he said with a smile. 'I wasn't expecting to see you today. You're looking well. What can I do for you?'

Anna's hand trembled ever so slightly when she picked up her cup. 'I don't usually watch the TV news. Too many negatives. I've got enough stress in my life without that. But I was in the lounge yesterday evening when my dad switched it on. I saw Laura Kesey talking about the murdered girl, the one found on Pendine beach.'

Lewis lowered himself into the room's only other seat, planting his feet wide, taking the pressure off his lower back to ease the discomfort.

'It's an ongoing investigation,' he said, wondering where the conversation was leading. 'Is there something you want to tell me?'

Anna touched a temple while closing her eyes for a beat. 'I recognised her, the girl, I'd seen her before. And the name Carly, that rang a bell too. Then

I realised I'd seen a photo of her and Mark together on his Facebook page. It's still there. They were in a relationship.'

Lewis arched his back, pushing out his chest, trying to get comfortable.

'Yeah, that's right,' he said. 'Carly was the daughter of a fellow officer. A mate of mine. Shady was with her after you.'

Anna looked away, averting her eyes to the wall. 'I'm so sorry she's dead.'

Lewis nodded twice. 'Yeah, me too, love, me too.'

Anna took a series of quick breaths as if building up to something. 'I'm sure you've guessed what I'm going to say next.'

Lewis suspected he very probably did. 'I'm listening.'

'I told you Mark had death fantasies. And about what he liked to do to me. Put his hands around my throat, choke me. I really think he might have killed Carly. The more I think about it, the more that makes sense. I'm still having nightmares. And it was even worse than usual last night. I could see Mark's face just inches from mine. It's awful! The thought of him killing that poor girl. Do you think it could have been him?'

Lewis thought, *Yeah, I do.* But he didn't say it,

biting his tongue. 'Every possibility will be explored as part of the investigation, love. You can be confident of that. You have my word on it. But there is only so much I can say. You know, confidentiality and all that. I'm sure you understand.'

Anna seemed unable to stay still as her face reddened. 'If Mark did kill her, I pray he doesn't get off like he has every other crime. I couldn't stand it if that happened, not again, not after what happened to me. The man brings nothing but misery to the world. It's time that stopped. Even my dad says so. And he doesn't usually say very much at all.'

He's not wrong, thought Lewis as he looked at her with empathy. He crossed one heavy leg over the other, buying time, wondering how much to say. Maybe Anna had information that could help. 'Shady's not been seen since coming out of hospital. I've been trying to track him down. Just routine, that's all. Covering all the bases. Obviously, he can't stay at his place here in town. Not after the fire. Any idea where he might be?'

Anna was slow to reply. As if carefully considering her response. After a few seconds, she finally shook her head. 'Where he might be... Where he might be...' she whispered, almost as if repeating a rehearsed script. 'No, there's nowhere I can think of. But if I come up with any ideas, I'll let you know.'

'No close friends or relatives who might be putting him up?'

'I'm not sure he's got any of either. Or at least, none he mentioned to me. He sometimes used to talk about his mother. But I don't think it's a happy relationship. He seemed to hate her. Deep down, Mark's a bit of a loner.'

Lewis prepared to bring the conversation to an end, thinking it was reaching its logical conclusion.

'Thanks, love, very helpful. Any news on the compensation or injunction?'

Anna rose to her feet. 'The application's made on both counts. I'm waiting to hear something.'

Lewis crossed the room and held the door open. 'That's great; glad to hear it.'

'I'm going to donate some of the money to domestic violence charities. I spoke to the refuge manager here in town. They've never got enough to meet demand.'

'Good for you. But maybe treat yourself too.'

Anna turned her head to face him as they walked towards reception. 'If it was Mark who killed Carly, he *has* to be punished this time. He can't get away with it again. How many lives must he destroy before he pays a price?'

Lewis had asked himself the same question, sharing Anna's frustrations and mourning the system that let them down. But he resisted the temptation to share that reality. They were both affected by Shady's offending in different ways. The predator would always be a curse on their lives.

'Nice to see you,' Lewis said, trying to exude a brief air of positivity before she left the building. 'If there's anything else you want to talk about, you know where I am.'

'Thanks, Ray,' she said, touching his arm.

He forced a reluctant smile.

'You're welcome, love. I will get Shady one day. I'll nail the bastard if it's the last thing I do.'

'Any idea who caused the fire?' Anna asked, pensive.

Lewis shook his head.

'Not as yet. We might never find out.'

She frowned.

'It wasn't any of my family. You do know that, don't you?'

'Don't worry about it. I'm focused on finding Carly's killer. And that's all. It's a case of priorities.'

Anna smiled, looking suddenly younger as if a

weight had lifted. 'I'll let you know when the compensation arrives.'

Lewis returned her smile, glad to end on a positive. 'You do that. Always glad to hear from you.'

She raised a hand, touched his arm again, then
walked away.

34

Lewis found his thoughts turning to his daughter after Anna left police headquarters. And, unusually for the detective, he decided to ring Bronwen at her workplace as he sat at his desk, back on the computer with a mug of tea in hand. Not for a specific reason as would have been the case in the past. But simply to hear her voice and say hello. Like a good father should. Something he knew he hadn't done nearly enough of over the years. Maybe, he pondered, it wasn't too late to change. An old dog could learn new tricks.

Lewis was still deep in contemplative thought as he rang the King Street bank's direct number, which was not generally available to the public. He felt certain Bronwen would have contacted him had she heard from Shady again. She'd have been straight on the phone or called at the station full of anguished complaints. But he told himself he should ask anyway. Just to demonstrate an interest. To show her he was thinking of her. Because family mattered. She mattered. A lesson learnt far too late. It wasn't all about work, however important it seemed.

He smiled when she said, 'Hello, Lloyds Bank.' Very efficient, very professional.

'Morning, Bron, it's Dad. I was just wondering how you're doing.'

He thought she sounded surprised when she replied. As if he was the last person she thought would call.

'Oh, hi, hang on, give me a second. I'll close my office door... There, that's better.'

'How are you doing?' he asked again, repeating himself. 'Are you still staying at Mum's?'

'No, I'm back home now. I only stayed the one night. I need my own space. And I haven't heard any more from that ghastly man, if that's what you're wondering. It looks like he's lost interest. Typical troll. He must have moved on to somebody else.'

Let's hope so, thought Lewis.

'Well, if you do hear from the fool again, I want

to know immediately. Get straight on the phone. Because he's dangerous. Never forget that. Am I clear?'

For a second, he thought she might be giggling.

'I don't think I said anything funny,' he said, perplexed.

'Sorry, Dad, I was just thinking about something else. Do you mind if I ask you something?'

'I guess not,' he said, screwing up his face.

'Do you remember Millie?'

He took a gulp of tea to clear his tobacco-ravaged throat. 'Millie? No, not that I can think of.'

'Of course you do. Millie Frost – you played rugby with her father. They lived on our estate when I was a kid. In the same street.'

'Oh, yeah, Frosty's youngest. I think she trained as a nurse. What about her?'

This time, Lewis was sure Bronwen was laughing. 'She told me she saw you at the cinema with a rather glamorous woman with black hair.'

Lewis was quick to reply as an unexpected flush crept across his cheeks. He knew it was ridiculous. A man of his age and experience blushing again. But for some reason, he felt nothing but embarrassment, so far out of his comfort zone.

'She's just a friend from work.'

'Really?'

'Yes, *really*.'

'Millie said the two of you looked close. You were holding hands at one point. And you kissed her cheek. You are a dark horse; my dad back on the dating scene. Who'd have thought it? She sounds like a bit more than a friend to me.'

It was the kind of conversation Lewis had never had with Bronwen before – the sort of thing she'd usually only discuss with her mother. Lewis felt acutely aware of that. And his embarrassment aside, it felt good. It seemed they were making a connection.

'Okay, you've got me,' he said, sighing. 'I've been seeing one of our civilian staff. She works in our social club behind the bar. I'll introduce her to you at some point if it lasts. I'm sure you're going to like her.'

'I'm pleased for you. Really, I am; it's about time.'

He felt he had to ask. And he was pleased to take the focus off himself.

'What about you, love? Any developments on the romance front? It's been a while since the split-up.'

'There is some news, as it happens. I met a man online. It's all the rage these days. Lots of my friends met their partners that way. And I've got a date tonight. From what I can gather, he's a bit of a hippy with long hair and a beard, who lives off-grid. Not my usual type. But he seems nice enough. And I thought, why not?'

The detective's protective instincts kicked in immediately, an inevitable result of policing. It was hard not to be cynical after all he'd encountered. 'So you don't know much about him?'

'Only what I've told you. And he's from Northern Ireland. Oh, and he's about the same age as me. That's about it.'

'Have you got his name?'

Bronwen was quick to reply. 'It's a date, Dad, not an investigation. I don't want you checking up on him. There are some good guys out there. Not everyone is a criminal.'

Lewis had heard the irritation in his daughter's voice. He decided not to push it. 'Well, will you at least meet him somewhere public the first time? Somewhere with plenty of other people about. Until you get to know him better. Better safe than sorry. I worry about you, love, that's all.'

'We're meeting for a meal at the veggie place I sometimes visit at lunchtime. It's popular and always fully booked. So you can relax.'

'Okay, good choice. Have a great time. And make sure he pays. He's lucky to be spending time with you. He should see it as a privilege. None of this split-the-bill crap.'

Bronwen laughed again. 'I can pay my own way, you know. It's not the 1980s.'

'I don't suppose you're going to give me that name? Just in case I know it?'

The sound of her blowing out air. 'It's a busy morning. There's stuff I need to be getting on with.'

'I guess that's a no.'

'You got that right.'

'One last question. Who contacted who first? You or him?'

'Bye, Dad, got to go.'

And with that, she ended the call.

35

Bronwen decided on a smart but casual outfit for her first date since her relationship break-up. She was keen to appear reasonably attractive but not overtly sexy. She had no intentions of getting physical, not so soon. She kept intimacy for loving, long-term relationships, of which there had only been one. She was happier that way. It worked for her.

She pulled on a pair of dark blue size sixteen jeans, surprised to find them feeling a little tight despite the elasticated waist. It seemed the diet wasn't going as well as she'd hoped. Damn! Too many carbs. Maybe, she pondered, she should get on the scales more often. Just to keep an eye on things. If anything, it seemed she'd put on weight. But at least she knew her new red top fitted perfectly. It had been well worth trying it on before buying... Yeah, nice, that looked great, hiding the bulges she didn't want him to see. Now for her winter boots and a warm jacket, and she'd be good to go.

Bronwen applied what she liked to think was subtle makeup before she left her home. Just light red lipstick, purple eye shadow, and a little mascara to make her brown eyes pop. She thought she should probably have trimmed her fringe as she looked into the hall mirror. It could be a little shorter. But it was far too late for that. Time was getting on. The taxi would be arriving soon. So she'd have to do as she was. And anyway, her date didn't look like he worried too much about appearance. All that beard, long hair, and glasses. And he seemed keen, maybe too keen. Perhaps she should have said no. Possibly, they weren't suited at all.

Bronwen came very close to cancelling her cab and standing her date up. Just not going. Staying in with the telly and a microwave meal. But she reminded herself how she'd feel were her date to do that to her. It had happened to her once as a teenager. And she'd felt like crap.

She heard the sound of a car horn, three sharp beeps, a minute or two later, and she again urged herself on as she opened the front door, feeling no less conflicted. *Come on, Bronwen, the cab's outside and waiting.* And her date would be waiting soon too. So what if they didn't get on? What did one evening matter? What was the worst that could happen? She could always make her excuses and leave. He might even be a lovely guy. She might enjoy herself. There was potentially everything to gain and nothing to lose.

It had started raining by the time the taxi dropped Bronwen off in Carmarthen's King Street, close to the iconic Lyric Theatre. She was still feeling somewhat apprehensive as she paid and exited the car, crossing the one-way street and avoiding the many puddles with quick-moving feet as she entered Merlin's Lane. And for a second time this dank February evening, she considered cancelling – just walking away. But she pictured her date sitting alone and waiting for her. And that was enough to encourage her on.

Bronwen glanced around her as she entered the familiar orange-painted café with its eclectic mix of artwork by local artists covering three of the four walls. The room was busy, full of chatting people of various ages and descriptions, but she still quickly spotted her date seated on one of two black leather sofas at the back, close to the serving counter. A pot of tea and a half-eaten dark chocolate brownie were on the low table in front of him. One of her favourite treats. He stood with a broad smile on his face as Bronwen approached, revealing strikingly white teeth that looked strangely at odds with his persona. But she was surprised to find herself thinking her overall first impressions were good. There seemed to be a friendly warmth about him. An approachability. Maybe, she said to herself, the date was a good idea after all.

'Hi, lovely to meet you in person,' he said, reaching forward to hug her. And she didn't feel the desire to pull away before he released her. A second surprise: this one even bigger than the first.

'Nice to meet you too,' she said, wondering if her teeth should be whitened like his. 'I've never been here in the evening before. Only lunchtimes. Thanks for inviting me. It's been a fair while since I've been on a date. I'm feeling a little nervous.'

He sat, smiling again when she sat on the two-seater settee opposite him. He handed her a menu.

'Me too,' he said, 'but I'm sure we'll have a lovely

time. I already love this place. Great choice. I think I might become a regular.'

Bronwen glanced at the menu before quickly putting it down. She had the same thing every time. Mushroom burgers with an organic mixed salad. A creature of habit.

'I'm new in town,' he said. 'I came over from Belfast to lecture at Trinity. And I haven't really got out much until now. What with settling into my new place and work. It's good to make a friend.'

She liked that he was well-educated but wondered if he suffered from eczema. His facial skin looked so very red, which could be the reason for the beard. Maybe he wasn't the best-looking guy in the world, but his personality made up for it. And his eyes – there was something about them, something she found beguiling even with the glasses.

'Have you decided what you're going to have?' she asked, fidgeting with the cuff of her jacket. 'Hope you're not too full after your brownie.'

'No, not at all. It was on the table when I arrived. You've been here before. What do you recommend?'

She told him what she was having, and he said he'd have the same. That anything good enough for her was good enough for him.

'What about a drink?' he asked. 'Do you fancy sharing a bottle of wine?'

Bronwen quickly decided the alcohol might help her relax. 'Good idea, that would be great.'

He smiled again, flashing those teeth. 'Red or white? I'm happy with either.'

She appreciated him giving her the choice. He seemed sensitive, thoughtful, and considerate.

'They do a lovely house red, all organic,' she said, gaining confidence. 'French, I think.'

He waved to a passing blue-haired waitress.

'Okay, perfect, then red it is.'

The two continued chatting after he gave their order. Her asking him questions and him reciprocating. And the more they talked, the more Bronwen enjoyed it. She felt he was a gentle soul. And he seemed genuinely interested in her and her opinions, so unlike the gym-obsessed, self-focused man who'd so severely let her down. She felt glad she hadn't cancelled as she drank her wine and ate the tasty food. She initially saw her date more as a friend than a potential lover. But the more they talked, the more she liked him. And after half an hour or so, she decided to keep her options open. Maybe he was boyfriend material after all. Perhaps she'd won the relationship lottery.

'Another glass of wine?' he asked, picking up the bottle.

'Yes, lovely,' she replied, 'but I'll just pop to the bathroom first.'

Bronwen picked up her full glass on her return, wondering why he seemed to be watching her so very closely as she raised it to her lips and drank.

'Are we going to have dessert?' he asked, looking down at the menu, taking his focus off her. And the question helped her relax.

'I wasn't planning to, but I'll have some if you are. I'm supposed to be on a diet, but I guess once won't do any harm.'

He pulled his head back as if she'd said the craziest thing he'd ever heard. 'A diet? What on earth for? You've got to be kidding me; you're beautiful as you are.'

Bronwen started feeling dizzy as she slumped slightly in her seat, placing her glass down for fear of spilling the remains of her claret. And then an overwhelming tiredness suddenly hit her, of a kind she'd never experienced before.

'I'm... I'm not feeling very well,' she said. 'I think I need some fresh air.'

He stood, helped her to her feet, and then paid

in cash, leaving the money on the wooden counter without waiting for the change.

'Come on, let's get you outside,' he said, taking Bronwen's arm. 'I think it's stopped raining. I've got my van with me. Parked in the quiet street at the bottom of the lane. It's best not to take any risks where health is concerned. I'll run you straight home.'

36

Three letters awaited Lewis on his hall floor when he arrived home from work at 7.20 p.m. two days later. Two with white envelopes were obviously from his bank and optician. But the third was in a larger brown envelope with his name and address written in bold capitals. And he was interested enough to carry it from the kitchen to the lounge along with a can of cold lager taken from the fridge, having discarded the other two letters on a countertop for later disposal.

The detective slumped into his favourite armchair and kicked off his scuffed shoes. He switched on the TV and took a long drink of beer, then looked down at the brown envelope still in his left hand. He could see it was postmarked Narberth, a lovely little Pembrokeshire market town a few miles from the coast, which gave no clue about its contents. So he opened it, ripping the brown paper and allowing the contents to fall onto the low coffee table in front of him.

Lewis stiffened, then swallowed hard. What the hell? There were three photos in total. Three small square shots of the type produced by instant cameras. A kind he hadn't seen in years.

Lewis dry-gagged once, then again, as he picked up the first celluloid image, holding it close to his bloodshot eyes with a shaking hand. There was a young woman in the photo. A naked female, hunched over and weeping in a darkened room with her hands and ankles bound. Like something out of a horror film. The kind of movie Lewis would never choose to watch.

Lewis was desperate not to believe the evidence of his eyes as he fought not to vomit. But as he studied the captive's face, he knew it was true. It was Bronwen. There was no room for doubt. No room for denial. And he felt certain Shady had taken her as his rage and anguish surged to a new and savage high.

Lewis used the end of a plastic biro to reposition

the other two photos on the table rather than use his fingers, keen to maintain evidence, almost on autopilot. He felt his heart pounding as he stared down at each likeness in turn, looking for clues. Anything that might help find her, anything at all.

Both photographs were much the same as the first. Just taken from different angles. Bronwen was handcuffed. That was clear. And the walls of what-ever building she was in were made of stone. That was worth knowing. That might help. He screamed out, swore revenge on Shady, then threw his half-full can of beer at the nearest wall.

Lewis took his mobile from a jacket pocket as he paced the room, first one way, then the other. He dropped the phone on the floral carpet, cursed loudly and crudely, then picked it up to dial.

'Laura, it's Ray. He's got her. He's fucking well got her!'

'Slow down, take a breath. And tell me, who's got who?'

Lewis wiped the sweat from his brow, his chest aching. He rushed his words. 'Shady, he's got Bronwen. The bastard sent me photos. Three of them. Here at my place. She's naked and hand-cuffed, totally terrified. We've got to find her, and fast. If I'm right about him murdering Carly, Bron could be next. And that's if he hasn't killed her already.'

He could hear the urgency in her voice. 'Oh, shit, so sorry, Ray. Let's take this one step at a time. How do you know it was Shady? We don't want to be looking in the wrong direction.'

He kicked the empty lager can across the floor. 'It was Shady. I'm telling you. It was him. I just know.'

'Okay, we'll check for fingerprints as soon as possible. But for now, let's assume you're right. Where were the photos posted? Do we know?'

'Narberth, yesterday.'

'Where's that? I know the name, but I can't think.'

'A few miles inland from Tenby.'

'Any idea if Shady owns any property down that way?'

'I checked the database after Carly went missing. There's only the restaurant building in his name; that's it, nothing else. Maybe he knows somebody who owns a place. And it has to be somewhere remote. Bron's not gagged in the photos. So he's not worried about her shouting out.'

'Unless it's soundproofed.'

Lewis grimaced, a small amount of acidic vomit

rising in his throat. He swallowed before speaking, fighting to focus, struggling to hold it together.

'It doesn't look that way.'

'Are you certain he hasn't used any bank cards?'

Lewis continued pacing, now out of breath, repeatedly panting like a dog needing water. He pulled his shirt loose at the collar, popping two buttons, which fell to the floor.

'I'll check again, but I'm not hopeful. I'm guessing the bastard planned for this. That's why he withdrew the cash. And his mobile hasn't been used either.'

'Anything in the photos that gives up any clue where they were taken?'

'Looks like an old stone structure. Could be an outbuilding, or maybe a farm, certainly nothing built recently. Just bare walls. Not even plastered. And the floor looks like concrete. It's better than nothing, but it's hard to tell.'

'What about Shady's Merc?'

'Still at the garage. Waiting for him to collect it. Whatever he's driving, it's not that.'

'When did you last see or hear from Bron?'

He gave her the full facts.

There were a few seconds of silence.

'Are you still there, love?' he asked.

'Yeah, sorry, Ray, I was just thinking. How much do you know about the guy you said she met for the date?'

'Fuck all, really. Just what I told you at work.'

'We need to find out who he is. At least check him out. See if he's got any sort of record. Because he might have. I know you're sure with this Shady thing. But our mystery man wouldn't be the first predator to target a victim online. We can't afford to ignore him. I'll get myself down to the café and ask a few questions. I'll do that now. And I'll put out an all-force alert in the hope someone comes up with something useful.'

'Thanks, Laura. We need to start searching.'

'Pembrokeshire is a big county. It'll take a lot of officers. Even limiting the search to older buildings. And that's assuming Bron's being kept in the same general area where the photos were posted. Which she might not be. I'll give Halliday a bell. Get him to approve an overtime budget.'

'Thanks, this isn't like anything I've ever dealt with before. It's different when it's personal. Whoever has done this, even if it's not Shady, I'll tear him a new arsehole when I get hold of him.'

'Right, Ray, I'd better make a move. I'll give you a

ring with an update if I find anything out at the café.'

'I can come with you if you want?'

'No, leave this one to me.'

Lewis quickly drank a second can of lager when his call ended. But for once, the alcohol didn't improve his mood. He was seriously considering driving to Narberth just to look around in the hope of finding inspiration when he decided on a second call. More out of desperation than anything else.

'Hi, Anna, it's Ray, I'm hoping you can help.'

Her tone sounded perplexed when she replied. 'What, you want my help? In what way?'

'This is between me and you, love. I think Shady might have abducted my daughter. And I need you to think very carefully before answering my next question.'

'Oh no, your daughter! How awful.'

'I know we talked about this before. But can you think of any old stone building Shady might have access to? Anywhere at all? Please take your time. As long as you need.'

There was a surprisingly long silence before Anna spoke again, somewhere between twenty and thirty seconds. When she did speak, she sounded hesitant, which Lewis thought probably down to nerves. 'I'm so very sorry, there's nowhere I can think of. I only wish there was.'

Lewis let out a small groan as his legs buckled under him. The pressure was finally too much as another avenue of hope slammed shut. He said his goodbyes while prone on the floor. It was several minutes later when he realised he'd had his first panic attack. He couldn't unsee those images. They seemed imprinted in his brain, never to be forgotten. Some things were too much to bear.

37

Anna had seriously considered telling DS Lewis about the ramshackle stone building Mark Shady had once shown her high in the Preseli Hills, on the far edge of the Pembrokeshire Coast National Park. Holding the information back seemed seriously at odds with all that was right. But in the moment, instinctively and with some regret, she had kept the information to herself. Not because she didn't want to help. But because she did. What use were the police? What good had they done her? None at all. Ray had failed her. That was the truth of it. And what was to say he wouldn't fail again? If she wanted something done correctly, she had to do it herself.

Her psychologist had said as much. Or, at least, something along those lines. She had to take responsibility for her life. If Mark was the guilty one. If he was going to be punished this time, it was up to her to make it happen. And then, when she could prove his guilt, when she had all the evidence she needed, Ray could take over. She'd tell him everything then. That way, not even a jury could get things wrong.

Anna sat alone in her farmhouse bedroom half an hour or so after the detective's urgent call, with the door shut against the world and a cup of calming chamomile tea in hand. And she used the quiet time to continue thinking. To try to make sense of her motivations and actions, just as her therapist had advised. What exactly had Mark told her? His mother owned the building, sometimes living there, but often not, as she travelled in India, or lived at some commune, or with one man or another. He seemed to think this had its potential advantages. But for some reason, he'd never explained why.

Anna came close to returning the detective's call more than once. To tell him all that. To put him in the picture. Because the information seemed relevant. And his daughter was missing, after all. But in the end, Anna decided against it for all the previously identified reasons. She told herself that all the legal system ever did was let victims down. Victims like her. Even Ray seemed to think that. And Mark could get away with murder. Of that, she had no doubt. Unless she took matters into her own hands again. Unless she acted on her knowledge and did the necessary things the situation demanded. Yes, she had to forget the police; it was up to her.

Anna repeatedly relived the events of recent months in her increasingly confused mind as she drove the forty-five-mile journey from Brechfa to the Preseli Hills along the A40, making her memories vivid. She shuddered as she thought about the rape, Mark's hands around her throat, restricting her breathing. She cried as she remembered the court case and not-guilty verdict. All the awful things the defence barrister had said. And then she laughed out loud as she recalled throwing paint stripper over Mark's car. She knew that would have hurt him. He so loved his shiny cars. Far more so than any living person. And the arson. What about the fire? Such fun. She almost had him that time. He came so very close to paying for his vile crimes. But he somehow got away then too. Slippery like an eel.

That was Mark. And maybe, for once, that wasn't such a bad thing. If he had died, it would all have been over far too quickly. Something she hadn't adequately considered at the time. Far too easy. He should be locked up and left to rot.

Anna's nerves jangled, sweat forming under both arms as she manoeuvred her car along the hilly, stone-strewn track, the dilapidated building now in sight for the first time, illuminated by her headlights. She came close, stopping and reversing when she saw the old rusty blue van parked close to the ramshackle entrance. It wasn't at all how she'd pictured events in her mind. And now she had doubts. Uncertainties she struggled to silence. A van! Who the hell had a van? Was she wrong? Was Mark somewhere else entirely? Perhaps, or maybe not. Maybe using such a vehicle to trick the police was precisely the kind of devious thing Mark might do. That was a genuine possibility. And she'd come this far, so why not find out for sure? Her therapist had told her to trust her instincts. And carrying on with her plans now seemed right.

She thought she saw a face at a window, seemingly staring out at her, as if the sound of her car engine had signalled her arrival. And then what seemed only moments later, as Anna exited the car,

Mark Shady suddenly appeared at the rundown building's wooden door with a long-bladed knife in hand. Anna quickly retreated to the vehicle's rear. In an instant she knew she was correct, and driving off wasn't an option she was willing to consider despite her fear. With trembling hands, she took one of her father's three side by side shotguns from the car boot, hurriedly loading it with two buckshot cartridges and switching off the safety catch as he strode towards her, his eyes dark and flinty.

Anna nearly lost her nerve as Mark raised the knife high above his head, picking up his pace, now only seconds away. She was frozen in indecision for the briefest of moments, but then she heard a high-pitched female scream for help inside the building. Anna could see the surprise painted on her oppressor's reddened face as she raised the gun to her shoulder, threatening to fire. And that was enough to stop him. At least for the moment. A small victory. But a victory nonetheless.

'Drop the knife,' she shouted, hopefully loud enough for the captive to hear.

Mark lowered his arm but didn't heed her demand as the blade caught the winter moonlight.

'Oh, come off it, Anna. You're a weak, pathetic little mouse of a girl, not a brave lion like me. You haven't got the guts for revenge. Leave violence to the bigger people. You're better at cowering and pleading. I'll give you five seconds to throw down your popgun. And if you don't, if you're even one second late, I'll cut your throat from ear to ear.' He pointed behind him. 'And then I'll kill that bitch in there too.'

Anna had heard enough as she felt herself squeeze the trigger, and then, bang, the force of the shot knocked her back as Mark fell to the ground, his right shoulder peppered with lead pellets.

'You crazy bitch!'

Anna slowly approached him, carefully out of his reach, one step, two, three. Because she knew what he was capable of. He'd attack if he got the slightest chance, even in his injured state. Of that, she was sure. She feared she might lose control of her bladder as she spoke again, striving to sound suitably assertive despite her fears.

'Get up,' she shouted, her mouth dry. 'On your feet, come on, up.'

He climbed slowly to his knees, the knife no longer in hand.

'Look at me,' he demanded. 'What the hell have you done?'

Anna held the gun a little tighter, finger back on

the trigger. 'You're going to stand up. You're going to go into the building. And then you'll set free your captive. Do it now. Because this time, it's me who's losing patience. And there's only so long I'll wait before firing again.'

Mark's blood seeped into his clothing as Anna followed him as far as a dank, darkened room in which she saw a naked young woman bound and hunched in a pool of bodily waste. Anna looked first at the woman, and then at her ex, tears running down her face as she took it all in for the first awful time.

'Are you Ray's daughter?' she asked. 'Sergeant Lewis?'

The young woman looked up with pleading eyes, nodding.

Anna focused back on Mark, keeping the gun on him, never looking away. 'Undo her handcuffs and untie her. Do it now. Or my next shot will blow your balls off.'

'I'm bleeding; I need help. Can't you see I'm bleeding?'

'Now!'

He did as he was told this time, using his uninjured arm to take a small metal key from a trouser pocket. Within a minute or two, his captive was free of her bindings. She drew her hand back, slapping him hard in the face on standing. Mark Shady groaned as he staggered backwards, Anna pointing the long steel barrels at him the entire time.

'Bronwen,' she said. 'I want you to take my mobile from my jacket pocket, then I want you to switch on the recording function, and finally, to listen as a witness. Mark is about to make a full confession.'

'My clothes. I need my clothes,' Bronwen said, trying to cover herself with her hands.

Anna turned her attention to Shady. 'Where are they?'

'They're gone.'

'Gone where?'

He glared at her. 'I burnt them.'

'You did what?'

'You heard me.'

Anna drew her lips back, snarling. 'Strip naked. Let's see how you like it. If she can't wear her own clothes, she's going to wear yours.'

Mark was reluctant to undress initially, but after further aggressive prompting, he finally acceded, wincing whenever he moved his badly injured arm. He sat on the cold hard floor as his victims had before him, bloody and shivering as the two women sat opposite him, about twelve feet away. Anna didn't speak again until Bronwen had covered her nakedness, a look of disgust on her face as she donned the bloodstained clothing. The mobile recording was now operational.

'Okay, Mark,' Anna finally said, still pointing the gun in his direction. 'Now you're going to admit to every crime you've ever committed. I want you to name all your victims one at a time and then say exactly what you did to them, when, and where. And that includes what you did to me. I'm talking about the full details. Not some simplified account minimising your guilt. And then, when you're finished, in however long that takes, we're going to ring Bronwen's father. And he's going to arrest you. And this time, there's nothing at all you're going to be able to say to get yourself off.'

Just for a fraction of a second, after he'd been speaking for about fifteen minutes, Anna thought she had seen the hint of a smile flashing across his face.

'What's so funny?' she barked, hating him with a burning intensity.

'Do you really think any of this shit is going to be admissible in court?' he asked, now clearly amused. 'With you pointing a gun at me? Not a fucking chance.'

And in that moment, as she considered his mocking words, Anna felt sure he'd uttered the truth. There was every danger he'd get off again. Even with all the evidence. And even with Bronwen's help. Because that was what Mark did. He evaded justice. He slithered away like the snake he was. It happened every single time. She couldn't let that happen. Not this time. Never again.

Anna stood, walked to within six feet of Mark Shady, pointed the gun at his head and pulled the trigger. His body slumped to the floor, his face a red, bloody, tangled mess of flesh and bone.

Bronwen looked ashen as she picked up Anna's mobile, gagging at the sight of the bloody corpse but unable to look away.

'I'm going outside to ring my dad,' she said, sobbing. 'Where... where should I tell him we are? Thank you so much for saving me. I thought he was going to kill me. I'm so very grateful. You saved my life.'

Anna gave Bronwen the required information, including a postcode, as she followed her outside. The gun was now empty of cartridges.

As the two women sat together on the grassy

ground, Anna felt resigned to whatever came next. She had no intention of running. No plans to try to escape. If she went to prison, so be it. Mark was dead. Her world a better place. And incarceration a price worth paying. She'd have to be satisfied with that.

38

Ray Lewis hurriedly exited his unmarked police car, lifting up and hugging his daughter tight after she ran barefoot to greet him. He'd never felt more glad. Never more relieved. And he had a good idea why Bronwen had insisted he come alone when he saw Anna seated on the ground close to the building's door, the shotgun at her feet. The weapon told its own story.

Lewis released his daughter, stepping back and staring at her bloody clothing, his mind racing.

'Are you all right, love? Do we need to get you to hospital?'

Bronwen was quick to reply. 'It's not my blood.'

He gave her a knowing look, reaching out for mutual comfort. 'Shady's?'

Bronwen looked at her father with unblinking eyes.

'He was going to kill me, Dad. He did awful things, truly terrible. And it would have got even worse, just like Carly Flowers. Anna shot him. It's her father's gun. She saved my life.'

Lewis felt his gut twist. There were many things he thought to ask his daughter. About things he knew would be challenging to hear, as evidenced by the photos and her haunted eyes. But such things could wait. He looked across at Anna and shouted, 'Thanks, love, I owe you everything,' meaning every word.

Anna smiled thinly as Lewis approached her, but didn't reply.

'Is the gun loaded?' he asked.

Anna shook her head. 'Not any more.'

Lewis took a breath. 'Where is he?'

'Mark? He's inside,' Anna said, 'in the room to the right of the kitchen. If you can call it a room. It's more of a cell. He admitted to everything, including what he did to Carly, me, and all the others. I recorded it. It's on my mobile.'

Lewis silently pondered that a picture was

emerging. The pieces of the jigsaw were slowly fitting together.

'Is he dead?' he asked.

Anna nodded twice. 'Dead, and in hell.'

The very sight of the room was enough to make Lewis shiver. Not so much the naked body prone on the floor. He was well used to such things after a long police career. But the fact that his loving daughter had been kept there, so very close to death. He looked at the bloody mess that had once been Shady's face, and grinned. Sometimes, he said to himself, there was justice in the world. No need for courts. An eye for an eye. Just occasionally, things worked out right. And as he stood there, he felt wholly and utterly determined to do whatever it took to ensure Shady didn't ruin any more lives. To hell with the rules. Screw the law. For once, the real victims had to come first. Shady, he said to himself, got precisely what he deserved.

Lewis addressed both women when he returned outside, glad of the fresh air. He spoke up, clearly enunciating each word, stressing the importance of what he was about to say. It didn't come easy. His policing instincts ran deep. But once he committed, his determination didn't waver. Not for a second.

'Okay, the two of you, listen up. This is what's

going to happen,' he began, looking from one to the other. 'Anna, we can't argue self-defence. You brought a weapon, and then you shot him twice. That's likely enough to convict you. So we're going to have to adopt a different strategy. You're going to take the gun home. Put on some gloves. Clean it of any fingerprints. And then put it back exactly where you got it from. And your phone. You can give it to me, and I'll get rid of it. You don't need to know where.'

Anna nodded and said, 'Okay.'

'I won't ring this in until you've had enough time to get to your parents' place. The police are going to be swarming over this area once I do. And in the unlikely event that anyone ever asks, you've never been here. You've never heard of the place. Am I clear?'

Anna nodded again, looking never more surprised as Lewis turned his attention to Bronwen, whose mouth had fallen open like a goldfish in a bowl.

'And Bron, as soon as we get back to Carmarthen, you're going to tell your story as it happened, making a full written statement to Laura Kesey. And when you do, you're going to stick as close to the truth as possible with one crucial exception. You make no mention of Anna. You say Shady was shot and killed by a man previously unknown to you. A man who freed you, stripped Shady and gave you his clothes. You can give a vague description of the killer, saying it was too dark to see him properly. Just decide on something and then stick to it. And I'll say I received an anonymous call from a blocked number telling me where to find you. I know Laura is going to be dubious. She'll want to know why I didn't call for backup. She'll have all sorts of questions. But if we both stick to the story, however hard she pushes, we'll be okay. And I'll say I dropped my phone somewhere, but I don't know where, so it can't be checked. If we do all that, there'll be no evidence to justify seeing either of us in any way as suspects. Whatever the DI's doubts, she'll have no option but to accept what we say. So sticking to our story would be key. No deviation, just tell our version of events with confidence. Do you think you can do that for me? And think hard before answering. Because if you say yes, there's no going back. We'll all be in it for the long haul. This is well outside the law. But I don't want to end my career with Anna banged up for God only knows how long. Not for a shit stain like Shady. So, both of you, have we got a deal?'

The two young women looked at each other and then at Lewis, indicating their agreement.

Bronwen began to weep, speaking between sobs.

'Thanks s-so much, Dad,' she said with feeling before hugging him again, her arms wrapped around his big torso.

'Yeah, thanks, Ray,' Anna added when father and daughter parted. 'I'll never forget this. You're my hero. And I'll always be grateful. If only there were more good men like you. The world would be a better place if there were.'

39

SIX MONTHS LATER

Lewis stood beside Tanya, stirring a large wok of heart-healthy Thai prawn curry simmering on the gas cooker and smiling.

'You moving in is the best thing that's ever happened to me,' he said with a smile. 'I was dreading retirement. But look at me now, almost two stone lighter, off the booze, and looking forward to our future together. I really do love you to bits. I'm the luckiest man in the world.'

Tanya gave a little laugh. 'Concentrate on your cooking, you silly sentimental old thing. Bronwen will be here soon. It would be nice to have everything ready and waiting. Then we can all relax and enjoy ourselves.'

'That's the plan.'

Tanya pecked his cheek. 'How do you think she'll take the news?'

'I think she'll be pleased for us.'

'Sure?'

Lewis nodded. 'Of course, why wouldn't she be? I really don't know what you're worrying about.'

Tanya approached the fridge. 'I want everything to go smoothly, that's all.'

'How's the fruit salad looking?'

'All ready. And there's plenty of soya cream. I bought two cartons.'

Lewis laughed. 'If anyone had told me I'd end up liking that stuff after dating you, I'd have thought they were mad.'

Half an hour or so later, Bronwen had arrived, the preparations were complete, and the three sat around the dining room table, drinking alcohol-free wine from crystal glasses and enjoying their delicious food.

Lewis looked across at his daughter with a grin he couldn't hide. 'Me and Tanya have some big news for you, love. We wanted to tell you together.'

Bronwen met his eyes. 'Ah, I was wondering. I thought there must be something with you going to all this effort. It feels like a special occasion.'

Lewis cleared his throat before speaking. 'We're engaged. And we're going to get married in Italy. Lake Como, somewhere Tanya's always wanted to go. And we want you there as our special guest of honour. All at my expense. My treat. I don't want you spending a thing. What do you think?'

Tears welled in Bronwen's eyes as she stood to hug them both, her dad first. She asked Tanya to show her the ring, which she did with evident pride. A single diamond on a gold band.

'I am so chuffed,' Bronwen said. 'Congratulations, I'm delighted for you both. I really couldn't be happier.'

Lewis wiped away a tear as his daughter returned to her seat. 'Let's have a chat about some potential dates later over a coffee. A bit of Italian sun will do us all some good.'

The next twenty minutes passed with happy, convivial conversation, but then the mood changed, and Bronwen looked more serious. Lewis knew things hadn't always been easy since her abduction, and her sudden, sullen expression came as no surprise.

'What's up, love?' he asked with genuine concern. 'I can see there's something.'

'I... I saw Anna in town yesterday morning. For the first time since, well, you know when.'

Lewis stiffened as tension filled the room. 'Did the two of you speak?'

Bronwen nodded but said nothing.

'It's all right, love. I've told Tanya all that happened. There are no secrets between us. You can talk openly. How's Anna doing?'

Bronwen shifted in her seat, a look of surprise on her face. '*Everything?*'

'Just as I said.'

Bronwen looked away, speaking without meeting his eyes. 'Anna's back at university. And she's doing voluntary work at the women's refuge here in town. I thought she looked well. Much better than before.'

Lewis smiled. 'Good for her. I hope things work out. She deserves some happiness. And we do, too. All of us. None of us must ever forget that.'

'Anna said she's still surprised we got away with it.'

Lewis nodded his acknowledgement. 'But we did. And we did the right thing. I'll always be certain of that. Shady had ruined enough lives without Anna's too. Things aren't always black and white.

Life is more complicated than that. That took me a long time to realise. But I got there in the end.'

Bronwen nodded as Tanya fetched the fruit salad from the fridge.

'Right,' Bronwen said with conviction. 'That's enough talk of the past. Sorry to lower the mood. What month have you got in mind for the ceremony?'

Tanya looked a little uneasy as she put the glass bowl on the table, as if talk of Shady had unnerved her. 'I thought May or June,' she said. 'Before it gets too hot.'

'That sounds lovely,' Bronwen said, speaking slowly, clearly enunciating each word, as if for fear her emotions might overflow. 'It'll be a wonderful new start. And let's never talk of Mark Shady ever again. Let's all agree now and never mention his name.'

'Agreed!' said Lewis with gusto, lifting his glass to his lips as tears began to flow. 'I'll drink to that – a toast to our future. The bastard never existed. Onwards and upwards. We're going to have the best year of our lives.'

* * *

MORE FROM JOHN NICHOLL

Another completely addictive psychological thriller from John Nicholl, *The Holiday*, is available to order now here:
www.mybook.to/TheHolidayBackAd

ACKNOWLEDGEMENTS

With thanks to my editor Isobel Akenhead and to the rest of the brilliant Boldwood Books team.

ABOUT THE AUTHOR

John Nicholl is an award-winning, bestselling author of numerous darkly psychological suspense thrillers. These books have a gritty realism born of his real-life experience as an ex-police officer and child protection social worker.

Sign up to John Nicholl's mailing list for news, competitions and updates on future books.

Visit John's website: www.johnnicholl.com

Follow John on social media:

ALSO BY JOHN NICHOLL

The Sisters

Mr Nice

The Cellar

The Student

The Cop

The Victim

The Bride

The Holiday

The Boyfriend

The Carmarthen Murders Series

The Carmarthen Murders

The Tywi Estuary Killings

The Castle Beach Murders

The Dryslwyn Castle Killings

The Galbraith Series

The Doctor

The Wife

The Father

THE
Murder
LIST

**THE MURDER LIST IS A NEWSLETTER
DEDICATED TO SPINE-CHILLING FICTION
AND GRIPPING PAGE-TURNERS!**

**SIGN UP TO MAKE SURE YOU'RE ON OUR
HIT LIST FOR EXCLUSIVE DEALS, AUTHOR
CONTENT, AND COMPETITIONS.**

SIGN UP TO OUR
NEWSLETTER

BIT.LY/THEMURDERLISTNEWS

Boldwood

Boldwood Books is an award-winning fiction publishing company seeking out the best stories from around the world.

Find out more at www.boldwoodbooks.com

Join our reader community for brilliant books, competitions and offers!

Follow us
@BoldwoodBooks
@TheBoldBookClub

Sign up to our weekly deals newsletter

https://bit.ly/BoldwoodBNewsletter

www.ingramcontent.com/pod-product-compliance
Lightning Source LLC
Chambersburg PA
CBHW010857130726
47900CB00017B/2747